D0297416

THE COLUMBUS CDE

a Novel

THE
COLUMBUS
CDE

a Novel

MIKE EVANS

WORTHY®
PUBLISHING

Published by Worthy Inspired, an imprint of Worthy Publishing Group, a division of Worthy Media, Inc., One Franklin Park, 6100 Tower Circle, Suite 210, Franklin, TN 37067.

WORTHY is a registered trademark of Worthy Media, Inc.

HELPING PEOPLE EXPERIENCE THE HEART OF GOD

eBook available wherever digital books are sold.

Library of Congress Control Number: 2015931768

For foreign and subsidiary rights, contact rights@worthypublishing.com

Published in association with Ted Squires Agency, Nashville, Tennessee

ISBN: 978-1-61795-484-9

Cover Design: Brand Navigation
Cover Photography: Dreamstime, iStock
Digital Illustration: Mike Chiaravalle

Printed in the United States of America
15 16 17 18 19 LBM 8 7 6 5 4 3 2 1

To my son, Diego, that you may know the truth and be set free.

As I came of age, I heard rumors about lands lying to the west, on the far side of the Ocean sea.

I heard reports and stories about sightings . . . canoes washing up on the Azores . . . bodies of strange-looking people appearing ashore after storms. Many people who lived near the sea believed there were people and land farther to the west, in some uncharted place.

I heard sailors talk of their deep desire to sail to the west, to explore these stories, to see if land did indeed exist there. No soul ever did. Some had the idea that they could sail west, all the way round to the East—that perhaps they could open a more accessible route for trading with partners there.

The idea seemed good and right to me, Diego, yet some resisted . . .

—Christopher Columbus

Winters ran his hand over his damp upper lip. His nerves were on overdrive, jacked up on adrenaline and five cups of coffee. Raids used to be the thing that kept him from getting bored. He actually looked forward to them. But today dread was more the mind-set than anticipation.

Time to do this thing. He pushed open the car door and stepped out. He could feel his hair stand up in the wind, even as short as he kept it. You could always count on wind in the Bay Area. Wind and hills and fog.

But today was sunny. Eye-burningly clear. Still nippy, though. There was always that chill in the air. Who was it, Mark Twain, who said the coldest winter he ever spent was the summer he spent in San Francisco? Winters grabbed his jacket from behind the seat, shrugged it on, and walked toward a black SUV parked farther up the street.

The neighborhood was situated not far from the East Bay. Most of the houses were built in the 1920s Craftsman style. Bungalows, really, although any of them could be sold for seven figures now. It was all about location.

Winters' hands felt tacky as he rubbed them together. In his twenty years in the Secret Service he'd participated in more clandestine raids, more down and dirty arrests, more classified operations than he could remember. This one, though . . . He glanced around for the nearest bush in case his stomach rebelled.

The passenger door of the SUV swung open and Taylor Donleavy stepped out, sunglasses in place, shaved head oblivious to the wind. He was a computer forensics expert who spent most of his time in the Service's technology lab, immersed in a world of terabytes and programming code. Donleavy should have been the one ready to throw up in the shrubbery. But he looked the way Winters used to feel before this kind of operation—chomping at the proverbial bit but trying not to look like it.

"Did they show you the house?" Winters asked.

"Yeah." Donleavy had a raspy voice. If he hadn't been a buddy, Winters would have called him a geek. Actually, he did.

"It's that one, right?" Donleavy gestured to a low, one-story bungalow four houses away, near the center of the block.

"Come on, Donleavy, don't point."

Donleavy looked cluelessly at his index finger, then shrugged and went on. "Looks too peaceful, doesn't it?"

It *was* hard to believe that in that unassuming two-bedroom abode, half a dozen Russians had infiltrated the online transaction system for worldwide retailer Galliano's and had obtained millions of credit-card numbers and associated user information files. While the neighbors thought the Russians were making borscht and tending the roses, they were actually using day-trader software hacked from some low-budget investment firm to generate millions of small investment purchases. What the neighbors didn't know, a retired schoolteacher from Spokane did—or at least he got suspicious enough to file a complaint with the Secret Service.

"It's not gonna be peaceful on the inside," Winters said close to

Donleavy's ear. "Just do your thing and get out. I know you're all hot after being part of this but—"

"I know. Seize the—"

"Shut up, Donleavy." This was why Winters hated taking a non-agent on a raid. But he had to. Only somebody like Donleavy could make sure the computers were seized intact so the whole case wasn't a bust.

Another car door slammed across the street and Lonnie Smith joined them. Although he was an agent, he looked a lot less obtrusive than Donleavy in a plaid flannel over a green T-shirt and a Giants ball cap taming a mop of curly, prematurely gray hair.

"It's a go," he said, grinning. Smith always smiled, no matter the circumstances. It stretched his gray mustache into an almost-grimace.

"You sure they're in there?" Winters said.

"Yeah. All eight of them."

Winters tried not to let his eyes widen. "Eight? I thought there were only five."

"Snipers have been in place since yesterday," Smith said as if he were expanding the guest list for a dinner party. "They count eight."

Winters began to sweat again—this time the icy, barely wet perspiration that paralyzes every muscle. "There can't be eight," he said through his teeth. "I'm not ready for eight."

Smith's mouth extended into a mirthless, white-toothed grin. "It's eight, buddy. If you can't handle it—"

"No, I can't! I *can't!* It's not what I signed up for!"

❖ ❖ ❖

Winters thrust his hands forward, reaching for what, he didn't know. His heart raced and panic seized him at the thought of entering that house, but his fingers grasped nothing except thin air and the pale light slitting between the slats of the bedroom blinds. After a moment, he rubbed his eyes with the heels of his hands, trying to remember where he was, then collapsed back on the bed and pulled his pajama-clad knees into his chest. What was it now—fifteen nightmares since the raid? He wouldn't have counted them if Archer hadn't told him to. She'd also told him to report to her when he had another . . . what did she call them? Episodes? It was a dream, not a psychotic episode. And he wasn't calling her.

Winters glanced at the alarm clock on the bedside table. He was surprised the thing still worked, seeing as how it had awakened him every morning in *high school* and he was now forty-five. Mom never changed a thing.

It was only 6:40 a.m., which meant it was 3:40 in San Francisco. Dr. Archer wouldn't appreciate a call from Winters at this hour unless he was suicidal. Not that she hadn't questioned him about that possibility after every session for the last two months.

Besides, this day wasn't about him *possibly* dying. It was about Mom actually dying, which she'd done two days before without giving him, Ben, or Maria any warning. Three days ago she'd called to tell him not to forget Uncle David's eightieth birthday. Now he was waking up in his boyhood room on the day of her funeral.

"Yo, Johnny," a husky voice called. "You awake?" That question was followed by a loud banging on the door.

"I am now," Winters replied.

The door was forced open, the settling of the house over the last fifty-five years having rendered it jammed. His brother, Ben, younger by fifteen years, entered with his usual swagger. The kid still carried himself like the Bowie High football captain—head cocky, arms held out to the sides in half circles because they were too buff to touch his ribs, blue eyes making sure everybody was looking at him.

"You were passed out when I got in last night," Ben said.

"I wasn't 'passed out.' I was asleep like normal people." Winters threw back what covers were still in place after the dream and swung his legs over the side of the bed.

Ben stepped forward, playfully batting at Winters' head. "No, man," he quipped, "you're not normal people. You're Secret Agent Man. S. A. . . ."

Winters stopped listening and stifled a groan. Ben had been ten years old when he joined the Service and back then it was cute when his kid brother bragged about his status and talked about it nonstop when they were together. Now it bordered on obnoxious. No, actually it had gone beyond obnoxious, especially since Ben had decided to follow in his footsteps.

Winters got to his feet and gave Ben a halfhearted hug.

"You hear anything?" Ben asked.

"About what?"

"About my challenging that last set of interviews."

Winters feigned a yawn and squeezed past him. The room had gotten smaller since they were kids. "No, I haven't, and nobody would tell me anything anyway."

"I was hoping you'd know something."

Winters stopped, hand on the doorknob, and turned toward him. "Ben. Brother. We came here to bury our mother and all you can think about is your job interviews?"

"No, man, I'm thinkin' about Mom, but—"

"Give it a rest," Winters said. He pried the door open, then walked down the hall to the bathroom. It was pointless to add that during Ben's endless stay with him in San Francisco, Ben had bombed the preliminary interviews because he went into them acting as if he were already an agent packing heat. His rejection was a done deal, but there was no convincing Ben of that.

When Winters returned to the bedroom, Ben was sitting on the edge of the bed, studying a family photo taken on the day Winters graduated high school—back when Ben was two. He was now looking more like a guy who had just lost his mother.

"I never felt like I knew her as well as you did," he said. To his credit, his voice was thick and soft.

Winters leaned against the dresser. "I think we knew two different Moms. She changed a lot after Pop died. And how old were you when that happened? Five?"

Ben gave a glum nod. "She was all into the past. Last couple of years I lived here she spent more time in the attic than she did down here."

Winters shuddered involuntarily. Ben made it sound as if the feisty, food-pushing mother he knew had turned into something out of one of filmmaker Brian De Palma's psychological thrillers. "What do you say we celebrate her in her best days?" he said.

Ben wiped his nose with the side of his hand and nodded. His eyes were already mischievous again. "Hey, did you get grayer since I was out there?"

Winters ran a hand over the hair he knew was turning more salt-and-pepper daily and glanced over at his brother. "Did you lose more of yours?"

Ben had their father's receding hairline, though he was far from bald. He reached out for Winters' midsection. "Is that a little soft spot there? What happened to your six-pack?"

Winters' face was impassive, but the comment struck home. If they didn't let him get back to work soon he was going to lose his edge. "I hope you brought a suit," he said, changing the subject.

"Oh, yeah. Hugo Boss, brother. Mom would be proud."

No, Winters thought, she would tell him he was a moron for spending money he didn't have. "Put it on," he said instead. "We need to get there early."

"Hey, is Maria here?"

Why didn't he just push all of Winters' buttons? Were they that obvious? "She's meeting us at the church," Winters said. "And she'll beat us there if you don't get a move on."

Winters was lying, of course, though it seemed Ben didn't notice. He knew Maria would wait until the last possible moment to show up. And not because she didn't love her grandmother.

Maria Winters looked up through a panel of thick hair and glared at her assistant. "What are you *doing?*" she asked.

Austin wafted a lanky arm toward the door—again—and said, "I'm trying to get you out of here, ma'am."

"Do *not* call me 'ma'am,'" she said, though she knew it was useless. He was not only from Mississippi, but he loved to needle her. "I want to finish this travel stuff," she continued. "I'm barely going to get back before we leave for Barcelona."

His eyes narrowed, making his already thin face look even skinnier. Spikes of hair the color of bran completed the effect: Austin looked as if he were about to levitate to the ceiling with her briefcase in his hand.

"I can finish the travel stuff. It's my job to finish the travel stuff. You shouldn't even be touching the travel stuff." Austin set the red briefcase on the desk and tapped it. "You're just stalling."

Maria dragged her fingers through the loose curls that would droop the minute she hit the sidewalk. It had been drizzling in DC all morning and probably was in Maryland too. Why did it always rain the day of a funeral? Couldn't people be buried when the ground was dry?

"Seriously," Austin said.

She looked at Austin again. For a twenty-three-year-old guy, he was pretty sensitive. She'd wondered more than once why he was working in a high-pressure law firm when he should be doing grief counseling or something. He'd been counseling her ever since Friday when she'd received the news about *Abuela* right here in this room.

"You need closure," he said now.

"I know. What I don't need is my family."

"But they probably need you."

"I doubt that very seriously. What they need is the opposite of me."

"Whatever. I already called you a cab. You have just enough time to make your train." Austin's hazel eyes softened. "You can do this. You know you can."

"'Can' is one thing," Maria said. "'Want to' is another." She stood and took her spring trench coat from him, then picked up the briefcase. "Promise you'll finish this?"

"If you don't go I'm going to cause a scene."

Maria couldn't stifle a smile, though it faded as soon as she stepped into the hall and plowed headlong into Bill Snowden. She didn't have time for one of Snowden's monologues, but you didn't put off the boss. Not this one, anyway.

"Where are you off to?" he asked, dark eyebrows tending toward each other. Maria was sure the man had them waxed.

"My grandmother's funeral." Maria backed toward the elevator as she added, "I sent you an e-mail."

"Oh, right," he said as he nodded. "Sorry for your loss."

Uh-huh. There was no "sorry" in Snowden's dark eyes. The striking contrast with his very-white hair should have made him handsome, but Maria never found cold men attractive.

"Well, here, take this with you." Snowden thrust a sheaf of papers into her hands. "Final details for the Catalonia meeting. You'll go straight there when you land in Barcelona, so take some Ambien or something for the flight. You'll want to sleep on the way over."

Maria bit off an *As if* and nodded, still making her way backward to the elevator. She also forced herself not to say, *You couldn't have sent me this by e-mail?* She didn't have to look at the pages to know that most, if not all, of it was handwritten in his inimitable scrawl—in pencil, no less. That was why she went to law school and was hired on at this prestigious firm at age twenty-five—so she could decipher her boss' handwriting like a 1940s stenographer.

"See you in Spain," he said as she stepped onto the elevator.

The doors closed, squeezing him out of sight. "Bye-bye," she whispered.

Yeah, she sighed to herself, *sometimes it is, as Austin would say, "wa-a-a-ay hard" to be professional.*

✦ ✦ ✦

The closer the MARC train drew to the stop, the less Maria wanted to think about going to *Abuela*'s house without her there. She had always been there—before and after the event by which Maria marked everything. Her mom's death. *Abuela* had been a constant—the summers when Maria went there to stay *after*—the Christmases the whole family spent there *before*. The house would still smell like paprika and saffron. Abuela had been making paella for a church supper the last time Maria talked to her. Maybe her smell would still be there too. Dove soap. Jergens lotion. Downy. But without her there, it would only taunt—Maria knew that.

And then there would be her father . . .

Him she couldn't think about or she'd head straight back to DC. Maria's fingers shook with anger even now as she opened her briefcase and pulled out the papers Snowden had given her. But as her eyes scanned the pages, her mind turned to work and very quickly her body relaxed.

Maria's firm, Gump, Snowden and Meir, represented Catalonia Financial, an international corporation with headquarters in Barcelona, Spain. Catalonia was currently acquiring Belgium Continental and wanted Snowden there to finalize the deal. Snowden never went anywhere without a full entourage, and he'd asked Maria to be part of it this time. It was her first overseas trip since she joined the firm in December, fresh out of law school, and even though his invitation had been last minute it still seemed like one of those only-happens-once things—until she lost *Abuela*.

"You're doing so well!" *Abuela* said to her on Easter weekend when she'd heard about the trip. They'd spent the weekend coloring eggs and eating ham and putting lilies on the grave of *Abuelo*, the grandfather Maria never knew. *Abuela* had taken Maria's face in both hands and said exactly what Maria knew she would say. "Your mama would be so proud."

Fourteen years after the fact and they were still crying. *Abuela* had always grieved as if Maria's mother, Anne, was her own daughter. She definitely grieved more than Dad had . . .

Maria blinked away the blur in her eyes and went back to the notes. Emilio Tejada, president and CEO of Catalonia Financial, would conduct the meeting himself and she would have to take notes rather than record the session. "Tejada's a tough bird, set in his ways," Snowden had written.

She couldn't think about "tough old birds" right now either. That was how her Uncle David referred to *Abuela*. Everything was leading back to her.

Maria's mind continued to wander and finally she crammed the papers into her briefcase, then sat quietly watching the raindrops stream sideways on the window of the racing train. She almost knew more about *Abuela* than she did about herself. Her father had even suggested during their stilted phone conversation that she should give the eulogy.

Was he the most insensitive creature ever to inhabit the planet? Maybe he didn't know that this was the first funeral she would attend since that awful September day when they buried Mom.

Or maybe he didn't know her at all.

3

Saint Peter's Episcopal Church was a ponderous old place that had changed as little as Winters' mother had in the years since he had been an acolyte there. He had carried the cross up the aisle nearly every Sunday because he was the only teenager left in the parish. The congregation had consisted largely of octogenarians back then, mixed with the few faithful younger people like Olivia Winters who were devoted to the denomination. He couldn't imagine what was still holding it together.

But it was actually a fairly young priest who met him at the door when he and Ben arrived, dripping umbrellas in hand. He might have been Ben's age, though he was visibly more mature. But then, who wasn't?

"Hello," he said. "I'm Father Todd. Is the family all here?" he asked after the introductions had been made.

Ben brushed past him and peered between the swinging doors into the sanctuary. "I don't see Maria," he said.

"How long do you want to wait?" Father Todd asked.

"Until my daughter gets here," Winters answered.

"Uncle David's in there," Ben said when the priest had left them. "How'd he get here?"

"They brought him over in the van from the nursing home. His wheelchair wouldn't fit in the trunk of my rental car."

Ben gave him a lopsided grin. "You're still cheap."

Winters had spent only four hours with his brother and he was already wishing he'd—

Just then, the door to the narthex opened and a figure clad in a white trench coat and carrying a red briefcase slipped in and tossed back a mass of honey-colored curls. Winters' throat tightened. His daughter looked just like her mother—liquid gold eyes peering through the semidarkness, head held high and almost haughty, hand reaching for her hair. Just as Anne had, Maria signaled her mood by whatever her hand was doing to her hair.

When she saw him, her fingers clawed at it and any hope of a smile disappeared from her face. That was too bad, because Maria had a marvelous smile that Winters thought upstaged the sun.

"Hey," he said and walked toward her. She didn't pull away from the kiss he placed on her forehead, but he felt her stiffen. "You okay?"

"Am I okay? No, Dad, I'm not okay."

Winters sucked in air. "I meant from the trip up here. You were cutting it a little close and I thought maybe you ran into trouble."

He was lying and she knew it. He saw the disbelief flicker through those limpid eyes. It wasn't what he wanted to see.

"Are we ready?" Father Todd asked.

"We are." Maria crossed to him and put her arms out. To Winters' astonishment he pulled her into a hug and held on.

"She loved you," he said into her hair.

She nodded, suddenly sobbing. Winters felt a sinking sensation in his chest.

✦ ✦ ✦

The service was everything *Abuela* wanted, Maria was sure. Traditional Episcopal liturgy. The same hymns they'd sung together at Easter. A sermon by Father Todd, whom her grandmother always referred to as "the young rector."

"You captured her beautifully," she said to him afterward.

"That wasn't hard to do," he said. "What you saw was what she was." His eyes misted. "And what she was—that was something."

Maria could have hugged him again. He might have been "the young rector" to *Abuela*, but he was pretty much her fount of wisdom when it came to God. She wished they had more time together.

"Come to the house, Father?"

Maria bristled at her father's voice. Brusque. Clipped. As if every word were part of an order.

Father Todd declined. Maria wished she could, but there was no getting around the reception at *Abuela's* house. The women in her circle had probably already descended on the place with cream-of-soup casseroles and comfort desserts. And if her Uncle Ben had anything to do with it, the wine would be flowing freely. At the very least she wanted to keep him from getting plastered for *Abuela's* sake. She'd convinced her friends her younger son had all but, to use an Austin phrase, "hung the moon."

Abuela had always said she didn't want anyone at the graveside, watching them "drop me into that hole," so the limousine took Maria, her father, and Uncle Ben directly to the house. The ride would have been silent if Uncle Ben hadn't bantered the entire time about absolutely nothing. Maria watched the muscles twitch in her father's cheek. For once they were in sync.

She'd been right about the food and the elbow-to-elbow crowd crammed into *Abuela's* two-story clapboard house. Her ancient great-uncle, David, was already ensconced in his wheelchair in the living room with a glass of merlot in one hand and a cigar in the other. Maria marched toward him and removed both, replacing them with a kiss on the cheek.

"That stuff won't kill me!" he protested. "Smoked and drank all my life and never sick a day. Now they put me away in some home and look at me—sitting here like a fossil."

Maria didn't bother to argue with that logic and headed to the dining room to fix him a plate. As she rounded the corner, she all but collided with her father, who was standing in the dark hall with his forehead pressed to the wall.

"Dad?" she said.

He recovered well. He always did. His penetrating dark eyes came back from wherever his mind had been and he slid his hands into the pockets of his slacks. Maria steeled herself for the prying questions and the lecture about whatever answers she gave him, no matter what they were.

"Nice service," he said.

Maria nodded. "Just what she would have wanted."

"You'd know that better than I would."

Was that a trace of regret she was hearing?

"Did you know?" he asked.

"Know . . ."

"That she was sick?"

"She wasn't. Not that I was aware of."

"So she just died in her sleep at seventy-two."

"It was the way she would've wanted that too." Maria pulled her hair back in a handheld ponytail that collapsed the moment she removed her hand. "She always said when it was her time to go, she just wanted to fall asleep one night and not wake up."

"She usually got what she wanted," Winters said. "I wish you'd agreed to an autopsy, though."

"I didn't want her cut open. She died with dignity and I wanted to keep it that way."

He gave a soft grunt. "The apple doesn't fall far from the tree."

"What does that mean?"

"You get what you want, too, don't you?"

Maria brought herself up to her full five-eight height. "No, Dad," she said. "I don't." She spun around and started toward the kitchen.

By the time she got back to the living room with Uncle David's plate of starch and sucrose, the old man was waving a gnarled hand and hollering, "Johnny! Johnny, come over here and sit down. I want to say something to you."

If Uncle David intended for this to be a private conversation he was going about it the wrong way. He refused to wear hearing aids and, as a result, he shouted like a foghorn.

Ben was sitting on the ottoman next to Uncle David's wheelchair but he got up and moved to the love seat. Everyone else found an excuse to scurry out of the room, which left only the four of them. Uncle David's reputation for interminable tales must have preceded him. Maria put the plate on the table beside him and started to join the group of rats who had abandoned ship but he caught her arm with one of his claws.

"You need to hear this too, girlie," he said.

Maria sat beside Ben on the love seat. Winters stood with one elbow on the fireplace mantel. "What's up, Uncle David?" he asked.

"It's not what's up—it's what's down!" the old man hollered. "Now that Olivia is in the ground."

Really? *Really?* Maria thought.

"Although if you believe like she did, her spirit is up, not down. Never could figure out why she still bought into all that."

"Did you call us all in here for a theology lesson, Uncle Dave?" Ben asked, furtively nudging Maria with his elbow.

"Theology lesson? No!" Uncle David looked blankly at Ben. "Who said anything about theology? I was talking about the will."

Maria was sure she felt Ben's pulse quicken. *Abuela* had told Maria several visits ago that she had stopped sending Ben money every time he asked for it. In Maria's opinion, that was something she should have done about fifteen years ago.

"She told me she was leaving all this to the three of you," Uncle David went on, giving the room a flourish with his stiff arm. "But I'm sure she didn't tell you about the hidden family treasure"—he paused for effect. For a moment Maria thought he had fallen asleep, then he finally finished, "In the attic."

"What are you talking about?" Uncle Ben asked. "Is there money hidden up there or something?"

Maria was ready to grab him should he suddenly launch himself from the love seat and head for the stairs.

"Something better than money." Uncle David nodded sagely and fell into another endless pause. "That's where she kept the family history."

Uncle Ben sagged. Maria wanted to smack him.

"And I do mean 'kept.' She has that third floor locked up like Fort Knox. Wouldn't let anybody else in there to look at that stuff."

Maria saw her father exchange glances with Ben.

"Told you she spent all her time up there," Ben said.

"No she didn't!" Maria snapped.

"All right, I'll bite." Winters lifted his chin at the old guy. "What's up there, Unc?"

"The proof!"

"Proof of what?"

"Proof that this whole family is Looney Tunes," Uncle Ben whispered to Maria.

Uncle David squinted suspiciously at the doorway before he said, in a quiet voice, "Proof that we are direct descendants of Christopher Columbus." He gave a deep nod and settled back in the wheelchair, visibly ready to enjoy watching the rest of them take it in.

Ben's shoulders shook until Maria jabbed him in the ribs. He put his lips next to her ear and said, "Told you they were Looney Tunes." Out loud he said, "It must be a thing right now, all you baby boomers trying to prove your roots."

Uncle David didn't appear to hear that, which was fortunate on two levels as far as Maria was concerned. He was a well-meaning old man who didn't deserve to be pooh-poohed. And who in this room could be considered a baby boomer?

Maria stood up and smoothed the creases in her skirt. "I have to get going," she said and looked at her father. "I'll come down and go through *Abuela*'s clothes if you want, when I get back from Barcelona."

She wanted to bite off her tongue. At the root. Why did she mention Barcelona? She pecked both uncles on their respective cheeks and, as she could have predicted, her father followed her out of the room.

"You're going to Barcelona," he said.

Maria stopped at the bottom of the stairs, arms folded. "I am. On a business trip."

"You'll be careful."

"I'm not in the kind of business you're in," she said.

She would have left it at that if she hadn't seen him wince. It might have been imperceptible to anyone else, but it was clear to her.

She'd spent eight years after her mother's death studying his face so that maybe she could know what he was feeling. Old habits died hard.

"What?" she asked. "You're still with the Service, right?"

"Why wouldn't I be?"

Maria rolled her eyes. "Never mind."

She turned to leave but he caught her arm. When she looked down at it, he let go, but she stayed. He exhaled as if he'd been holding his breath all day.

"I'm on paid leave right now," he said.

"Why?" She watched his Adam's apple bob, something that had delighted her as a kid. Now it looked painful.

"Lot of things stacked up," he said finally. "Then a raid went bad and I . . . got a little depressed." She waited. The apple bobbed some more. "They've got me seeing a doctor," he continued. "She clears me, I go back to work."

There was a whole lot more to it, Maria was sure of that. But she was also sure that was all she was going to hear right now. It was the longest conversation they'd had in probably five years and she didn't want it to end on a sour note. Not today. Not with *Abuela*'s spirit still so near.

"Won't be long now," he added.

"Good," she said.

"Johnny! Johnny, you heading for the attic?" Uncle David called. "Wait a minute and I'll go up there with you."

"Bye," Maria said.

And she fled for her sanity.

4

Winters stayed in Maryland for a week dealing with his mother's estate. Ben was initially enthusiastic about helping, but after twenty-four hours he took a flight for Phoenix to return to whatever pressing matters awaited him. Winters still couldn't figure out what Ben actually did there and had an uneasy feeling he didn't want to know.

By Friday he had things pretty well wrapped up. Maria sent him an e-mail listing the things she wanted and those were now in a storage unit where she could pick them up when she got back from Barcelona. Winters would have the maple bed and dresser shipped to his place in San Francisco. The rest of his mother's belongings had been sold. All the paperwork was signed, the lawyer had the process in motion, and the only thing left to tackle was the attic.

Winters had put that off for two reasons. First, Ben's comment that Mom spent a lot of time up there frankly gave him the creeps. His mother was usually a stable woman, making sure everybody was fed, sending birthday cards with ten-dollar bills tucked inside, continually trying to build a bridge between him and Maria. But she did have— he guessed what people would call a "spiritual side." Mom still carried on conversations with her long-deceased husband, Winters' father, and said she "knew" things about Anne's condition in the afterlife.

He was half-afraid he'd find some kind of ritual altar up there. If not worse.

The other thing that kept him out of the attic was Uncle David's pronouncement that it contained "proof" that they were direct descendants of Christopher Columbus. Where had *that* come from? He knew his mother kept photo albums that went back to the Civil War days when photography was first used and she would tell him the name of every fifteen-times-removed relative in those pictures until his eyes glazed over.

But she'd never mentioned a thing to him about Christopher Columbus. Uncle David was probably getting senile. Maybe that was what made Winters reluctant to go rooting around in trunks—the fact that it might not be true. But now that it had been suggested, it was actually intriguing. Curiosity—coupled with too much time on his hands after everything else was done—finally drove Winters to the third floor with a flashlight and a portable vacuum cleaner.

Winters was surprised to find it well lit—an upgrade he had known nothing about. An old velvet couch he remembered used to be in the tiny room off the kitchen Mom called her "parlor" was the only thing not packed away in the expected trunks. Five of them were lined up neatly under the dormer window. The rest of the space was empty.

Winters tossed the unneeded flashlight onto the couch and watched for a cloud of dust to puff up from the cushions, but there was none. That made the portable vacuum superfluous too. The tops of the trunks were dirt-free as well. Mom must have cleaned up there recently. Who dusted and vacuumed their attic?

Although the air wasn't at all chilly, Winters shivered. She'd saved him a lot of work, getting rid of all the detritus of their past lives he'd seen the last time he'd been there. Either she'd known she was going to die, or . . .

Since he couldn't come up with an alternative, Winters went to the first trunk, lifted the lid, and glanced down at the contents inside. Uncle David was wrong so far. She didn't have anything locked down like Fort Knox. In fact, there was an envelope on top of a stack of overstuffed photo albums. His name—*Johnny*—was written across it in Mom's precise handwriting.

He tested the stability of the couch and perched on its edge to read the letter inside the envelope.

Dear Son,

If you're reading this, I'm probably gone. I hope I had a nice death. I always wanted to save you boys and Maria the kind of grief we had when your father passed away. I'm with him now, so be happy about that.

Since I'm in Paradise where all things are clear to me, I know for sure what I've searched for years to prove—that we are the direct descendants of Christopher Columbus. I'm sure this will come as a surprise to you, the fact that I have been researching this for a long time. You remember my trip to Salt Lake City? That was all about genealogy. I didn't share this part of my journey with you because it just seemed that it should be between God and me. After all, that's where the idea came from—one of those rare times when God whispered into my thoughts, "Olivia, you must do this." I heard it when your father proposed to me and when I took Maria for the summers after Anne died and you couldn't care for her, so I know I can trust it.

So far I haven't found proof of the direct link and I haven't discovered the reason God is having me do this. I know only that it's your job now to continue the work. In this trunk you'll find all I've discovered so far. I'm trusting you to take care of it. The other four trunks are all family photos and documents—baptismal certificates, marriage licenses, your baby teeth, and locks of Ben's hair, that kind of thing. Maria is the keeper of the keys on those items. She'll need a bigger apartment for them, I'm sure, but as well as she's doing, I have no doubt she can afford it. Be proud of her, Johnny. She is a wonderful combination of you and Anne.

I can be content here in heaven knowing you'll pick up where I left off. Again, I don't know why it's important. I know only that it is, and that you are the man to do it. You won't be alone. I am always with you.

Love,
Mom

Winters read it twice more before he returned it to the envelope and stared at the open trunk. She'd never shown any signs of dementia and the letter was certainly lucid—except for the parts about God talking to her. That had never been his experience. But the rest . . . the rest of it stirred him. He almost felt as if she were sitting beside him waiting to see if he'd do this thing for her.

He couldn't see himself poring over genealogical documents for hours on end. If he wasn't already nuts a little bit of that would put him there soon. She had probably hit a dead end or there would have been no need for the letter.

Still, looking at what she'd found was the least he could do and then he could pack the stuff away in good conscience.

But he sure wasn't going to look at it up here. The air in the attic was starting to feel heavy. Whether that was his imagination or not, he was taking the books downstairs.

Half an hour later Winters had it all transferred to the

bedroom—the only room in the house that was still furnished. He stacked the books on the dresser and propped up on the bed to peruse the first of what turned out to be memory albums with pages full of his mother's writing glued into them, along with documents and letters written by long-gone relatives. It actually made for interesting reading.

Port of entry documents from the Washington Avenue Immigration Station in Philadelphia. A quarantine order. A quarantine release, for three people listed as Esteban, Magdalena, and Antonio de Torme. Esteban and Magdalena were adults. Antonio was a minor. Apparently someone thought they had smallpox.

So Antonio became Winters' grandfather, his mother's father. That made Esteban and Magdelena his great-grandparents. If they truly had contracted smallpox, Winters probably wouldn't be here.

He flipped through a few pages of receipts for items they bought as they settled in the States, and a picture not attached to a page popped out. It was a photograph of a young boy and a man, both looking every bit the pitiful refugees. Winters looked on the back, where the words "Alba de Tormes, Spain" were scrawled. "This little boy is Antonio Torme," his mother had written on the page. "The man standing next to him is Esteban Torme."

The only thing Winters could think of was Mel Tormé singing about chestnuts roasting on an open fire.

"Okay," he said to the empty room. "Just because our ancestors came from Spain doesn't mean we're related to Columbus." Every American with a Spanish last name must claim that. And even if they were, what was the big deal?

Winters got up and went to the window where he'd stood hundreds of times growing up, watching for his dad to come up the driveway from work with a newspaper under his arm; trying to get a glimpse of Heather O'Neal, who lived across the street and whose bedroom directly faced his; waiting for the mail carrier to deliver his acceptance to Georgetown.

The trees were bigger now and even with only a few pale early spring leaves they obliterated his view of Heather O'Neal's old room. His view of everything was different from what it had been back then. Only now it was blocked by old tragedy and fresh grief, neither of which he knew what to do with.

Maybe this Columbus thing was part of both. Or maybe he was just as unstable as Julia Archer said he was. She'd told him to stop sailing, stop biking, stop pursuing his pilot's license in case he had an "episode." But what harm could he come to going through the dusted-off dreams of his overspiritual mother? Maybe he would just die in his sleep too.

He went downstairs to find a box in which to ship it all to San Francisco.

5

Emilio Tejada fixed his gaze out the narrow window onto the shining waters of the Mediterranean two blocks away. The tiny village of El Masnou, northeast of Barcelona, spilled sleepily away from the coast below. Its residents were unaware that an urgent meeting had been called in the stucco building known to the villagers as *la casa del extrano hombre de edad*—the house of the strange old man. Abaddon was a mysterious figure to the uneducated people of the village. No one knew where he came from or how long he had been there. The folks made guesses about him when they thought of him at all, and over time they appeared to think of him less and less. Tejada didn't see how that was possible, and yet it was a good thing.

"Emilio," a ghostly voice said, "will you join us?"

Tejada turned away from the window and crossed the cool room. He approached the carved teakwood, high-backed chair and bent low, gently kissing the knotted hand of the man who sat in it. The old man's eyes were closed and a shock of his white hair, still streaked with the black of his youth, fell over his forehead. Tejada could feel the envy of the twelve men seated on Andalusian cushions behind him. They would never admit to coveting Abaddon's obvious favoritism, but Tejada knew, and he tried not to enjoy it. They were, after all, a brotherhood.

Tejada took his place on the one empty cushion to Abaddon's right. A spear of sunlight from the narrow window cut directly into his face. He didn't wince. All faces remained emotionless as Abaddon led them in the ritual.

"With the ancients who came before us," they followed in unison, "and for the future of our own creation, we pledge our lives and our fortunes to the Master."

Each of the thirteen, Tejada included, reached toward the small purple pad on the floor in front of him and picked up a ring, which each man slid onto the ring finger of his left hand. The customary silence fell—so quiet that even the warblers beyond the windows seemed to hush themselves until Abaddon spoke.

"We have a singular purpose here," he said, voice thin. "One that has been unfolding for centuries . . ."

During the dramatic pause, one of many Tejada knew Abaddon would take, Tejada noted how weak his old Master's speech had become. The words were still strong, the force behind them invincible. But at times the voice itself became breathless, as if he, too, were fading off into the centuries.

"Now," Abaddon continued as the thirteen leaned in to hear, "the dreams dreamed ages ago and the plans made by past generations will come to fruition. Now!"

He had managed to summon up a sonorous tone and several of the men jerked back in surprise. Tejada remained still. He'd learned to flow with Abaddon's fluctuations.

"You are privileged not only to see it but to participate in establishing it." Abaddon's eyes, dimmed by age and the darkness in which he preferred to dwell, swept the circle. "Count it as the privilege of your lives." He nodded at Tejada. "You have the orders I have asked you to pass down?"

"I do, Abaddon," Tejada said.

"Please proceed." Abaddon closed his eyes.

Tejada guessed speaking those few sentences had exhausted Abaddon. He hated to think that this abrupt move to put the plan into place was linked to Abaddon's fading energy. The man was of some indeterminable age above ninety and until recently had been as robust as Tejada himself. It was difficult to think of him any other way, or to think of him not there at all.

"Emilio?" Abaddon said, eyes still closed.

"Yes," Tejada answered and turned to the twelve sitting before him—his brothers of *el Grupo de Barcelona*. If they resented this delegation of Abaddon's authority to him, they didn't show it. He met no resistance as he gave them their individual instructions.

✦ ✦ ✦

The sun had begun to spread its pinks and oranges over the Mediterranean when the meeting concluded with another chorus of the vow. Each man kissed the hand of the venerated Abaddon and took his leave. Tejada was last, and when he grasped the old man's fingers in his, Abaddon held on. His frail voice notwithstanding, his grip was still powerful.

"Stay a moment," he whispered. "Sit here."

Tejada pulled his cushion closer to Abaddon's chair and lowered himself onto it. Abaddon leaned forward, so that his face was almost level with Tejada's. Emilio could barely see it in the gathering darkness.

"You think the meeting went well?"

"Yes, Lord Abaddon," Tejada said. "I think it went very well."

"Good. I would hate to know that the others would take the pledge and not follow through."

Tejada felt his brow lift in surprise. "Why would you think that? Didn't you sense their agreement? Their unity of purpose?"

The old man nodded and twisted the ring on his left hand, mumbling the Greek letters across the top, "*Chi, rho, omicron,*" and the inscription beneath them, "*Ferrens.*" He looked sideways at Tejada. "You remember the day you took the ring?"

Tejada had no idea where this was going. "Yes I do," he said.

"I installed you myself, and do you know why?"

Tejada shook his head, although at times he'd been sure he did know.

"I gave you all my power."

Only the society's principle of maintaining complete aplomb kept Tejada from crying out. He'd known it, yes, but to hear it from Abaddon was another matter entirely.

"I did that for a purpose." Abaddon's voice seemed to be gaining strength now that the others were gone. It had its original rough, gravelly texture. "Do you know what that purpose was?"

"I do."

"Then do not forget it."

Tejada stirred uneasily on the cushion.

"You're troubled," Abaddon said, eyes closed again. "Why?"

"Do you suspect that there is something afoot to thwart us?"

"Not some*thing*, Emilio. Some*one.*" His eyes opened and met Tejada's. "Be alert, and report any deviation to me immediately."

Tejada agreed, though he couldn't fathom anything interfering with Abaddon's well-laid plan, a plan born from centuries of preparation. Though his voice might falter, he possessed a force seemingly without end. He was aged, but not diminished. Tired, but not overcome. Somewhat unkempt of late but still attractive, in that way that all charismatic people remain—though, Tejada thought, far more than any other.

The plan would proceed as it had been prepared. In Tejada's experience, no force could compete with the innate and burning energy of Lord Abaddon.

And now he knew he also had that power. He would use it for good.

6

Maria ignored Bill Snowden's advice to take a sleeping pill on the flight and she was glad she'd followed her instincts. She slept soundly in the business class cabin and was awake enough when the plane touched down to appreciate her first sight of Barcelona—the diamond-blue Mediterranean, the bright tile roofs, the spires of the Sagrada Família.

A thick-necked driver with a close shave holding a sign with her name on it met her outside customs and swept her, along with her luggage, off to a waiting car. After Maria's failed attempt to use her college Spanish on him, he scowled at her. When she whipped out her phone to pull up the Spanish/English translation app, he became absolutely sullen. She forgot him when she slid into the backseat of the limo and bumped hips with a young woman about her age with dark, curly hair and a bright smile.

"Elena Soler," she said, in elegant British English. "I'll be your assistant while you're here since I understand yours was unable to come."

"Unable to come" didn't quite describe it. Austin would have had his cat at the kennel and his mail stopped within minutes if Snowden had asked him. Their assumption was that Maria was going to be

Snowden's assistant while she was there and wouldn't need one of her own. She guessed he'd had a change of heart.

"Your first visit to our city?" Elena asked.

"Yes." Maria nodded, eyes riveted on the passing scenery. "Look at this architecture. Oh, my gosh, is that a Gaudí?"

Elena's eyes—a silvery gray—widened. "Not many people our age appreciate that."

"I love buildings. Love. Them."

"I'll take you sightseeing if you want," Elena said.

"Like I'm going to have time."

Elena had a knowing look. "We don't drive ourselves the way Americans do. You might just learn how to live while you're here. Besides"—she gave a dainty shrug—"I plan to take care of all the minor details so you can enjoy your stay."

Maria didn't know where Snowden had found this girl. In fact, if he knew she was this accommodating he'd probably take her for himself.

"That's where we're going," Elena said, pointing.

Maria looked in that direction and let an old expression of *Abuela*'s—"holy cow!"—slip out. Elena put her hand to her mouth, obviously to hide a smile at the untraveled American.

But seriously? The Catalonia Financial complex looked more like a university than the location of the world's largest investment company. Situated on a lush green campus of manicured lawns, the buildings were all glass and polished steel and graceful lines that spoke more of elegance than business.

"*Señor* Tejada likes things nice," Elena explained.

"This is way past 'nice.'" *Actually, try overkill,* Maria thought.

The limo pulled up to a gleaming tower, the tallest on the site, and the sulky driver alighted from the front seat to open Maria's door almost before the engine stopped running.

"*Gracias*, Louis," Elena said.

Louis grunted in response as they slipped from the car and made their way past.

"What's with him?" Maria muttered.

"You mean the Mount Rushmore face? He's not supposed to flirt with any of the women he drives."

"Flirt? He looks like he wants to slit my throat."

Elena once again drew her hand over her mouth.

"It's okay to laugh," Maria said. "I'd be offended if you didn't. This is some of my best stuff."

"You *are* funny," Elena said.

When Maria was nervous she went into her stand-up comedy routine, and that morning she was in rare form. She didn't want to appear to be anxious, but it couldn't be helped. This was her first opportunity to prove herself to Snowden. Until now he'd treated her as nothing more than his go-to gal for grunt work, and she had not graduated Harvard Law for that. That wasn't what her mom would want her doing either. Maria hoped her nerves would settle down while joking with Elena.

An elevator took them to an upper floor and from there Elena led her to a pair of double doors made of intricately carved Spanish cedar.

"More 'nice'?" Maria whispered.

"You haven't seen anything yet," Elena whispered back.

When they slipped between the heavy doors, Maria saw Snowden rise to greet her, but she still had a minute to take in the room. Men occupied every chair around the massive horseshoe-shaped table. The walls were cream stucco, the floors hand-painted ceramic tile. One whole wall contained tinted windows overlooking Barcelona, while on the others were heavily framed portraits of what must have been Catalonia's forefathers. One of them even wore a *conquistador* helmet. Maria had thoroughly researched the history of the company, but she didn't recall it going back *that* far.

"Good flight?" Snowden asked at her elbow.

She knew he wouldn't wait for any answer so she didn't bother replying.

"They're about to start," he continued. "You'll sit directly behind me, and remember, no recording. I told them you were trustworthy, so they won't ask for your phone."

"What about Elena?"

Snowden had a puzzled look.

"My assistant?" Maria added.

"Oh. Yeah . . ." Snowden gestured toward a row of chairs. "She can sit beside you."

He returned to his chair. Maria presumed the other chairs were occupied by the Catalonia board of directors and the representatives of Belgium Continental. All the men wore Armani-type suits and subdued ties. The air was heavy with the smell of men's cologne.

Maria and Elena followed Snowden and took their places in chairs along the wall behind him. They were barely settled when the double doors opened and a tall man entered the room—back straight and head held high, as if it were momentarily bereft of its crown. The only thing missing, Maria thought, was a trumpet fanfare to announce his entry.

"Emilio Tejada," Elena whispered.

Yes. The CEO of Catalonia Financial. Maria had never seen a picture of him. She had imagined him as older, more sedate, less interesting. In reality he was handsome, though not outstandingly so. As he moved through the room, touching shoulders and shaking hands, it was apparent that his attractiveness came largely from his charm. He had the look of someone who remained cool even in the pit of summer when everyone else was bathed in his own sweat. Wavy, dark hair. Deep-set eyes. Maria watched him lean his head in closer to a few of the men around the table and nod solemnly, then break into a reassuring smile. There was nothing aloof about him, and yet it was clear he was a breed apart from everyone in the room.

Elena slid a piece of paper onto Maria's laptop. *Fascinating, isn't he?* it read.

Maria nodded. *Abuela* would be saying he was "quality" while nudging her in the rib with her elbow. The man wasn't her type, but yeah—he was intriguing.

Tejada took his place at the head of the table and Maria looked at the door, waiting for the rest of his staff, but no one else followed. So this was it for legal representation—Snowden, two male secretaries, and her? Emilio Tejada was either trusting or a cheapskate, and from the looks of this place, it wasn't the latter.

Then one of the doors opened again and a muscular, broad-shouldered man with a bald head stepped in. He was built like Uncle Ben but looked a whole lot scarier.

Maria raised her eyebrows at Elena, who scribbled, *Carlos Molina. Head of security for Cat. Everywhere.*

That made sense. Who would mess with him?

As Tejada took his place at the table, the room quieted. He raised his hands in a stand-up gesture and Maria started to get to her feet, but Elena put a hand on her arm and whispered, "Just them."

Twelve men stood and at a nod from Tejada, said in unison, "*Con los antiguos que vinieron antes que nosotros, y para el futuro de nuestra propia creación, nos comprometemos nuestras vidas y nuestras fortunas con el Maestro."*

Before Maria could utter a "Huh?" Elena passed her a note that said simply, *Don't ask.*

Yeah, she was definitely going to have to work on her Spanish. And she was going to ask Snowden if they did that every time they met. It would be nice to be prepared so she didn't make some huge cultural error.

For the first hour, the board conducted regular business, all in English, which Tejada said, with a nod toward Snowden, was for the benefit of his American colleagues. There was a lot of receiving and approving of financial reports, most of which Maria only summarized in her notes. Gump, Snowden and Meir represented Catalonia in all aspects of its business, but its main purpose here was the Belgian deal.

Finally the discussion turned to the pending acquisition and Maria came to attention. As each document was passed to Snowden, he in turn handed a copy back to Maria, and she read it with the keen—and fast—eye she'd learned to use in her nine months at the firm. She then typed the main details on her laptop and e-mailed them to Snowden, who could talk intelligently as questions arose from the Belgian contingency.

"You're good," Elena whispered at one point.

Maria gave an appreciative nod. She hoped Snowden thought so.

The meeting broke at two for what Elena told her would be a two-hour lunch.

"I wish," Maria said. "Is there someplace I can work while maybe you run out and get us something?"

Elena all but rolled her eyes. "I wonder how any of you Americans live to retirement. There's office space for your whole firm, but you'll be the only one in there. *Everybody* goes out for a meal."

"Okay," Maria said, "but only for an hour."

"Louis will drive us."

"We can't walk? That's the best way to see a city."

Elena pulled her aside and lowered her voice. "I guess no one explained this to you."

"Explained what?"

"Louis isn't just your driver. He's your bodyguard while you're here."

"*Body*guard!"

Elena put her finger to her lips, but Maria was having a hard time going with that. "I do *not* need a bodyguard."

"It's not like you have a choice. Everyone who comes here in association with Catalonia is assigned one."

"Well they can give Happy Face Louis to someone else." She brushed Elena's shoulder with her fingertips. "Don't worry about it. I'll talk to Mr. Snowden."

"That won't do you any good," Elena said. "These are *Señor* Tejada's orders."

And he started giving *her* orders when? Maria switched her briefcase to the other hand, plastered on a smile, and said, "So, where are we going for lunch?"

7

When the meeting ended, Tejada retreated to his office. Snowden followed and watched as Tejada eased into the throne-like armchair behind the desk, then took a seat across from him. "You're certain you don't want a drink?" Tejada asked.

Snowden shook his head and twitched his lips in a half-smile. "Your people almost drank me under the table at lunch. I'm good."

"I have never understood that expression."

"That's because you Spaniards never get drunk enough to fall out of the chair—and I chalk that up to the fact that you start feeding your kids Madeira at birth."

"Then I'm sure a cigar is out of the question."

"You're killing me, my friend."

Tejada smiled. "An excellent meeting today, yes?"

"I agree," Snowden said with a nod.

"Anything further we need to discuss about the acquisition?"

"I'll know more after I've had a chance to go over the documents, but for now, no."

"Good. Then I want to turn to the other matter." Tejada glanced at Snowden to read his reaction before continuing. This was the important part. There could be no mistakes. "You'll have the agreement to me by the deadline."

"Yes," Snowden replied. "That's the plan."

"Of course it's the plan," Tejada said calmly. "The question is whether you can carry it out."

"If I have the funds, then yes, absolutely." Snowden shifted in the chair. "My concern is—"

"If your concern is whether there will be enough money, no worries, my friend. Projected reserves will be in place."

"So they aren't now?"

Tejada chuckled, a sound he seldom made unless he was truly amused. "Would you keep that kind of money in an accessible account before you needed it?"

"No, of course not," Snowden admitted.

Tejada folded his hands lazily on his lap. "This kind of concern is what I appreciate about you," he said. "But on a different note, I see that your Congress is approaching another vote on the debt limit."

"Yes." Snowden appreciated the change of subject. "They're at it again," he said with a short laugh. "They're telling us the federal government will run out of money in a few months, which we've heard before."

"I have an opinion about that," Tejada said.

Snowden sat back in the chair. "Love to hear it."

"I think the International Monetary Fund needs to apply pressure to the economies of several different countries that hold large amounts of US debt. Experts at IMF think a gesture from the US Congress that indicates a firm resolve not to continue borrowing would help exert that pressure." This was the matter that interested him most about Snowden's visit.

"So why don't they?"

"The director of IMF doesn't want to approach the US Treasury secretary directly on the matter with an overt request."

"They don't want a paper trail."

"Correct."

Snowden smirked again. "And you know all of this through your nephew."

"He keeps me informed."

Tejada steepled his fingers under his chin and focused his gaze on Snowden, reading his reaction once more. If Lord Abaddon's plan was to work, this piece of the strategy had to go precisely as planned.

"The problem with not raising the debt limit," Snowden said, "is that some of the bills will go unpaid—at least in the short term." He seemed to warm to the subject. "The government can't pay all of its obligations without borrowing, and if the debt isn't raised, something will go without funding."

"In the short term?"

"Yes," Snowden replied. "After the first thirty days the cash flow from revenue would even out and the government could meet its basic obligations, including debt service. But even then, large portions of the budget would be unfunded."

Tejada nodded. "And that would bring chaos to the American economy. Can I bring you into my confidence?"

"Since when do you have to ask?"

Tejada gave it a beat before he continued. "IMF is facing an imbalance in several of its accounts." That wasn't true, of course, but he knew Snowden wouldn't notice—or care. "They look at this as a supply-and-demand problem."

Snowden's forehead wrinkled in a frown. "I don't follow you."

"The price of US debt trades at par because the US keeps producing so much of it."

"Interesting way to look at it."

"That the US might do otherwise and limit the availability of its paper would suggest a limit on supply and most certainly drive up the price, helping the IMF get things back in balance."

"You're looking at a huge risk there," Snowden said. "Doing that will raise doubt about whether the debt will be repaid and drive the price down rather than up, making things worse."

"That is a risk I would be willing to take," Tejada said. "If it were up to me." Tejada could see the tension working in Snowden's neck. He must remember to challenge him to a friendly game of American poker. "Perhaps you should talk to Michael Stafford about this."

"The lobbyist?" Snowden said.

"We like to use him in political matters."

A knock on the door interrupted them. Tejada had sent his administrative assistant home for the day and everyone else had been instructed to stay away. It must be—

"Come in, Molina," he said.

The door opened. "It's not Molina," a female voice said.

A head of loosely curled hair appeared in the doorway.

Tejada stood. "And you are?"

"Maria Winters, *Señor* Tejada," she said. "I'm with Gump, Snowden and Meir."

"I know—"

"Maria," Snowden snapped as he rose from his chair to face her. "What are you doing in here?"

"I just wanted to—"

"Whatever it is, we'll talk about it later."

"I just—"

"It's okay," Tejada said, cutting them off. "What did you need, Ms. Winters?"

"I just wanted you to know that I do not need a bodyguard, so you can call off your *Señor* Louis before I—" She paused to take a breath. "Before I dismiss him myself. I'm sure you would rather do the honors."

Tejada fought the urge to smile. He suspected this was not a young woman one laughed at. Still, he couldn't resist the temptation to play with her a little. He turned to Snowden. "How do you feel about this, Bill?" he said. "Should we turn her loose alone in the city of Barcelona?"

"We can't afford an incident," Snowden replied. "Perhaps it would be better if he—"

Tejada expected her to backpedal but was surprised when she said coldly, "I was told the bodyguard was *Señor* Tejada's idea."

"And so it was," Tejada said. "Most women who visit us here are grateful for the protection." He smiled at her. "But clearly you are not most women."

"I don't need protection," Maria repeated, "so if you'll relieve Louis of his duties I would appreciate it."

"Done," Tejada said.

"Thank you," Maria replied as she backed out the door.

When she was gone, Tejada looked over at Snowden. "What was her name again?" Tejada said.

"You don't want to know," Snowden said as he slumped into his chair.

8

As a psychiatrist, Julia Archer couldn't have been more of a stereotype, at least how Winters pictured one. Dark-rimmed, rectangular glasses. Hair pulled into a severe bun. Sweater set and Aigner loafers. She was the caricature of all therapists he had seen in movies and television shows, and if she asked, "How do you feel about that?" one more time, he would seriously—

Like *that* was going to get him back to work. He chomped at the inside of his mouth and surveyed her across the short space between his chair and hers. At least she didn't have a couch in here.

Archer tapped her pen on the pad that lay in her lap. "Do you realize that we've been at this for two months—"

"Oh, yeah," he said, nodding. "I'm well aware of that."

"—and we haven't made what I would consider any measurable progress?"

"I feel fine."

"I don't." She took off the glasses and parked them on top of her head. Winters could never figure out why she did that. "Jim Rebhorn was right to ask me to take you on. The kind of trauma you underwent can change a person—"

"I was captured," Winters defended, "and our people rescued me—"

"Not before your captors held a knife to your throat and threatened to slash it—"

"But they didn't."

"And yet the nightmares continue." Archer put her glasses back on. "The last thing Jim needs is an agent trying to deal with emotional pain on the job and failing at both."

Winters shifted in the chair. "So you've said."

"And I'll keep saying it. Your return to active duty is subject to my approval and so far, I'm not seeing much effort from you to get it."

He hated throwing her even so much as a crumb, but she was right. He would return to work when she said so. His supervisor, Jim Rebhorn, had made that abundantly clear each time Winters had called him, which was every week since the first "episode." The last time, Rebhorn hadn't answered at all. "I did one thing you suggested," he said.

"And what was that?"

"I took up a hobby. A 'calming hobby.'"

"Skydiving?"

"Cut me some slack here, Doc. I'm not that crazy."

"Then what hobby did you find?"

"I'm researching my genealogy."

She seemed surprised. "You're kidding."

"You don't approve."

"I don't disapprove. I just expected something else. Golf, maybe. Or tennis. Not genealogy. Where did that come from?"

Winters crossed his legs. Now he might be getting somewhere. "My mother believed we're direct descendants of Christopher Columbus."

Archer had a skeptical expression. "Is this a joke?"

"She didn't think so."

"But do you?"

Winters shook his head. "Actually, I'm finding out some pretty interesting stuff. Did you know, for instance—"

"John." Her face was sober.

"What?"

"I told you to find something to soothe your nerves—so you can face the issues you have to confront to get well. Have you had any more episodes?"

"I had another *dream* when I was in Maryland."

"Understandable. Your mother's death was yet another stressor. Was it about the raid?"

"The dream?"

"Yes."

"Yeah." Winters nodded. "It was about the raid."

"How far into it did you get?"

"Not far."

Winters stood, walked to the window, and looked down at the Mission District. It was a peculiar location for a psychiatrist's office. Behind him, Archer waited patiently. "Look," Winters said finally, "I know what happened that day."

"And it wasn't what you wanted to happen."

"It wasn't what *should* have happened. But stuff like that does go down. You move on."

"And that would account for the breakdown you had in your supervisor's office."

"I didn't have a breakdown."

"You shoved everything off the man's desk, kicked his chair across the room, punched a hole in the wall, and broke the window when you threw your gun at it."

Winters turned to face her. "All right. I got upset when they put me on leave."

"I think there was more to it than that."

"Like what?"

"Like the trauma of that raid."

Winters shoved his hands into his pockets. "Have you ever been in a life-and-death situation?"

"No, but you have—more than a few times. It was your job to be in those situations. If we can figure out what happened in here"—Archer put her hand to her chest—"then you'll have a chance."

"To get back to work."

"To get back to yourself."

Winters hated it when she said stuff like that, but once again he held back. Archer was right about one thing. If he didn't work with her, he had no chance at all. "Okay," he said. "What do you want to know?"

"Did you seek counseling after your wife died?"

The air seemed to go out of the room and Winters glared at her. "What happened to my wife has nothing to do with this. Are we clear on that?" His face was tense and the muscles in his jaw flexed. "Don't bring it up again."

Archer rose from her chair. "I think that's enough for today."

For once, he agreed with her.

Outside the building, Winters unlocked his bike from the handicap rail and sped up Nineteenth Street, breathing in the smells of every restaurant he passed. He was several blocks into the ride before he stopped imagining ways to have Archer fired, along with the monologue he would deliver right before he told her where to put her psychological services.

Avoiding pain? Of course he was avoiding pain. Who didn't?

Yes, he was worried about his career. Yes, he wanted to get back to work. Why did she think he kept coming to see her every week? To look at her legs? They weren't *that* great.

Winters erased that last remark. He didn't go there with women. He didn't go anywhere with women—because he'd had the best and lost her.

The shrill sound of a truck's horn snapped him back to the present and he swerved the bike to a halt. His heart slammed in his chest. He had to get a handle on this. His career was all he had. Maria obviously didn't want a relationship with him.

But if getting a handle on it meant talking about Anne . . . that wasn't happening. That wasn't happening at all.

✦ ✦ ✦

The light was already shifting by the time they actually got started. There was the matter of personnel to consider.

"We got enough people?" Winters asked Smith.

"Oakland PD has the area cordoned off, four blocks in every direction. SWAT is ready to join our guys at the front door. An ATF team is waiting for you in back. And the sheriff's office has men patrolling the perimeter just in case."

"Might not be enough," Winters said.

A grin tightened Smith's moustache, but only briefly. "You don't really think we need more."

"I think if we get in there and find out we're shorthanded, it'll be too late to matter."

Smith adjusted the bill of his ball cap. "You want me to get some more guys up here? FBI would be all too glad to dive in on this case. They've been lobbying for it for two months."

"Never mind," Winters said. "I'd rather close this one by myself than ask them for help."

"You sure?"

Winters had almost forgotten Donleavy was there. His previous bravado had faded, and the skin around his mouth had gone pale.

"We're okay," Winters said.

He let his eyes dart to the five Secret Service agents gathered near the curb. Donleavy nodded, although he didn't look at all relieved.

"You carrying?" Winters asked.

Donleavy patted his right hip, and Winters smothered a groan. He could be a little more conspicuous—maybe.

"Okay," Winters said. "Make sure you stay behind us when we go in."

"Right."

"And have that pistol handy."

"Okay."

Winters mentally checked the magazine of his pistol, which he'd already done five times since he'd loaded it. "Let's do it," he said.

Winters and Donleavy led the way up the driveway of the house next door. They paused at the back corner, then darted through the backyard into an alley that ran parallel to Patterson Avenue. Eyes alert, Winters moved cautiously with Donleavy close behind him, and came to a stop behind the house occupied by the Russians.

"This is it," Winters whispered to him.

Donleavy nodded. All color had left his face but his eyes seemed alert and focused. He'd be okay.

Winters started across the backyard. Concrete steps led up to the back door. All he had to do was make his way up and kick in the door.

But his legs were paralyzed. "I can't move!" he shouted to a world gone cold and dark. "Help me! I can't move!"

This time Winters woke to find himself on the floor beside the couch in the living room, clutching at his legs like the crazy person he was now convinced he was becoming. He used the coffee table to pull himself up and knocked his laptop over. The screen lit up.

It was a dream, he told himself. *A dream and nothing but a dream.*

Winters used his sleeve to wipe the sweat from his face and looked at the time on the computer screen. Two o'clock. No sense trying to go back to sleep. Not that he wanted to.

After a moment, Winters pushed himself up from the couch, stumbled to the kitchen, and poured a ginger ale. Glass in hand, he returned to the living room and propped up on a pillow with the laptop resting on his knees. He'd read everything his mom had found, and his research into Christopher Columbus had been interesting but not helpful, genealogically speaking. When he'd fallen asleep he'd been trying to contact a Spanish genealogist he'd found online. College professor. Specialized in connecting people to their Spanish ancestors. Probably a dead end.

Not that he was desperate. This thing had taken hold of him in Mom's attic and hadn't let go since he'd been home. But maybe it was just another thing like the sailing, the flying. Banned from those pursuits until he was cleared by Archer, this filled in the gap. Could just be a matter of time before he let this go too.

And then what?

The old anxiety sizzled under his skin. It was a feeling he couldn't stand. Winters took a long drink from his glass and forced himself to check his e-mail.

One message. From Sophia Conte. The genealogist.

Dear Mr. Winters,

I found your e-mail interesting, if somewhat misinformed. Christopher Columbus made four voyages, not three. And he did not make a fortune as you have supposed. Ferdinand and Isabella promised him 10 percent of everything he found, but once they realized he had discovered something of immense value, they worked to take it from him. He, and his family after him, litigated their claims for several hundred years.

And no, he was not Italian. He was born in Genoa but he lived in Portugal first and then Spain. We lay claim to him.

But don't let your enthusiasm be dampened.

Winters stopped reading to snort out a laugh. "Dampened"?

The problem with studying Columbus is that he left a great deal of false information, probably so no one else would find out about his discoveries. For example, most of the directions in the voyage logs are skewed so his route couldn't be followed.

And she knew that how?

There is much more I could tell you. Do you Skype?

Winters blinked. She wasn't shy, that was for sure. Probably a middle-aged spinster starved for company.

It sounded familiar.

He'd think about it.

9

"You realize, of course, that I'm having to run twice a day to stay ahead of my caloric intake." Maria looked at Elena over the plate of *caracoles* they were sharing. "But it's so worth it."

They were sitting across from each other at Los Caracoles, so named because it was famous for its snails. Elena pushed the plate toward her and tapped its edge. "The last one is for you."

"Let me think about it . . . yes." Maria popped the morsel into her mouth and closed her eyes.

"I have never seen anyone enjoy food as much as you do," Elena said.

"I don't really have time to at home."

Elena's eyes widened. "You work harder there than you're doing here? I can't see how you could. You are a workaholic."

Maria refrained from spattering a laugh. Elena's English was flawless, and rightfully so. She'd been educated in England before attending the University of Pennsylvania. Which made Maria wonder why she was working as a freelance assistant to an attorney who was little more than an assistant herself.

That wasn't quite true, though. For some reason, Snowden had given Maria more responsibility here. In fact, he was seldom around except to give her more files pertaining to the acquisition, and even at that, most of the time he sent them through Elena. At one point he'd even flown back to the States for a couple of days.

"Where have you gone?"

Maria blinked her way back to Elena. "Rabbit trail," she said. "Sorry. Did I miss something?"

"I was saying that I want to take you to Sagrada Família, since you are so into architecture."

"I do like buildings. Well-built ones."

"Then I definitely want to show you this one. It's controversial here, and it's still under construction so . . ."

"So . . . what? I'll need a hard hat?"

Elena didn't answer. Maria started to turn her head to follow Elena's gaze, but Elena stopped her with a hand to Maria's wrist.

"What?" Maria said.

Red blotches appeared on Elena's face and neck. "*Señor* Tejada," she said.

Maria hadn't seen him for more than a week. Not since the day she'd barged into his office. Snowden had given her the *What were you thinking?* lecture, but Louis had been removed from bodyguard duty so she didn't see an issue with running into the man. Elena, on the other hand, looked as if she'd been caught in a crime.

"This is a delightful surprise," Tejada said in his Mediterranean accent.

Maria suspected he didn't actually have a trace of one—that the elongated e's were part of his natural charm.

"I see you are enjoying one of our best restaurants. You saw the stone rotisserie outside?"

"It was hard to miss." Maria smiled at Elena, who was now a study in shades of red. "*Señorita* Soler is seeing to it that I get a taste of the best of everything."

Tejada nodded as if they were having a deep conversation about the meaning of life. "Then she has surely taken you to Botafumeiro."

"Actually not," Maria said. "I understand that's a bit out of my price range."

"Then you must allow me to take you there."

It flowed so naturally from his lips, Maria almost burst out, *Let's do it!* But wait. Was he asking her out? On a date?

She looked at Elena, who was no longer making eye contact. No help there. Not that Maria needed any. She shook her hair back. First of all, she made it her policy not to date people she worked with. And second of all, no. Smooth, wealthy, powerful Spaniard with enough charm to attract any woman he wanted? Not happening.

"Have I offended you, *Señorita* Winters?" His eyes looked genuinely concerned.

"Not at all," she said. "I appreciate the offer. But no worries. Elena is taking good care of me."

If that offended *him,* he showed no sign of it. He looked as if he'd expected that answer to begin with. She'd never encountered a man so unflappable.

All the more reason to turn him down.

Tejada nodded to each of them, wished them a good day, and departed. Maria watched him until he reached the door where Molina was waiting. "Did they have lunch here?" she asked.

"I have no idea," Elena said. "I didn't see him when we came in."

"He's so . . . mysterious."

Elena gave a soft grunt. "There was no mystery about that conversation. He wants to take you out."

"I think he was just being polite."

"No, I think he came in here specifically to ask you to dinner."

Maria pulled in her chin. "You're not serious. Are you saying he followed us?"

"Not necessarily."

"Not *necessarily?*"

The blotches were beginning to bloom on Elena's face again. "All I'm saying is that *Señor* Tejada doesn't waste his time. He might seem polite—he is—but everything he does has a motive."

Maria felt her eyes narrow. "You mean he wants to use me for something?"

"I mean he didn't just stumble in here and ask you to dinner. That's all."

"That's kind of creepy," Maria said.

Elena tilted her head. "'Creepy' is not a word I would use to describe him."

"So . . . if he had asked *you* to dinner, you would have accepted?"

"Completely moot point," Elena said. "I am not in his class. Shall we order our next course?"

"Let's have that wonderful thing with all the mussels in it," Maria said. "And by the way, you have more class than just about any woman I know."

✦ ✦ ✦

Maria was packing her briefcase when Snowden stopped by her office. Elena had offered to take her out to a few clubs, but Maria declined, preferring to continue working in her hotel room. The details of the Belgian acquisition were mind-boggling.

Tell me you don't have another file for me, she wanted to say to him.

Instead she pushed her hair back over her shoulder and smiled. "More work?"

"No. Just thought I'd check in." He lowered himself into the chair opposite the desk in her temporary office, which was twice as large as her permanent one in DC. He sat back and folded his hands as if they were about to have a father-daughter chat.

Maria's antennae went up. Snowden didn't "just check in" and the closest thing he came to paternal was when he handed out the holiday bonus checks.

"I understand you ran into *Señor* Tejada this afternoon," he said.

The antennae rose further. "Word travels fast. He told you I was having the snails?"

"He didn't tell me anything. Molina did."

Maria zipped her briefcase and tried not to look startled. She had never exchanged a word with Tejada's security guy, but now he was passing on information about her as if she were somehow *his* concern?

"Don't get all worked up about it," Snowden said.

"I'm not getting worked up."

"He only mentioned that he saw you—"

"And?"

"And he said you declined a dinner invitation from Mr. Tejada."

"What is this, middle school?" Maria raked a hand through her hair. "Ooh, did Tejada ask Molina to ask you to find out if I like him?"

Snowden's eyebrows ran together. "You have to be careful here, Maria. We can't afford to make a social faux pas."

"'We,' sir?" Maria said. "Don't you mean me?"

Snowden rearranged himself in the chair. "I don't think it would hurt our relationship with Catalonia for you to let *Señor* Tejada show you his favorite restaurant."

Maria had to bite down on her lip to keep from saying, *What am I, a call girl now?* She took in a long breath and stared at the El Greco print on the wall before she said, "If *Señor* Tejada wants to take all of us out to his favorite dining destination, I'm all for that. But the two of us sharing suckling pig by candlelight—I don't think so. Not unless you have something specific related to the acquisition you want me to discuss with him, in which case Elena and I can meet with him in his office."

Snowden looked a little stunned, which irritated her more than anything. She'd worked with him for nine months and he still knew virtually nothing about her as a person.

He sat for a moment longer. She wondered if he was trying to decide what message to give Molina for Tejada. *Pass him a note in the locker room,* she wanted to say.

He left before she was tempted to actually say it.

Winters was concentrating on an article Sophia Conte had e-mailed when his doorbell rang. He peered through the peephole.

Donleavy.

He hesitated. They'd talked on the phone a few times after the raid. Gone for coffee once. They hadn't clicked like they used to, and he toyed now with the idea of not answering.

"Winters? Hey, buddy, I was in the neighborhood—"

Oh, for Pete's sake.

Winters pulled the door open. "Don't quit your day job, Donleavy," he said to his startled face. "That's the worst line since 'Come here often?'"

"What?" Donleavy said.

Winters let him in. "How could you possibly just be in the neighborhood? You live at the other end of town."

Donleavy's shaved head turned red. "Okay, you found me out." He shrugged. "I just miss you, man."

Winters nodded. "You want coffee?"

"Is it made?"

"It's always made. Come on in."

Winters went to the kitchen and turned on the Keurig. Donleavy followed him and parked himself at the table where Winters had been working with his laptop. "What's all this?"

"Just some work I'm doing to pass the time."

Donleavy turned a book on its side to check the cover. "You taking a course or something?"

"Something like that. You still take half cream, half coffee?"

"Yeah."

"I don't know why you even bother."

Winters opened the refrigerator and pulled out the half-and-half. When he closed it, Donleavy was looking at him, eyes drooping at the corners.

"What?" Winters said.

"I don't know. We used to talk, that's all." Donleavy spread a long-fingered hand over the piles of papers and books on the table. "You're obviously heavy into something here."

Winters sighed and put a full mug in front of him. "It's some genealogical stuff I'm doing. Laugh and I'll slug you."

"What am I going to laugh at?"

Winters put his own lukewarm cup in the microwave and, leaning on the chair opposite Donleavy, told him what he knew so far. As he should have expected, Donleavy was far from incredulous. He was a portrait of fascination. Once a geek, always a geek.

"So, no link to your family yet," he said.

Winters shook his head. "But the stuff I'm learning about Columbus is pretty interesting. Not at all what they taught us in school."

"Nothing they taught us in school was interesting."

"Or necessarily true. You know the whole thing about the *Niña*, the *Pinta*, and the *Santa Maria*?"

"The three ships the king and queen gave him."

"They only gave him two. He had to provide the third one himself. Established shippers didn't want him to take the trip and made it as hard for him as possible. They were actually afraid he'd find a quicker route to Asia."

"I thought they *wanted* a quicker route. That doesn't make sense." Donleavy wiggled his eyebrows. He loved things that didn't make sense.

"They controlled the known routes," Winters said, "which gave them a monopoly on Eastern trade. Since they refused to help, Columbus turned to another group of guys." He stood and reached for the microwave. "You really interested in this?"

"Do I look bored to you?"

Winters knew what bored looked like on Donleavy. And this wasn't it. He sat down and continued, glancing at the legal pad on the table. "Luis de Santángel, Gabriel Sanchez, and Don Isaac Abrabanel gave him an interest-free loan of seventeen thousand ducats. Close to two million dollars in today's money."

"Impressive." Donleavy leafed through one of the books. "You get all that info out of here?"

"No. I've been e-mailing a professor. Genealogist type in Barcelona."

"He an expert?"

"She."

"Ahhhhh."

Winters shook his head at the grin in Donleavy's eyes. "There's no 'ahhh.' She's a resource. I'm Skyping with her tonight."

"Good to see you getting out."

"Shut up, Donleavy."

Winters let him take a few more sips before he leaned across the table. "Okay, so now you want to tell me what you're really doing here?"

The bald head went crimson again. "What makes you think—"

"I haven't totally lost my touch," Winters said. "You never leave your lab in the middle of a workday. You never come over here unless I invite you. And you might be a geek, but nobody cares this much about Christopher Columbus except me and the professor. So what's going on?"

Donleavy ran his hand across the back of his head. "Rebhorn wanted me to talk to you. Not that I didn't want to see you, man, because—"

"Talk to me about what?" Winters knew his tone was testy but right then he didn't much care.

"It's about your brother," Donleavy said.

Not what he expected. At all. "What about him?"

"He's been calling the office, bugging anybody he can get to."

"About re-interviewing."

Donleavy nodded. "Everybody's been told not to take his calls. *He's* been told not to *make* any more calls, but his number comes up on an average of twelve times a day."

Winters was sure he'd calculated it.

"Rebhorn wants you to tell him to back off," Donleavy said. "Otherwise they're going to issue a restraining order against him."

"I'll talk to him, see what I can do." Winters zoned his eyes in on Donleavy's. "Why didn't Rebhorn call me himself?"

Donleavy shrugged. "He knows we're friends—"

"Don't play that with me, buddy. Why didn't he call me?"

"You really going to make me answer that question?"

Winters stood and looked away. "He thinks I'll blow up at him.

He told Archer I had an 'emotional breakdown.' That's what he's afraid of."

"He didn't say."

"It's okay. I know." Winters went back to the table. "What about you? Do you think I'm crazy?"

"No! Nobody thinks you're crazy, man."

"What word is he using then?"

Donleavy stared at his hands.

Winters knew he'd pushed him far enough. "Look, I appreciate you coming by, seriously. I'll talk to Ben, get him to leave everybody alone." He stood up straight. "Do me a favor, will you?"

"Sure, buddy."

"Tell Rebhorn I'm not unstable. I think that's probably the word he's using."

"Sure," Donleavy said. But he didn't meet Winters' eyes.

✦ ✦ ✦

Winters wasn't in the mood to Skype with Sophia Conte at 2 a.m. It wasn't that he'd rather be asleep—he wasn't doing much of that anyway. But after Donleavy's visit, it was hard to care about Columbus or his ancestry or anything except the rumors being passed around about him at the office. Winters was writing an e-mail to Conte to cancel their appointment when Skype signaled an incoming video call. Okay, so he would keep it short.

When her face sprang into view, Winters was taken by surprise. As he had expected, her hair was gathered into a loose bun, but it was dark and tending toward frizzy, which created a soft halo around her face. No glasses pinched her nose. Her dark, deep eyes were bright with intelligence. And she couldn't have been more than thirty-five.

"Mr. Winters," she said. "You're younger than I expected."

The words *So are you* pushed against his lips but he didn't let them go. You didn't say that to a woman. You also didn't say, *You're better-looking than I imagined.*

She was obviously waiting for him to say *something.* Her face was turned slightly to the left, as if she was leaning in to hear better.

"Nice to meet you," he said. "John Winters."

"Yes," she said. Her English was very good, laced with a soft accent. "This is the time we arranged, no?"

"Yes. Yes, it's perfect."

"Good. I thought I had caught you off guard."

Actually she had, and he was having a hard time getting back on track. "Thanks for meeting with me," he said finally. "I know you must be busy."

"I always find time for the things I want to do. Shall we get started?"

All business. He could use that right now.

"Before we begin," she said, as if she were opening a class in Columbus 101, "I would like to recommend a book to you."

Winters sniffed at the stack already on the table. "I'm up to my— uh, my earlobes in books."

"You may not have come across this one—the *Book of Prophecies?*"

"Whose prophecies?"

She gave him a smile. "Those of *Señor* Columbus."

"About the New World?"

"No. About the *end* of the world. These were linked closely to the book of Revelation, and he was convinced the end would come by 1650."

Okay, she was sounding more "spiritual" than his mother.

"You're familiar with the book of Revelation, Mr. Winters? From the Bible."

Yeah, he'd studied it in Sunday school. Eons ago. "'Familiar' might be too strong a word," he said, "but I know the basics."

"*Señor* Columbus writes about the things he felt would have to happen before the world could end, or more specifically, before Christ could return." She held up a graceful finger. "For instance, he believed that the Garden of Eden had to be found again."

"So, he thought the New World was Eden?"

"Perhaps. Another example, he believed that there had to be one last crusade to recapture the Holy Land. There is conjecture among scholars that one of the reasons for his first voyage was to find enough gold to finance that crusade."

"Any proof of that?" Winters asked.

"No. I find it interesting only because his willingness to engage in creative speculation helps us to see how our current culture influences our view of prophecy. We still struggle with the idea of one world leader. Columbus thought there must be someone to fight for the freedom of Jerusalem, which was one of the conditions he saw for Christ's return. He thought King Ferdinand and Queen Isabella might be such leaders." She smiled again. "He believed we were to prepare the world for battle with the Antichrist—actually he believed the Antichrist to be a group of people, though *Señor* Columbus never said who that group was. He was reluctant to speak about it openly."

Winters tried not to squirm. Sophia must have sensed that because she lightened her voice and said, "But we do know that *Señor* Columbus was passionate in his opinion that the world was about to end, and he was not alone in that belief. Several noted theologians of the day supported him. They were convinced the world would last a total of seven thousand years, counting from the creation of Adam through the books of the Bible to the birth of Christ and calculated that time to be 5,343 years."

"Ah," Winters said. "So he added the fifteen hundred years up to the time he lived and expected the world to end around 1656." Donleavy would be impressed, although Winters didn't know why he wanted this woman to be.

"*Sí*. Yes." Sophia gave the almost-imperceptible smile again. "As we know, of course, he died before that. And the world did not end."

"Seems to happen a lot with these prophecies," Winters said. "So, are we saying he was nuts?"

"I am sorry." Her eyes laughed. "I am not familiar with that expression."

"Was he crazy?" Winters asked.

"There is a long line of scholars who think he was. I prefer to think of him as zealous. Completely—how do you say it—sold out to the mission he had undertaken. Not unlike you, Mr. Winters."

"Crazy?" he said. "Or sold out?"

Her eyes laughed once more, and she folded her hands under her chin. "That is as far as it goes—the prophecies and the belief that they would come true. You can read more about this in the *Book of Prophecies*. I thought you might find that interesting. However—"

"I don't like howevers," Winters said.

"I understand. Speculating about this area of inquiry is a nice mental exercise, but it brings us no closer to finding the next generation of your family."

"What does?"

Sophia shuffled through papers in front of her and looked back into the camera. "I may be able to show you an established genealogy of Columbus that runs down to within a few generations of your grandfather."

Winters came back to life. "You can?"

"Yes, but I must take a few steps back first."

"Okay," he said, nodding.

"I have looked at the immigration records you sent me. Officials often listed the names of immigrants incorrectly. Most of them could not read any language other than English. When your grandfather gave his name and hometown, the immigration officials, it seems, could understand only part of what he said—in this case, the name of the town. And because that came last, they wrote it down as his last name."

"Is that good or bad?"

"Neither. It simply means your grandfather was thereafter known as Esteban Torme, instead of Esteban from Torme, Spain." She glanced down at a paper. "Actually, it says Esteban Torme from Huelva, Spain, which was the town they sailed from, not the town they lived in." She smiled, again in the smallest way. "You will like this, though."

"Why is that?"

"Huelva is the same place *Señor* Columbus sailed from on his first voyage."

"Sounds like a lot of people sailed from there," Winters said. He was strangely disappointed.

"Yes," Sophia said. "However—and you may appreciate *this* 'however'—that means the reason I have been unable to trace the name Torme to the Columbus line may be because that was not their real last name."

Winters nodded. "So how do we find out what it was?"

"It may be difficult, but knowing where they were originally from is helpful. Alba de Tormes is a famous place in Spain and a link like this, if it proves correct, could make it possible to connect your family to a known genealogy of *Señor* Christopher Columbus."

"Could," Winters said.

"Yes. We have only to connect your Esteban Torme to the third duke of Liria, Jacobo-Franscisco Eduardo Fitz-James Stuart y Colón."

"Say again?"

"And . . . you can only do that here in Spain."

Winters sat back in his chair. Until now Sophia seemed like a woman as passionate about her obsession as Donleavy was about his. At this point, though, he smelled a lure to spend money.

She was waiting, patiently it seemed. Winters decided to tread lightly. "Why is that?" he asked. "Why can I only do it from there?"

Sophia turned her head to listen as she'd done before. "We must find the ship's original manifest. The one created on this side of the voyage. It should have their names listed correctly. We know three people traveled together—your Esteban, Magdalena, and Antonio—and that makes it easier."

"I can't do that online?"

She shook her head. "I have already checked. The online sites do not have that information and if they did, we cannot trust that they are reliable."

"Why?" He knew he was pressing, but as intrigued as he was becoming, he couldn't let that sway him from knowing whether this was on the up and up.

"The entries will be handwritten," she said. "Someone would have to read them, translate them, enter the information on the website. Too many opportunities for error. Far better to see the actual documents."

"So you're saying I have to come to Barcelona." Winters ran his hand over his face. "Don't take this the wrong way, Ms. Conte, but why can't I pay you to do it and send the results to me?"

"You can," she said.

"However . . ."

"I am not certain I could be as effective as you, Mr. Winters."

"I don't follow."

The faint smile reappeared. "Because people don't say no to a man like you."

Winters looked for a trace of a tease, but there was none. She was waiting again, and he had the feeling she'd wait half the night for a response.

"I'll give it some thought," he said.

"And I will give it some prayer," she said. "Good night, Mr. Winters."

"Good night, Ms. Conte," he said.

But she was already gone.

11

"Is it customary for *Señor* Tejada to hold business meetings in his home?" Maria asked.

Elena looked at her from across the seat in the limousine. "I've never known him to do it, but then I don't know everything about the way he works. No one does."

"And you're sure Snowden is going to be here with his mi—his two guys."

"I don't know that either."

"What good are you then?"

When Elena didn't respond with the usual laugh behind her hand, Maria leaned forward.

"That was a joke."

"I know."

"Then why the stressed face? What aren't you telling me?"

Elena leaned her head back against the leather seat. "If I knew anything I'd tell you. That's why I'm stressing. I don't like not having the information you need."

"I don't need information. I have that in here." She tapped the red briefcase at her side. "I'd just like to know what I'm walking into so I don't make another social 'faux pas.'"

Elena did laugh then. "Just about everything you do is a social faux pas, Maria. I haven't been able to teach you anything."

"I beg to differ. You've taught me how to eat barbecued leeks. And that seafood with its head still on—"

"I mean something that doesn't have to do with food."

Maria felt a sudden—and unfamiliar—shyness. "You've taught me that another woman can be trusted."

"I'm sorry?"

"Most of my friends are guys. Okay, both of my *real* friends are guys, and one of them is a priest. I haven't had a girl friend since middle school." She smiled at Elena. "Until now."

Elena ducked her head and turned to look out the window.

Maria decided to give her a minute and gazed out the opposite window. They'd left the city proper and were now rounding a long, sweeping curve. A three-story mansion came into view, its sandstone-colored stucco bright in the sun. It was capped with the kind of rich tile roof Maria had come to love about Spanish architecture. As they drew nearer, she saw that a second-floor balcony roof formed a patio for the top floor. Perched on the side of the mountain and bathed in light, the house seemed to tower over the region.

"Wow," she said.

"Yes," Elena responded.

"Can't you imagine *Señor* Tejada standing on that balcony like the lord of the manor?"

"No," Elena said, voice low. "I see him standing right there ready to open the car door for you."

The limo rolled to a stop, and Maria grabbed her hair with one hand and her briefcase with the other. Tejada opened the door, leaned down, and nodded. "Welcome to *mi casa*, Ms. Winters," he said.

If he said, *Mi casa es su casa*, she wasn't getting out of the car.

Since he didn't, Maria slid across the seat and extricated herself without accepting the hand he offered her. He had the grace to offer the same hand to Elena, who took it like the mistress of protocol she was.

Tejada seemed far less imperious in his own home than he was on the Catalonia campus. Although he ran the meeting with his usual businesslike crispness in an airy, sunny room that screamed good taste, it was over in half the time allotted and he was offering all of them drinks—Snowden and his minions, the two gentlemen from Belgium Continental, plus Elena and Maria. Maria opted for mineral water and turned to follow the group out to a portico for appetizers. Tejada touched her lightly on the elbow and said, "I would like to show you my home."

Maria glanced at the rest of the party but Tejada said, "They have all toured the house before."

Snowden nodded at her. Maria narrowed her eyes at him but she could see there was no getting out of this. She considered summoning Elena to go with them, but that would seem rude, even to her. "Lead on," she said.

Tejada guided her down a central hallway and into a large, high-ceilinged room with a panoramic view of the city. The lights of Barcelona were beginning to wink in the distance as the sun's descent purpled the sky. "I never tire of it," he said gesturing to the vista.

"I wouldn't either," Maria replied.

"You love my city, then?"

"Do you own it, too, *Señor* Tejada?"

As soon as she said it, she could imagine Snowden snarling at her, but Tejada's dark eyes sparkled.

"Much of it," he said. "The rest . . . no one can possess. It is for all of us."

"All of it is lovely," Maria said. She nodded toward a painting on the opposite wall. "That's a Picasso."

Tejada followed her to it. "*The Old Guitarist*. Quite different from his cubist paintings."

Maria put her hands behind her back to keep herself from touching it. "He had a broader range than most people realize."

"You are familiar with his work?"

Maria nodded, eyes still on the emaciated face of the old man as it bent to his music. "I grew up in New York City. We spent many a Saturday at the Met."

"The Metropolitan Museum." Tejada smiled. "I know it well. Several of the paintings I own are on loan there."

Maria searched his face for signs of arrogance, but there were none. Pleased, yes, but not proud. Either he was a superb actor, or she'd figured him wrong.

"I see you appreciate fine art," he said. "Perhaps you will enjoy these."

They moved through a doorway and into another, smaller hallway, although *smaller* was a relative term. It was wider than her apartment in DC and lined with portraits similar to those she had observed in Catalonia's boardroom. Each was heavily, yet tastefully framed and with museum-quality lighting. The first was the same *conquistador* she'd seen that first day in the boardroom.

"You like this fellow?" Tejada said.

"Who is he?"

"Sebastian e Colon. One of my ancestors."

Of course.

"His name is much longer but few of us remember it."

Maria doubted he had forgotten. "You're interested in history," she said instead.

"The parts that matter to me. Very much so. You?"

"Probably much the same way. My father was the history major."

"Yes?"

"When it comes to ancestors, though, that was my grandmother. She believed we are direct descendants of Christopher Columbus."

"Do you share that belief?"

"Not at all."

"Then I'm free to say this." His dark eyes twinkled again. "Every American who visits the Iberian Peninsula claims to be a relative of Columbus."

Maria wished she hadn't shared that. His response seemed like a slap at *Abuela*. It was time to return to the group anyway, but before she could turn in that direction Tejada was softly nudging her elbow yet again.

"And what do you know of the history of Catalonia Financial?"

She resisted the urge to say, *How much time ya got?*

"I know the corporation was formed in 1922," she said.

"Ah, but we go back much further than that." Tejada nodded at the other portraits on the walls. "Catalonia has been many different things over the years—an importer, a shipping company, an investment vehicle, even a religious institution."

Maria wondered if that accounted for the vow the board members had repeated at the beginning of their meeting. Before she could ask, Tejada continued. "It all began in 1382 as a group of Barcelona businessmen who simply wished to pool their resources for mutual benefit. We strive to maintain that attitude."

"Mutual benefit." She arched her left eyebrow.

"But then you wouldn't need to know all of this, would you?" he said. "You represent the corporation, and anything that transpired before the date it was formed would be beyond any applicable statute of limitations. Come then, meet some more of my elders."

Maria allowed him to steer her along as he talked, but her mind was still back on "statute of limitations." Why would he use that term? Were they into some shady dealings way back then?

She resisted the urge to shrug. What corporation wasn't into something questionable even now?

They'd fast-forwarded in history from portraits to a series of photographs, most of them circa nineteenth century. "These are our past directors," Tejada said. "The photos go back as far as 1860."

"They seem like a dignified group," Maria said. Actually people in those old photographs always did with their stiff postures and stern expressions. As a kid she'd often wondered when smiling was invented.

"They were quite a group," Tejada agreed. "But just as with our directors today, they were not famous men. At the time, the men you see here were among the wealthiest in Europe. Unlike the Rothschild bankers or your own American industrialists of the same period, not one of these men was known to the public."

"That kind of anonymity would be impossible today," Maria said.

He stopped at the end of the hall, eyes shining down at her. "You think so?"

"The Internet makes everyone visible."

"Then tell me. How many pictures of our current directors have you found?"

Maria studied the wall.

"You won't find them here," Tejada said. "Did you see their pictures before you left Washington?"

"No," Maria said. "I didn't." She'd never been able to find any on the Catalonia Financial website either.

Tejada bent his head closer to hers. "That is because no such photographs exist."

Maria didn't have a chance to ask why. Molina suddenly appeared in the hallway ahead of them. Was there a secret door? "Dinner can be served at any time," he said. His eyes never reached Maria but she felt the cold hostility that always chilled her when they occupied the same acre.

"We cannot be late for that, can we?" Tejada said. "We know how much Ms. Winters enjoys a good meal." And with another light touch to her elbow he ushered her to the dining room.

✦ ✦ ✦

These days never seemed to end, Tejada thought as he stood watching the two limousines crawl down the road toward the city. He would prefer to close this one here on the balcony with a cigar and a glass of Tempranillo, taking in the May air, rather than meeting with his nephew in the study. Anytime he was required to be with Philippe Prevost he felt as though he was being deprived of oxygen. He felt Molina in the doorway behind him.

"He is here?" Tejada said.

"He is."

Tejada sighed.

"I can put him off," Molina offered.

"No. This needs to be done."

Tejada waited until he heard Molina show Prevost into the study before he went inside. Prevost was already pacing. "Sit," Tejada said.

"I've been sitting all day."

Tejada sat in the chair behind his desk and stared at him. Finally, Prevost perched on the edge of one of the wing chairs.

"Sherry?" Tejada asked.

"You know I don't drink."

"Perhaps you should start," Tejada said. "It might improve your disposition."

Prevost nodded at the glass in Tejada's hand. "It would take something stronger than that."

Tejada drew a long breath in through his nostrils. Prevost's neuroses tried his patience. He might need something stronger himself before this meeting was over. "So," Tejada said. "Where are we?"

"We had another round of discussions. I think Germany is interested. France and Great Britain will agree if Germany does."

"And the Russians?"

Prevost stroked the pencil-thin moustache above his thin upper lip. "Russia remains reluctant."

"And the Chinese?"

"Showing interest, but so far noncommittal."

Tejada set his glass on the desktop. "Why only interested?"

"They still remember the hit they took in 2008 when the Americans nearly ruined the world's financial system."

"As well they should," Tejada conceded, "but if we had switched from dollar-denominated transactions before all that happened, they would have saved a great deal of value. Right now, the entire system— every nation on earth—is at the beck and call of the Americans."

"Yeah, well," Prevost sighed. "The Russians aren't our only problem."

"You're referring to the Chinese?"

"Yes."

"They should have led the fight to move us away from the dollar."

"They don't like the situation any more than we do, Emilio. But they know that commerce with the US is still a good deal for them. They have acquired a lot of technology through their joint ventures— a *lot* of technology—and they've been able to use it to push their domestic economy forward far faster than they could have developed it on their own."

Tejada nodded. "It would have been impossible for them without their US trade."

"Exactly." Prevost slid from the arm of the chair to the seat. "Which is a huge obstacle for us."

"We have no choice but to find a way around it," Tejada said, refusing to budge.

"Then what would you have me do? This right here," Prevost said, gesturing with both hands. "The effect of the US economy on their domestic economy is why they have not sold out to this idea of yours."

"Of mine?" Tejada arched an eyebrow.

Prevost's face tightened. "You know what I mean."

"Very well," Tejada said, "they are unsettled by the proposition of moving away from dependence on US demand. I see that. But their market is maturing. Convince them that they could sustain eight percent growth from their own domestic consumption."

"How do you get to that?"

"I wish you knew." Tejada got up, walked around his desk, and leaned against the edge of it, looking down at Prevost. "You are the director of the IMF, Philippe. It is your business to know about their investments in . . . South America, Africa—"

"I do know." Prevost's voice shook. "Africa is the last cheap labor pool large enough to replicate the kind of success China enjoyed when US manufacturing shifted to Asia. This is what I am trying to tell you. The Chinese think they will get the same boost when their manufacturing moves to Africa as the US got when it sent manufacturing to China."

"They want to do with Africa as the Americans did with them."

"Yes. Joint ventures with domestic companies. Transfer technology."

Prevost spread his hands. "They want to assume control of the world's economy. They want to take America's place."

Tejada stood. "And this is what I am trying to tell *you*, Philippe. That is the very reason you have to get them on board. *Now.* Before they move too far forward in their economic development and it becomes impossible for me to—" He stopped short, reached behind him, and retrieved his glass. "You know your next step."

Prevost rested his hands in his lap and closed his eyes. "Beijing," he groaned.

"Yes."

"They will want to know how the plan will affect their holdings of US debt."

"Tell them it won't at first."

"Still, they'll question it. You have no idea how these people can—"

"All right." Tejada could bear no more of the whining. "Tell them that Catalonia Financial will guarantee their losses."

Prevost's eyes popped open. "You have the board's approval for this?"

"I don't need it," Tejada replied.

Prevost sat up straight. "That's a lot to guarantee. Are you sure you can handle a pledge like that? The Chinese will expect you to be good for it."

"And you don't think I can be?" Tejada went to the wet bar and refilled his glass. "Do I need to remind you that Catalonia owns or controls a significant portion of the world's mineral assets?"

"No, you don't."

"Or that we have gold and diamond mines in South Africa and Indonesia and Australia? That our oil and gas reserves are the most extensive of any entity on the planet?"

"You do not need to remind me."

Tejada turned to him, refreshed drink in hand, and spoke softly. "Then why are you questioning me? We can cover any loss the Chinese might incur. All right, Philippe?"

"They hold one-point-two-trillion dollars in US debt."

"We will not have to pay the full amount. Even if there is a major correction in the market, US debt will not become worthless." He gave Prevost a nod. "Just worth less. You see?"

Finally Prevost seemed to. His eyes took on the intelligent gleam that had gotten him his position. "Catalonia will only have to cover the loss, the difference in value, not the face amount."

"Precisely."

"They will be intrigued by this. But they will not act on it until something forces their hand, and in the meantime they will bleed Catalonia for as much as they can get."

"I have something in mind that will motivate them."

"And that is?"

Tejada closed his eyes. "We each have our part of the plan to carry out, do we not? There is a reason why the left hand does not know what the right hand is doing."

He didn't add that only he had control over both hands. He had promised Abaddon he would not reveal that.

"Simply present the plan to Beijing," he said. "And get them to agree. I will take care of motivating them to act quickly." He pressed his hand on Prevost's shoulder. "*Nos comprometemos nuestras vidas y nuestras fortunas con el maestro.*"

12

Maria pushed her chair back from the desk and looked across the office at Elena, who sat at the table collating the report for that afternoon's meeting. "Would you take a look at this? I don't think I'm reading it right."

"That would be a first," Elena said.

"I'm serious. Something's weird here. Grab a chair."

Elena joined her at the desk. "What's up?"

"I'm reading over these notes I typed up for Snowden. Now that I'm looking at it, this doesn't make sense."

"Snowden actually took notes?" Elena pretended shock. "Wait— did I say that?"

"You did. I'm a bad influence on you. Read this sentence out loud, starting after, 'The matter can be concluded without reservations.'"

"Let me get the context first."

Maria watched Elena's eyes scan the paragraph she'd just written. *We are satisfied with the progress of the acquisition thus far. The matter can be concluded without reservations . . .*

"You want me to read the rest out loud?"

"Yes. I need to hear it."

"'The matter can be concluded without reservations and expectations can be met. An agreement will be in the hands of Catalonia

Financial by the anticipated date, at the price agreed upon, as long as the projected reserves hold up. Tejada will make certain that they do.'"

Maria watched Elena's eyes. As they scanned the paragraph again, her face blotched—the now-familiar signal that she was anxious.

"You see it, too," Maria said.

"What are *you* seeing?"

"That either Snowden wrote this after a two-Madeira lunch or something . . . not quite right is going on."

"You're talking about this." Elena pointed to the sentence *Tejada will make certain that they do.*

"Yeah. How does he have any control over the projected reserves? They're projected. As in, not there yet."

"It has to be a mistake," Elena said. "*Señor* Tejada has an impeccable reputation. I can't imagine he'd try to deceive a colleague . . . make him think there is real money on the books when it does not exist."

"So you think this was a mistake on Snowden's part?"

Elena shrugged, something Maria had never seen her do. "What's this?" Maria said, imitating her.

"I can't really say, Maria. You know Mr. Snowden better than I do."

"I don't know him *that* well. He plays it pretty close to the vest." She looked at Elena and waited for her to meet her gaze. "It's only a mistake if he didn't mean to put it in here. Right?"

"There's one other possibility. What if you read his original notes wrong?"

Maria shook her head. "I've been doing almost nothing *but* reading the man's hen-scratchings for the last nine months."

"It's worth looking again. Where's the original?"

"You have it. I gave it to you to file."

"Perfect. I'll go pull it. The files are in the other office."

"Thanks," Maria said. "And Elena?"

"Yeah."

"This thing is just between us for now."

"What thing?" Elena said. "Relax. We'll get it figured it out."

Maria hoped so. Because time could be running out on this deal. And on her job.

✦ ✦ ✦

Abaddon was in a black mood when Tejada arrived in El Masnou two days after his meeting with Prevost. He'd seen his lord in that state before, though few others had. Abaddon made it a point not to speak with anyone when the darkness descended within. At least, not with anyone other than Tejada.

This was one circumstance in which Tejada was not grateful for his closeness to the man. He would prefer to avoid the unpredictable state of mind that turned the very air to lead. Tejada could hardly breathe when he entered Abaddon's private chamber and squinted his way to the chair by the window where Lord Abaddon sat. The candle on the small wooden table was the only light except for the weak sunlight that showed through the cracks around the window frame.

"You have made me wait," the Master said, his voice gravelly and hoarse.

Tejada didn't say he'd come as soon as he'd been summoned. Abaddon brooked no defense even in the best of moods. Instead, he kissed Abaddon's hand and lowered himself obediently onto a cushion near the chair. He didn't have to see Abaddon's face to know he was scowling.

"You have reached an impasse with one of our players."

"As I explained," Tejada replied, "it is only a temporary issue. Prevost is in Beijing as we speak."

"I suppose it will not be a waste of time to continue as you are. The heart of a man is at times unpredictable."

"You're not referring only to the Chinese."

"I am referring to the Americans and their lunatic debates."

"I have placed Snowden on that," Tejada said. "I have no reason to believe he will fail."

"I don't trust him."

"He does have his limitations, but—"

"He has brought you a temptation."

"I don't understand."

"A woman."

A *woman?* Tejada was glad the old man couldn't see his face clearly. He didn't like to be completely defenseless in his presence, but what was he talking about?

"Why does Snowden bring an associate to close the deal with the Belgians?"

"It is a large transaction."

Abaddon swept that away with a stiff hand. "Snowden could handle it himself with a few clerks. Is she beautiful, Emilio?"

"She has her good qualities."

"Full of feminine wiles?"

"Hardly. Quite the opposite."

"Smart."

"She is that, yes."

"Then watch yourself, Emilio."

Tejada nodded.

"We are close to our goal. You *must* maintain focus!"

"You have my word, Lord Abaddon," Tejada said quickly.

"See that I do! Do not fail me! You cannot fail *us!*"

Even in the dark, Tejada saw the angry flash in his eyes. And not anger only. Something else. Something far more sinister. Something Tejada would do all in his power to avoid.

13

Julia Archer pushed her glasses farther down her nose and looked at Winters over the top of the black frames. "Please tell me you did not just say you're going to Barcelona."

"Is that a problem?" he asked.

"Not *a* problem, John. A *number* of problems, starting with the fact that you'll miss . . . how many meetings with me?"

"I don't know how many. I bought a one-way ticket. I have no idea how long this is going to take."

Archer dropped her pen onto the pad that rested in her lap and took off her glasses. He'd known she wasn't going to applaud the decision, but he didn't expect her to be this unsettled by it.

"Let me be clear about this," she said. "You haven't made a lot of forward progress, but this move is going to take you backward."

"How do you figure that?"

"Because you aren't facing your demons. You're running away from them. Emotionally before. Now physically with this trip."

Winters shook his head. "Look, this is the first thing I've been motivated to do. I'm starting to feel like my old self again."

Archer raised an eyebrow. "Which self?"

Here they went with the psycho-talk. Winters just looked at her.

Archer put the glasses back on and studied the pad. When she looked at him again, her gaze was searching. Winters felt as if he were being frisked.

"All right, here's the deal," she said finally. "If you take this trip—against my best advice—I'm going to have to report to Rebhorn that I've given this my best shot, you have been noncompliant, and I have to recommend that you not be reinstated."

Winters opened his mouth but Archer put up a finger to stop him. "Unless in this session right now you tell me exactly what happened in that raid, as you remember it."

The tightening of Winters' jaw sent piercing pain into his ears. "You're looking for some connection to my *deeper* self?"

"That's for us to discover as we talk."

"This reeks of blackmail. You know that, don't you?"

Winters' voice was low, almost menacing. Archer gave him a wry smile.

"Whatever it takes, John."

Sweat already dampened his palms and he rubbed them nervously against the arms of the chair.

"I'm not saying it's going to be easy," she said. "But that's the only way I'll agree to keep quiet about the trip."

Winters knew he could wait her out for the remainder of the session, but where was that going to get him? Not to Barcelona. And not back to his job. Not back to his identity.

He examined his knuckles. Archer still waited.

"All right," he said at last. "Where do you want me to start?"

There was no triumphant gleam in her eye. She simply adjusted her glasses and said, "In the last dream, you were about to kick down the door. Pick it up from there."

Winters fixed his gaze on a spot just above Archer's head, at the lower left corner of her framed certification. "I hesitated at the bottom of the steps to make sure Jamison and Stevens were in position at the rear of the house."

"They were other agents."

"Right. I motioned for Donleavy—computer forensics—to go to the corner of the house. We'd gone through it all before but he's not a field agent, so I pretty much had to hold his hand."

"Did that make you nervous?"

Winters shifted his gaze to meet hers. "Can we just get through this without you asking me how I felt?"

"It's what I do," Archer said. A trace of amusement crossed her face. "Go on."

"Donleavy ducked out of sight." Winters closed his eyes. He could see it as if it were happening right then. He had turned in a quick, forceful motion. As his body pivoted, his right foot came around in a sweeping arc, striking the door near the frame. It flew open with a sharp *crack* and Winters charged inside. He sensed Jamison and Stevens behind him.

If all went as planned, a team would hit the front door at the same time, and agents would pour into the living room.

Winters felt a flicker of anxiety, then he heard the door crash open and the house fill with commands . . .

Archer tilted her head. "And?"

"Three Russians were captured immediately. Two more tried to flee through the kitchen and ran straight into me and my team. Jamison took one down—Stevens was on the other one. We had the element of surprise on our side. And these were computer geeks, coming up against guys you don't want to mess with." Winters turned his gaze to Archer again. "You want the details?"

"Keep going. What were you doing while they caught the two guys?"

Winters swallowed hard. "Right about then I heard something under the floor."

"What kind of something?"

"Movement that shouldn't have been there. When I first hit the kitchen I'd noticed a door near the stove. I opened it with my left hand—my gun was in my right. There was a staircase going into the basement. The two Russians we'd just taken down were handcuffed to a radiator so I told Jamison and Stevens to follow me down."

"So you were basically in charge of this mission," Archer observed.

"I had point on it, yeah." He knew he'd told her that before. She was leading him somewhere.

"What happened when you got down there? Into the basement."

"There was a furnace at the bottom of the stairs. That gave us some cover, which was good because a gunman fired from the opposite corner. He got Stevens in the shoulder, just below the shoulder blade." Winters indicated with his hand. "He slid down against the wall."

Blood had splattered everywhere but he spared Archer that detail. He'd like to spare himself too.

"What did you do?" Archer asked.

"I was still behind the furnace, so I opened fire. Jamison was behind me but trying to get Stevens out of there."

"Is that protocol?"

"Yeah. Stevens was looking pretty bad so I told Jamison to get him upstairs and send Smith down to back me up."

"And Smith was?"

"Lonnie Smith. An agent on the front team. I had to cover Jamison so he handed me Stevens' pistol. When he had Stevens over his shoulder he shouted 'Go!' and I came out from behind the furnace . . . both pistols blazing, I guess you'd say." He tried a half smile on Archer. "Just like on television."

Archer didn't smile back. Again, she waited. Again, Winters swallowed.

"By the time Jamison got Stevens up the stairs, both magazines were empty. I dove back behind the furnace to reload. I stuffed Stevens' gun in my pocket. That's when . . . that's when I felt something cold and hard press against the side of my head. Guy had a thick accent."

"Guy?"

"The guy who said, 'Drop the weapon, please.'"

That had struck Winters as odd. The politeness of it. It made him want to grab the guy by the throat.

"I heard gunfire upstairs, which wasn't supposed to be happening. This guy says to me, 'Your comrades are not faring so well.' I thought he was bluffing. It was impossible for me to tell from down there who was coming out ahead." Winters forced himself not to shift in the chair. "I heard the floor creaking, footsteps overhead, and a door slammed. My assailant says something like, 'I do not believe your friends are coming to rescue you. Your only hope is in me. Now put down the pistol.'"

Winters over-imitated the heavy Russian accent—mugging the facial expression—but Archer showed no hint of amusement. "What was going through your mind?" she asked.

Another attempt to get at his feelings. Winters wasn't going there. "All I was thinking was where the . . . where was Smith? Had he called for backup? And what about Donleavy?"

"You had a gun to your head—you were clearly in trouble—and that's what you were thinking?"

"I'm trained to think, not feel," Winters said. "You give in to fear and you're done."

"Did you think you were going to die?"

"I suppose the thought crossed my mind."

"You'd been on a number of raids before this one. In any of those, did you ever think you were going to die?"

"No. Never."

"What made this one different?"

Winters gave a short, dry laugh. "Well, for one thing, the guy had a pistol to my head."

"But you've had other people point a gun at you, haven't you?"

"Yes."

"And you knew they were going to kill you if you let them."

"Yes."

"So what made this one different?"

"I'm about to tell you."

"Good," Archer said.

He wondered if the government was paying her to make this as tedious as possible. "I could hear people coming down the stairs," he said. "All speaking Russian."

"Do you know Russian?"

"Enough to get by. There were three of them and one of them grabbed the pistol out of my hand as he went past me. It was futile to resist at that point. I didn't have a plan yet."

Winters stopped. Not voluntarily. He hit the wall he always came to when he got this far.

"The rest is history," he said. "I stayed alive, obviously. That's first priority when you're in a situation like that. All the other agents got out okay. Stevens survived. He went back to work a couple of weeks ago." Winters refused to swallow. "All's well that ends well."

"And yet here you are," Archer said. "Refusing to look at what happened between the time those four Russians had you in the basement and you"—she glanced at the pad—"'stayed alive.'" She leaned

forward. "These are the very things you need to face
to take you apart. Even more than it already has. So
after they took your gun?"

"Some of this stuff is classified."

"I'm cleared for it."

"Then let's just say I'm a little claustrophobic," Winters said.

"Do you always do that?"

"Do what?"

"Mask your pain by making fun of it?"

"Is that what I'm doing?"

"Did you do that after your wife's death?"

Winters froze. "I told you that has nothing to do with any of this."

"I think it has everything to do with it."

"I'm not going there."

The room was suddenly smaller. The walls squeezed his chest. The
ceiling pressed the top of his head. The floor pushed at his feet and
forced him into a fetal position. Only by grinding his teeth into the
inside of his cheeks did he keep from screaming.

"Those other raids you went on—those were in New York,
weren't they?"

He nodded.

"You told me the first time we met that you had been on dozens
of raids since your wife died—"

"I never talked about my wife."

"I apologize. You said you'd been on dozens since 9/11."

"What about it?"

"Actually, the records show that you worked only ten cases between the time she died and the time you moved to San Francisco."

"So?" The metallic taste of blood filled his mouth.

"What the records don't show is that you sought any serious

nseling. Two sessions with the grief counselor the Service provided and that was it. That doesn't seem like much after such a tragic loss."

Winters spoke through clenched teeth. "Look, everybody process-es grief in a different way. I was distraught, I admit that. But I could function. I had to—I had a ten-year-old daughter to take care of. And the work didn't stop—in fact there was more to do after that than before. So I pushed ahead. That's what Anne would've wanted."

"For you to bury yourself in your work."

He clenched both fists and parked them on his knees. "I can't make this any clearer. I dealt with whatever I was feeling and I moved on as best I could. Sue me for not spending hours in some psychia-trist's office wallowing in my grief. That's not me."

"But you couldn't, could you?"

"Couldn't what?" Winters relaxed his hands and dried his palms on his thighs. He thought this hour had to be pretty much over.

"You couldn't move on, emotionally," she said. "Isn't that why you requested to be relocated here to San Francisco?"

"Okay, yes. Too many reminders of the past in New York. I didn't see the point in being constantly bombarded with the fact that she wasn't there anymore, taking our daughter to the museums, getting excited over finding fresh artichokes at the market—that kind of thing. Maria was out of school by then, so I asked for a transfer." He looked Archer straight in the eyes. "And it's been better here."

Archer nodded. "So after eight years, the reminders were still too much." She held up a hand as he started to protest. "That isn't a criti-cism, John. It's a statement of the fact that you may not have done as much healing as you thought. Will you consider that possibility?"

"Everything was *fine* here until that raid went south. But that has nothing to do with my wife's death. So can we just drop it?"

Archer glanced at her watch. "You're still determined to go on this trip?"

"The deal was, I open up about the raid and you don't use Barcelona as a reason to keep me from being reinstated."

"I'm not sure what you've told me today qualifies as opening up, but it's a start. Do yourself a favor and think about all this while you're gone."

"What are you going to tell Rebhorn?" Winters asked.

"That we're still working on it. That you're taking a break and you'll be back in a few weeks to pick up where we left off." She tilted her chin up at him. "Not too long, John."

"Or I'm in trouble with you?"

"No." She shook her head. "You're in trouble with you."

14

"Do I need to do anything else with this?" Elena said, holding the paper aloft.

Maria pulled out the pen she'd been using to keep her hair twisted on the top of her head and let it all fall down around her shoulders. "No, I'll handle it. It still baffles me, though."

"Me too."

"Thanks for doing this."

"I didn't really do anything."

"You're the one who thought of looking at the original. Saved me from making an idiot of myself."

"As if you could ever do that."

"You have no idea." Maria glanced at her phone to check the time. "Why don't you call it quits for the day?"

"What about you? I thought we could go to Restaurant Montiel for dinner—they have a gourmet tasting menu."

"I've got more to do here. Besides, I have to slow down on the whole eating thing. I can't afford to buy a new wardrobe."

"Stop it. You look amazing." Elena pulled her messenger bag out of the bottom drawer of her desk. "I have never understood American women's obsession with looking like anorexic models. You're sure you don't need me to stay and help you?"

"Positive. Take the night off. You deserve it."

"And you don't?" Elena slung the bag over her shoulder. "Never mind. See you in the morning."

When the door closed behind her, Maria kicked off her pumps and propped her feet on the desk. The light from the window behind her was fading. She snapped on the desk lamp and turned her attention once more to the file Elena had brought her.

It was definitely the same one Maria had typed from. Same stain from Snowden's dribbled coffee. Same pencil smudge in the right margin. If she brought it to her nose she'd probably smell the cologne he bathed in, but she wasn't doing that.

As she continued to study it she pulled her hair back up and secured it with the pen again. Same notes, but not the same. As Elena had pointed out when she'd presented it to her just minutes ago, the words Maria had typed—*at the price agreed upon as long as the projected reserves hold up*—were not the words on the page. Instead, it read, *at the price agreed upon, as the reserves projected have held up.*

There was no way she had made that mistake. Not that *and* the next sentence. She'd typed, *Tejada will make certain that they do.* The notes in front of her said, *Tejada has made certain of that.*

Maria smoothed the paper on the desk, moved her feet to the floor, and leaned closer. How could she have misread the whole thing? Snowden's handwriting was bad, but in this case it was slightly better than usual. She'd have to've been extremely tired to make that mistake. Maria rubbed her eyes and stared at it again. No, she'd done these in the morning, after two cups of that Spanish mud they called coffee.

The only possibility was one she didn't want to consider, but without Elena there to offer her always optimistic alternatives, Maria had to. Did Snowden change his notes *after* she'd typed them up?

She shook her head. That made even less sense than her reading it wrong in the first place. She hadn't given him the typed version yet. It was still right there on her desk. So what reason would he have to go back and change the notes?

And *had* they been changed? Snowden always wrote in that infuriating pencil, so he could have erased the original and made the change, but there was no evidence of that.

Maybe with a magnifying glass. She opened a drawer and pawed through the collection of gadgets and supplies Elena had filled it with. Maria found everything from a battery-operated staple remover to gold paper clips, but no magnifying device.

"What am I doing?" she muttered. This was ridiculous.

The question really was—were the reserves on which the entire Belgian acquisition rested merely *projected* reserves rather than actual? From what she'd heard in meetings and researched for Snowden, the powers at Belgium Continental were far too cautious to agree to that.

And the even more disturbing question was, how would Tejada make certain that the projected reserves held up? It was more like Snowden to say "Tejada will make sure of that," or "Tejada has that handled." He could pull out the proper grammar and impressive vocabulary when he had to, but he never did it in his notes. And Elena was surprised he'd taken any at all. He always had one of his minions do that for him.

So . . . this had to have been a private meeting. But why? If the acquisition was a done deal—the price was right and the reserves in place—why the need for some clandestine one-on-one discussion behind closed doors?

Maria shook her hair out the rest of the way. Okay, she was

getting carried away. Elena was probably right—she needed to take the night off too.

She reached to close the desk drawer when a tap sounded at the door. Before she could respond it opened and Snowden's white head appeared. "Got a minute?" he asked.

Maria felt her face flush and rose to her feet. "Sure," she said. "Come on in."

As Snowden crossed the office, she slid the folder into the top drawer and pushed it closed. "I was marveling over what was in here," she said. "Elena must have bought out Staples before I came."

Snowden seemed oblivious to what she was talking about. She was babbling, but he was obviously not focused on her or what she was doing. He looked as if he had veered off course on his way to somewhere else.

"Everything okay?" Maria asked.

"Yeah," he said.

Lying, clearly. His face was pale, playing up a five o'clock shadow she'd never seen on him before.

"I'm missing some paperwork," he said. He looked at her expectantly.

"Can you be a little more specific?"

"You'd know it if you saw it—seeing how it doesn't have anything to do with the acquisition."

Maria was surprised he didn't go straight to the desk drawer because the words *It's in there!* must surely have been written across her face.

And yet she wasn't sure. The notes *were* about the acquisition, private meeting or not. If she pulled them out now, he'd want to know why she was keeping them and why she had hidden them when he entered the room.

She could feel Snowden peering at her.

"I'm thinking," Maria said, "but I'm not coming up with anything. If you want to give me more details I can keep an eye out for it."

"Never mind," he said. "It's probably in my office somewhere."

"I can lend you Elena to look for it," Maria offered.

Snowden nodded absently.

"You lucked out hiring her."

Snowden looked puzzled. "What do you mean?"

"Hiring Elena for me. That was a good call."

"You're talking about your assistant?"

"Yes. Of course. Who did you think?"

"I didn't hire her," Snowden said, already halfway to the door. "Molina did."

"Molina?" Maria was astounded. "The security guy?"

"He does the staffing for Tejada. Makes sure everybody's vetted."

Maria felt prickly. "Tejada doesn't trust you to bring your own staff?"

Snowden *looked* prickly. "I wasn't going to get you an assistant. It was Tejada's idea." He ran his hand over his stubble as if he'd just realized it was there. "Forget about that paperwork. It'll turn up."

He turned away with no good-bye but left the door hanging open to reveal Carlos Molina waiting for him in the hall.

What in the world? she thought. Snowden needed the head of security to escort him to visit his own staff?

When they were gone and she heard the elevator doors shut, Maria took the file from the drawer, removed Snowden's notes, and tucked them into her briefcase.

✦ ✦ ✦

Tejada had his secretary set up coffee in his office before she left for the day. He wanted to handle Philippe Prevost differently this time. Not that he wanted to enable the whining and wheedling. He couldn't abide that. But he needed whatever information his nephew was bringing back from China.

The tentative knock on the door came at the stroke of seven. Prevost's punctuality always seemed like groveling to Tejada. From anyone else he deemed it considerate.

When his nephew came in, Tejada greeted him with the customary hug he'd left out the last time they'd met, poured him a cup of coffee, and ushered him to one end of the couch. Tejada occupied the other end. "Tell me of the Chinese," he said.

Prevost rubbed his eyes. He had come straight from the airport as Tejada had requested.

"I met with Zhang Yo," he began.

"Head of the Bank of China. He is a young man."

"Late thirties, but make no mistake, Emilio, he is genuinely gifted and incredibly intelligent."

"No more so than you," Tejada said.

"All of that is beside the point."

"Why?"

"The old guard leaders."

"What about them?"

"They think the US dollar will decline anyway and they want to hold out for the day when China becomes the dominant global economic force."

"You reminded Zhang Yo that day is not as close as the old guard thinks?"

"I did."

"You told him that in the meantime China may be exposed

to fluctuations in the price of commodities due to domestic US decisions—the ones we've talked about?"

"I did." Prevost's cup rattled on its saucer and he set them both on the table. "It was not the message he was opposed to, Emilio. It was me."

Tejada motioned for him to go on.

"Yo was actually in agreement with me, but he says many in the Chinese government are doubtful of my ability to deliver. They say I won't be in office long enough to get the job done. Rumor has it that I might be replaced this month."

"Rumors from whom?"

"The Russians. And the Americans."

Tejada waved him off, but Prevost leaned forward, eyes watery. "Is that true, Emilio? Is there a movement afoot to have me removed?"

If there was, Tejada knew nothing of it, but the idea was disturbing. "No," he reassured. "But there *is* a power play by the world's three strongest economies to wrest control of the IMF from my influence."

"From *your* influence?" Prevost said, his voice winding up. "This is *my* head we're talking about."

Tejada forced himself to relax. Even though they both knew Tejada was the real controller of the IMF, he couldn't lose his temper with Prevost. At least not until he knew all he had to tell. "I trust you talked to someone in the Chinese government," he said.

Prevost looked offended. "Of course I did. I had a meeting with the premier, Wang Peng."

"I know who he is," Tejada responded.

"He says they're still in discussion about the idea, but they had hoped I would be in favor of the yuan rather than your plan. I told him switching to the yuan creates more problems because other countries are as suspicious of China as China is of the US."

"And you presented that with complete diplomacy, I'm sure," Tejada said drily.

"What would you have me do? There is enough bowing and scraping with those people as it is. You want me to mince words too? Because they sure don't."

Prevost went into a spasm of coughing that stopped only when Tejada had poured him a glass of water and watched him drain it. His greatest concern about Prevost was apparently coming true. He wasn't strong enough for this.

When Prevost was able to continue, he said, "The premier kept bringing the conversation back to how long I would be with the IMF and how much control you have over me and, as a result, the Fund itself."

"And you reassured him, of course—"

"That's not all. He said if I vote for the yuan instead of a new—" Prevost looked around the room and lowered his voice.

Tejada smothered a groan. No one could be more obvious about not saying what Tejada had told Prevost not to say aloud. If anyone had a hidden camera in here they would know immediately what they were talking about. He could feel his patience thinning.

"If I do that, they will see that I remain on at IMF because they like my vision and loyalty."

They liked his malleability. Tejada was about to say so when Prevost went on.

"The premier wants me to say your—our—plan is not workable at this time and then in a few weeks he wants me to give my support to measures proposed by China and the OPEC nations that would move oil contracts from dollar-denominated transactions to yuan-denominated. When I pointed out that would show disloyalty to you, *he* pointed out that compromise is inevitable."

"Compromise is weakness," Tejada said. "How did you leave it with Peng?"

"We discussed your offer to guarantee their losses if they are generated by general market forces, not from losses generated internally."

Tejada nodded in surprise. "Good call, Philippe."

"He didn't think so at first. He said that would protect them from US whim but not from an IMF interpretation of how their losses occurred during the transition. He feels they are being asked to trust but are not being trusted in return."

That was why Peng was premier. Tejada felt the stirring of disappointment, and anger, with Prevost.

"I said, 'A simple guarantee to cover your losses during the transition is what I have to offer.'" Prevost pulled himself up to his full but diminutive height on the couch. "He said, 'So you are going to remain loyal to your uncle.' When I said yes, he said, 'It is that loyalty which I admire about you. The guarantee of our debt would be most welcome.'"

Tejada hid his relief. "He played you."

"Yes. He *tried* to play me."

"But we won."

"This round at least." Prevost picked up his coffee cup, looked into it, and set it back down.

"What else, Philippe?"

Prevost sighed. "Next time we talk, they will want us to offer them something new to make things right."

"Then we'll give it to them."

"And it will be one more thing after that. It will be a never-ending cycle. What we need is something dramatic to force their hand."

Once again Tejada was reminded of how Prevost had achieved his status. Here was another flash of his oft-hidden brilliance.

"Go on," Tejada said.

Prevost's pale eyes glimmered. "We need something that forces them back to us. An event that makes them want this deal and want it fast, rather than dragging out negotiations to see how long they can delay us or how much they can get out of us."

Tejada sat back. "An event like that would not be beyond the realm of possibility."

"You're not going to tell me what it is, of course."

"In time." Tejada rested his elbows on his knees. Time to end this before Prevost started to whine again. "You should gauge the Russians' reaction to all this. But don't meet them in Moscow. Some other location. Someplace less . . . obvious."

"I have to go to Brussels for a meeting of the G8 finance ministers. I'll see Dmitry Koslov there."

"Good," Tejada said. "See what you can find out." Tejada resisted the urge to pat him on the head. "You have done well, Philippe. The Brotherhood is indebted to you."

Prevost's eyes indicated the compliment fell short of what he expected, but he was gracious in making his exit from the room. Tejada sat looking at the closed door long after he left. The coming days would bring difficult decisions about his nephew, of that he was certain, but he did not look forward to what he already knew would be the result.

15

Maria walked from the hotel to the Catalonia Financial campus the next morning, a brisk ten-block trek. She'd been up most of the night and neither the coffee nor a four-mile run cleared her head enough to face what she had to do.

Around her the city bustled as produce appeared in bins on the sidewalks and the usual tempting aromas wafted from the cafés. She liked it here, and yet there was something—a feeling—as if what *Abuela* used to call "no-see-ums" were pressed into the shadows, lying in wait.

Maria shook out her hair and stood up straight. That was just lack of sleep. And the conclusion she had come to after studying Snowden's notes last night with a magnifying glass she'd borrowed from the concierge. She'd managed to get it out of him without having to promise to have a drink with him.

Her phone rang in the depths of her briefcase and she stopped at a sidewalk bench to fish it out. She caught Elena's call just before it cut to voice mail.

"Morning," she said, voice bright as usual. "I got your text. You still want to meet at El Magnifico?"

"Actually I changed my mind," Maria said. "I'm on a bench about a block from Catalonia, on Fontanella. Why don't you bring coffee here?"

"Is everything all right?"

"Yeah. I just want to discuss something with you and I feel like those walls have ears."

"They do," Elena said. "Didn't I tell you?"

While she waited, Maria took Snowden's notes out of her briefcase and scanned them once more. Even without the magnifying glass, Maria had noticed something late last night. The date at the top was the same as the day of their first meeting with Belgium Continental, the day she'd arrived. How could Snowden have written that the acquisition was a done deal when they'd only started the real negotiations that day?

The notes had to be about something other than Belgium Continental.

That in itself wasn't such a big deal. Gump, Snowden and Meir represented all of Catalonia's dealings and Snowden was involved in most of them. The veiled references in the notes could refer to anything, not necessarily the Belgium Continental transaction. But why would Snowden take notes if he wasn't trying to be specific? It wasn't like him to write down things he could just throw at her on his way out of the office for after-work drinks.

Maria looked across Fontanella. No sign of Elena yet. Either there was a long line at the café or the girl had cut and run. Maria had no reason to think she would, except for what the study with the magnifying glass had revealed. With some bright light and magnification the erasures were clear.

The original words were replaced with new ones. The less-condemning ones. And in Snowden's handwriting. Or someone who knew how to imitate it well enough to fool her.

It wasn't Snowden who did it. He was looking for the notes, Maria was convinced of that. He had never intended for her to get them in the first place.

Only one person knew Maria had them. Only one person knew she'd questioned them. Watching that person approach, coffees in hand, Maria resolved to find out why and what that could mean.

"Here you go—two creams, no sugars." Elena handed a cardboard-sleeved paper cup to Maria and sat on the bench next to her. "I like the way you eat and I like the way you drink coffee. Most Americans bring their latte habit with them."

"Does Molina hire assistants for all Americans who come here?" Maria said.

"That was an interesting segue."

"He did hire you, though."

"Yes, he did."

"To do what?"

Maria hadn't meant for it to come out so much like an accusation, She was reminding herself of her father.

Elena looked bee-stung.

"I'm sorry," Maria said. "I'm confused and I don't do well when I feel out of control. Let me start over." She set the coffee on the ground beside the bench. "Were you really hired by *Señor* Tejada to be my assistant, or to keep tabs on me?"

"Keep tabs on you?" Elena's eyes filled with tears and her voice quivered. "Why would he do that? Why would you think that?"

"I just want you to be straight with me."

Elena looked as if she wanted to run.

"Are you afraid of somebody?" Maria asked, pressing the point.

"*Señor* Tejada didn't hire me," Elena replied. "He doesn't even know me or anything about me. He probably thinks Mr. Snowden hired me."

"Look, I know Molina is the one who actually gave you the job, but I'm sure Tejada told him to do it."

"No," Elena said, shaking her head. "I'm just as certain he didn't."

"Why?"

"Because Molina is blackmailing me."

The words came out so softly Maria almost missed them. "*Blackmailing?*" she whispered.

Elena's eyes darted from side to side, checking suspiciously. Maria took her by the hand. "Come on," she said, "let's walk. Pretend we're talking about guys or something."

Elena looked bewildered, but Maria pulled her up and slipped her arm through Elena's. She grabbed her briefcase with the other hand and tugged at Elena to get moving.

"Your coffee," Elena protested. The cup still sat on the bench.

"Forget about it. Talk to me."

Elena waited while two men in shiny silk suits passed them, then she began. "I don't know what to do. He hired me—"

"Molina."

"Yes. He hired me to watch your work and tell him if you came across anything 'unusual.'"

"He didn't tell you what to look for?"

"No. He just said to get close enough to you that you would tell me about any *aberraciones*. Aberrations."

Maria stiffened. "How would you know what you saw was an aberration if he didn't tell you what he was looking for?"

"Look," Elena said. "I didn't try to become your friend because of that. All right"—she shrugged—"maybe I did at first, but the more we worked and did things together, the more I respected you and I didn't want to do what Molina said. I didn't think I had to really worry about it. Everything was going so smoothly and nothing came up that looked suspicious to me."

"Until I found that information in Snowden's notes and started asking questions." Maria still didn't know whether to trust Elena now, but she needed to learn as much as she could before they reached the office. She gave Elena a nudge. "Laugh."

"What?"

"Pretend you're laughing. It can't look like you're telling me this."

"You think he's watching?"

"You think he's not? Laugh," Maria insisted once more. Elena broke into a phony guffaw and they both giggled. "So, what happened when I asked you about Snowden's notes?" Maria said. "What did you do?"

Elena started to cry and Maria pulled her closer. "You can't break down," Maria said. "Keep smiling."

Elena didn't smile, but she took a deep breath and choked back the tears. "I went to the filing cabinet and got the notes. I was going to take them to Molina, but I couldn't." She glanced over at Maria. "Honestly, after all we'd done together and the friendship we've developed, I couldn't bring myself to do it."

"Why?" Maria said. "I wouldn't be the one in trouble. We didn't even know if anyone had done anything wrong."

Elena bit at her lip.

"Elena, what is it?"

"I don't want you mixed up with Molina," she said. "If he can blackmail me, he could threaten you too. He will do anything to protect Tejada's integrity."

"Again, what did you do with the notes?"

"I changed them," Elena whispered. "I thought that would be the end of it. But it wasn't, was it?"

"Don't consider a career in espionage," Maria said, in her dry, humorous voice. "All it took was a magnifying glass and a forty-watt bulb and I had it figured out. What I don't get was how you matched Snowden's handwriting exactly."

"I looked at his other notes."

"Girl of many talents."

Elena stopped abruptly and looked over at Maria. "Please don't doubt me," she said. "I took a big chance not telling Molina."

Maria looked around and spotted the El Corte Inglés, a department store. She pried Elena's fingers from her arm and took her by the hand. "In there," she said, pointing.

Elena's palm was tacky, her face sheet-white, as she let Maria lead her into the store and straight to the ladies' room. "They don't like you to use their facilities without making a purchase," Elena said.

"Don't worry, I'll buy something."

Maria checked all the stalls and turned to face Elena. "What does he have on you?"

Elena's face crumpled again and she began to cry. "Talk to me," Maria insisted. "Before someone comes in here. I may be able to help you. I'm a lawyer, remember?"

Mascara, eyeliner, and eye shadow had turned to a murky mix that now trailed down Elena's face. Maria reached for a paper towel. "You talk," she said. "I'll wipe."

Elena closed her eyes, as if somehow what she had to say to Maria would be easier if she couldn't see her. "I'm here illegally."

"I thought you were a Spanish national."

"I am. But when I was in the United States, I . . . got into some trouble."

"Legal trouble?"

"Yes."

"So we'll fix it." Maria replied. "I won't even charge you. What happened?"

"You can't fix this."

"I'm a Harvard graduate," Maria quipped. "I can fix it. What happened?"

"I killed someone."

Maria stopped mid-wipe. "You killed someone?"

"It was an accident, but even my lawyer said my chances of going free were practically nada."

"Then he wasn't worth the money you were paying him."

"I wasn't paying him. He was appointed by the court. I don't think he believed me."

"It shouldn't have mattered. So what did you do—you ran?"

"I knew someone who knew someone who could get me out of the States and back here. I gave them all the money I had saved for college. They gave me a whole new identity."

"How old were you?"

"Eighteen."

Elena stared down at the floor. Maria took a step back, towel still in hand.

"How did you end up with him?" she said.

"Molina?"

"Yeah."

"I gave them everything I had and I thought I was free when I got back. I'm from Madrid but I didn't want to live there where everyone knew who I really was. So I came here, to Barcelona. The city was all new to me and I didn't know anyone, but I got a job as a server at Botafumeiro and an apartment with some other girls who worked at the restaurant. I was starting to save for university again." Her eyes clouded. "And then Carlos Molina walked into the restaurant and took it all away."

"How did he even know about you?"

"Because he knows everything."

"How did he know about you?"

"I don't know, but he made it clear that if I didn't do what he said he would notify the authorities and I would be sent back to the United States."

"And nothing says 'guilty' like fleeing the country." Maria took Elena's chin in her hand and gently tilted up her head. "Has Molina made you do anything else besides spy?"

"No. If it had been prostitution or drugs or something, I would have killed myself rather than do it."

Elena's voice was so vehement, Maria believed her.

"Just keeping an eye on people who come here to work on special projects didn't seem so bad. Until you came." Her voice broke.

The attorney in Maria told her to get proof, not to assume Elena's innocence in this until she had more than just her word. But the woman in her told her she couldn't let this poor girl look over her shoulder for the rest of her life, working for a weasel like Carlos Molina.

"Okay, listen," Maria said. "This acquisition shouldn't take more than another week, if that long, and we'll be returning to the States. Just keep doing what you're doing. We'll act as if nothing happened. But if you want . . . I'll get things moving for you to leave with us. I'll hire an attorney for you—several of my friends from law school work for firms specializing in criminal cases, accidental homicide, all that." Maria squeezed her hands again. "You're in prison here and the only way out of it is to go back and work through the process."

Elena didn't say no. But she didn't nod either. A storm of indecision and shame and guilt raged in her eyes.

"Why are you doing this?" Elena said.

"Because I have to." Maria reached into her briefcase and pulled out her phone to check the time. "We are so late. Okay—here's the plan. I'm going to rush into work like I overslept and I'll tell anybody who asks that I sent you out for coffee." She dug in her pocket, pulled out a wad of euros, and peeled off several. "Do the coffee thing again and bring it in—*after* you reapply your makeup and *after* you settle down enough to look at people without crying."

Elena's eyes started to fill again.

"See what I mean?" Maria gestured with her hand. "I know once you get started it's hard to turn it off, but give it your best shot. You can't go in there looking like this. Tejada and everyone else will notice." Maria picked up her briefcase and put her hand lightly on Elena's damp cheek. "We'll get through this. You aren't alone. Okay?"

"I'll be all right," Elena whimpered. "Maria—how can I thank you?"

"By getting me a coffee. And one of those Magdelenas muffins. See you at the office."

She gave Elena's hand one more squeeze and hurried from the restroom. The proprietor's chilly gaze greeted her so she grabbed a scarf from the rack and tossed the rest of the wad of euros on the counter. "Keep the change," she said.

"Muchas gracias!" the woman called after her.

"*De nada*, lady," Maria muttered. She stuffed the scarf into her briefcase and walked to the Catalonia campus. Elena's situation crowded her mind, but there was room in there for Gump, Snowden and Meir's "situation" as well. If Snowden's original notes were for real—and why wouldn't they be?—was the firm into something it shouldn't be? She decided to find out.

16

Tejada glared at the small digital recorder on his desk. What did a man have to do to convince people that he didn't like recordings? Although he didn't believe it was true, he'd been assured it was the only secure way to get this information to him. It seemed more like laziness and lack of imagination to him.

He inserted the earbuds and turned his chair to face the window. Barcelona was treating them to a glorious day. It might do something to lighten his mood. He hoped the contents of the recording would as well.

The voice of Patrick McCarthy wasn't familiar to him, at least not on a personal level. He'd heard him on CNN, as he was a well-known political consultant. He spoke ironically, as if everything were fodder for satire. Sarcasm and cynicism snaked through every sentence.

"We need to discuss the pending congressional action to raise the debt limit," the familiar voice said.

"Ahh, yes," McCarthy replied, chuckling.

The chuckle was a sound Tejada rarely made himself and he didn't see the need for anyone but a clown to make it either. McCarthy, however, had always proven to be a very useful clown, having been financially rescued by Catalonia on more than one occasion.

"The regularly scheduled game of congressional charades," McCarthy went on. "Who are you shilling for this time?"

"This time the issue will be handled differently. Our friends want to hold the line on spending."

"Since when did they take an interest in our debt ceiling? I thought they loved our debt."

Tejada thought he heard ice clinking in a glass. Bourbon might move the conversation along or slow it to a snail's crawl. So far it was the latter. He tried to push aside his impatience.

"Things have changed."

"This isn't a budget debate, you know," McCarthy said. "It's a debt debate."

"It's all about spending, and Congress has proved unable to restrain itself, but if it limits the amount the US can borrow, then the spending side will take care of itself. They can't spend what they don't have."

"Either have another drink or get to the point."

Tejada nodded in agreement.

"No debt-limit increase."

McCarthy's voice flattened. "You want Congress to refuse to raise the debt ceiling."

"Yes."

"Okay. They'll all talk about it. About fifteen or twenty of them will take a stand—for a while. But in the end, enough will cave on the issue to pass an increase bill. Half of these guys are up for reelection. They're not going to tank the economy and then go home to face the voters, so why are we even talking?"

"Because the group that wants this pays my fee . . . and yours."

McCarthy was silent for a moment, then said, "Fair enough. But does 'the group' have a plan for making this happen? Because I'll tell you what's going to go down if they don't. The other side will trot out the debate rhetoric. Then one party will take the 'hold the line' position, the other one will stake out the 'default on the national debt would be catastrophic' point of view."

"That's where you come in. We need a coordinated effort to educate the public that not raising the debt limit is not the same as default."

"Too many 'nots' in that statement."

Again Tejada nodded.

"You have people who can make that argument in a more intelligible manner," Tejada's man said.

"A zoo has animals who can do that," McCarthy said. "But yes, we do."

More ice clinked. The pace of this conversation was beginning to make Tejada want a drink himself—and it wasn't even 10 a.m.

"In the first month there would be a technical default."

"A 'technical default.'" Tejada could almost see the wry expression on McCarthy's face. "I didn't know there could be such a thing."

"Something would be paid late—Social Security maybe, or government payroll."

"Incidentals."

"But after the first month the cash flow would catch up. There's easily enough to cover the debt service payment and most of the essentials."

"I'm growing old here," McCarthy said. "Cut to the chase. What exactly do you want me to do?"

"Go to the American people."

"Not Congress."

"No. Go to the American people. Make the argument for austerity. The government living within its means, just like every household in the country. Come up with a campaign. Get the American people onboard. Make sure they know that our future rests on their willingness to do more than just go along with this. We face a crisis and we need them to call, write, e-mail their representatives."

Tejada suppressed a grunt. The argument was factually correct but it lacked passion. Difficult to persuade anyone to do anything without emotion.

"We have to do something about our own financial condition before China's economy gets any stronger and they're no longer dependent on us. It begins with fiscal responsibility."

"That's the message you want me to give," McCarthy said.

Tejada didn't like the doubt in his voice.

"Yes, but in your own words. In a way that motivates voters to do something about it. Don't just give them numbers and information. Grab their hearts."

"You're breakin' mine," McCarthy said.

"Make them get up and act."

"Okay." Tejada imagined McCarthy shrugging. "But all of this will go nowhere unless Congress is willing to act. Or I guess in this case, they refuse to act."

"Don't worry about Congress. Just focus on the people. Work it like a political campaign. Voter drives, the whole nine yards. When the people back home speak up, the reps will get in line."

"You're talking about a big campaign. And I'm talking about substantial remuneration."

Tejada didn't wait for the crackling of the envelope, the flipping of the bills. He turned off the recorder and pulled out his trash can just as his phone buzzed.

"*Señorita* Winters to see you, sir?"

"Send her in," Tejada said.

He pushed the trash can back under the desk just as the door opened and Maria appeared. In spite of Abaddon's warning, Tejada found it difficult to take his eyes off her and even more difficult to send her away. Maria had made it plain she was not interested in him, which was perhaps another part of his fascination with her, but he was fine with merely enjoying the view.

"*Señor* Tejada," she said. "I wonder if your offer to show me your Botafumeiro still stands."

"It does indeed," he replied.

"Lunch today? If you're free?"

"I will clear my calendar."

"Fabulous. See you at two?"

"I will have my car waiting."

"Oh, no," she said, smile dazzling. "Let's walk, shall we?"

Was there any point in arguing? She was already halfway out the door and taking most of the air with her. "A walk it is," Tejada called after her. "Any other requirements?"

"No. Well, yes." She stopped in the doorway and glanced back at him over her shoulder. "No Molina. Just the two of us."

And without waiting for an answer she was gone.

Fascinating woman.

It seemed to Winters that there was more to getting ready to leave the country than there had ever been preparing a case. Reservations, packing, mail hold, and not least of all, trying to get in touch with his brother. He'd been e-mailing, calling, and texting Ben ever since Donleavy had visited him, and he'd been met with nothing but cryptic replies like, *Crazy busy, Secret Agent Man. Will get back to you ASAP.* Which he had yet to do.

Winters hadn't indicated why he wanted to talk so Ben shouldn't have any reason to put him off. In fact, Winters was surprised Ben didn't jump to the conclusion his brother knew something about his appeal to be re-interviewed by the Service and hop on the next plane from Phoenix to San Francisco. Every time Winters left to run an errand he half-expected to find Ben when he returned, hanging out in his living room with a bag of Cheetos. After all, he'd never returned the key Winters lent him the last time he was there.

When days went by and still there was no response, he decided to use Ben's desire for news of his application as bait and sent him a text message that said, *Got news about your interviews. CALL ME.*

Still nothing—and it was bugging him. What was Ben so "crazy busy" with that he couldn't punch in a number on the cell phone?

Winters Googled him to see if an association with a business popped up. All he found was a weeks-old Facebook status report that read, *Back from my mom's funeral. Life changing.*

After that, Winters was too ticked off to care about it anymore. Let Rebhorn get a restraining order. It might shake the kid up. Nothing else seemed to.

He was almost ready to depart for Barcelona—only needed to get a haircut and a good night's sleep before a zero-dark-thirty flight the next morning—when Donleavy called.

"Just getting ready to leave the country, buddy," Winters told him. "Going to Barcelona—and I don't want to hear any comments about the professor."

Winters didn't add that he and Sophia had been Skyping twice a week. Donleavy would have a field day with that.

"Wasn't going to make any," Donleavy said. "Can you meet me at that dive where we used to get coffee?"

His voice sounded tense and Winters wondered why.

"Sure," Winters said. "But when? I'm leaving in the morning."

"I'm thinking now would be good."

"Everything okay?"

"I'll see you in a few minutes," Donleavy said, and he ended the call.

Now Winters was worried. There could be only one reason for him to insist on a meeting—bad news. His mind whirred as he struggled to figure out what that news might be. Maybe Rebhorn got Archer's report about him leaving the country. Maybe Ben had called the office one time too many and pushed Rebhorn over the edge. Or, maybe it was something else.

✦ ✦ ✦

Donleavy was already at a table in back when Winters arrived. *He's been watching way too many movies.* They would have drawn less suspicion standing in line at Starbucks.

Winters ordered a cup of coffee and slid into a chair across from Donleavy. He looked more nervous than he had the day of the raid—perspiration gleamed on his shaved head and his thumbs rubbed his index fingers like they did at meetings when Rebhorn got long-winded. Not good. Winters decided to skip the small talk.

"What's this about?"

"Something I found." Donleavy glanced around nervously.

"Donleavy," Winters said, "stop looking like we're in a Matt Damon film. What's going on?" He leaned across the table. "I'll make it easier for you. They're not going to reinstate me, right?"

"No." Donleavy shook his head. "I mean, I don't know if they will or not. It's not about that."

Winters tried to conceal his relief. "Okay, then whatever you have to tell me isn't going to send me across this table." He looked more closely at Donleavy and saw fear in his eyes. "Are you in some kind of trouble, Taylor?"

"No," Donleavy said. "But you might be."

"You're killin' me here. What is it?"

Once more Donleavy's eyes darted around the room. Winters let it go this time.

"I've been working on some e-mails in connection with the Russian case," he said finally.

"On your own?"

Donleavy nodded. "Something about it keeps bothering me, you know? We should have known more about what was going down in that house before we got there. I just never could believe it was your fault you were caught that unaware."

"Look, I appreciate what you're trying to do but—"

"Wait. Just hear me out." Donleavy's voice dropped. "One of the e-mails was from a guy who, through a whole series of ins and outs, we know was working with the Russians, even though he isn't Russian. It was written to a source that's turned out to be a dead end—a screen name rather than a real name, IP address for a public computer in a library in Arcadia, Arizona—but what it said got me going."

Winters wished he would get to the point, but Donleavy was relaxing into it and he didn't want to mess with that. Otherwise they could be here for days.

"I didn't bring the e-mail—I didn't want to print it out—but I memorized it."

Of course he did.

"It said, 'Just connect it to his laptop's USB port. The file will open without you doing anything else.'" Donleavy hitched himself closer to the table. "Then he sends another one. 'Did you do it?' His next e-mail had the reply attached to it, which said, 'Couldn't. S.A.M. always around.' The next one was, 'Do it soon or all bets are off.' After that there was only one more, which said 'Done.'"

"What's that got to do with me?" Winters said. "Shouldn't you be looking for somebody on the case with the initials S.A.M.?"

"I already did that and I got nothin'. And this might *not* have anything to do with you, but you were point man on the case. Any chance someone had access to your laptop?"

Winters grunted. "Half the time *I* can't even get into my laptop, it's got so many passwords and hoops you have to jump through before you can check your e-mail."

"Are you taking it with you on this trip?"

"Wasn't planning on it," Winters said. "Too much of a hassle."

"You mind if I take a look at it while you're gone?"

"You'd be able to tell if somebody tampered with it?"

"Maybe. It would be worth a try."

Winters took a gulp of the now-tepid coffee and considered it. The whole thing was a long shot at best, but he appreciated Donleavy's loyalty. And examining the laptop couldn't hurt—if it did turn up something, maybe they would all get over it and let him go back to work.

"I don't have time to get it to you before I leave," Winters said. "But I'll give you the access code for the garage. You can get in the house from there."

"Write it on your napkin and slide it across the table to me."

"Why?"

"Because it's cooler that way."

"You're killin' me, Donleavy," Winters grinned. "Just killin' me."

18

Botafumeiro was everything Elena had described to Maria. Richly paneled walls. Silver ice buckets. Luxurious Spanish furnishings.

Something of its charm fell away, though, as the server fluffed out Maria's napkin and handed it to her and she thought of Molina coming in here and taking Elena's world away from her. Maria wondered if he'd ordered the spider-crab pie before he presented his blackmail plan. Or did he simply back her into a corner of the kitchen with one of his withering stares?

"Ms. Winters?"

Maria looked up to find Tejada studying her. He had a way of making his concern for the person in front of him appear to be his *only* concern. If it had been anyone else with a look like that, she would have blurted out the whole thing, beginning to end. Instead she smiled and scanned the menu. "I think I'm just perplexed by all these choices," she said. "Will you order for both of us?"

"I would be happy to," Tejada replied. "But I doubt you are ever perplexed about much, Ms. Winters."

She set the menu aside and looked over at him. "Let's settle one matter right now, *Señor* Tejada. If we're going to work closely together, I think you should call me Maria."

His brows rose. "Are we going to work closely together?"

"I hope so."

His eyes grew warm. "It was my understanding that you did not want to be 'close' to me."

"I said 'work,' not 'socialize.'"

"I stand corrected then. I thought this was a friendly luncheon."

"Oh, it is. I've never been one to believe that business can't be cordial."

"All right, then. Maria it is. On the condition that you will call me Emilio."

"I would," Maria said, "but I like the sound of 'Tejada' better. Gives me practice with my Spanish pronunciation."

Tejada's eyes smiled. "You could practice with Emilio just as well."

The server approached and Maria tried not to imagine Elena in his place. Although from the look of things, the actual servers were all male. The females were bussing tables and occasionally filling water glasses.

"Now, why do you keep drifting off to some mysterious place . . . Maria?" Tejada asked.

"Barcelona does that to me, I think," Maria said, turning back to the moment.

"You have fallen in love with my city."

"Which is why I have something to propose to you."

"I'm intrigued. First, may I order you a drink? A glass of wine, perhaps?"

"No. Thank you." She committed enough flubs when she was sober and she couldn't afford any in this situation.

"Good then. We will toast with water."

"What are we toasting?"

"This proposal you have in mind."

"You haven't heard it yet."

"Let's just say that if my instincts serve me well, and they usually do, I will find it to my liking."

Maria had to admit this guy was good.

"Here it is, then," she said. "The Belgium Continental acquisition is all but finished. A few i's to dot, a few t's to cross."

"Yes."

"Which means that we'll be returning to the States soon."

"Sadly."

"That is exactly the word I would use. I know that the Belgian deal is not the only case our firm works on for you and I also know that Bill Snowden handles all of that."

"He does."

Tejada was listening as if what she was unfolding was absolutely scintillating—and she hadn't even gotten to the point yet. He was definitely good. Among the best, in fact.

"I also know," she continued, "that Mr. Snowden represents other conglomerates as well."

"I make it a point to be aware of those things."

"As far as he allows you to. Mr. Snowden is a great deal smarter than he sometimes lets on. That," she added quickly, "is part of how he works."

"I am aware of that too." The trace of a frown appeared on Tejada's brow. "Should I be questioning your loyalty to your employer, Maria?"

"Not at all. As you yourself have said, you already know of all of this. What you might want to question is *his* loyalty to *you*."

Tejada became very still, so still that Maria could no longer read his face. This was where the waters ran deep. If she was going to get out, now was the time to do it.

Instead, she plunged ahead even deeper. "I'm actually trying to protect the firm—as well as you."

"Oh? And how is that?"

"Mr. Snowden made a slight mistake recently, one I caught and was able to correct without any need to bring it to his attention. I mention it to you only because I see it as evidence that he may have taken on too much. I would hate to see that affect what is obviously a good working relationship between our two companies."

"Go on."

"What I propose is that I be brought back to Barcelona to work with you in bringing any other open issues up-to-date. Just on a temporary basis, relieving Mr. Snowden of some undue stress."

"Have you discussed this with him?"

"Actually, I couldn't come up with a way to present it to him without offending him. Do I say to my boss, 'I think you're doing too much and you can't handle the load'? I couldn't see myself having that conversation."

"You might be demoted. Or fired."

"In which case I would look for another job. But I like where I am, and I like Barcelona, and I like working with Catalonia. And I think I can be of benefit to you and your corporation."

"I have no doubt of that." Tejada paused to let the server place a selection of clams and oysters on the table.

Maria made the expected appreciative sounds and tried not to slurp as she slipped an oyster into her mouth. Surprisingly, it turned to cardboard on her tongue. Nothing she was saying was untrue, but it felt manipulative in that way she disapproved of when anyone else did it. She reminded herself to keep thinking about Elena.

After he made sure everything was to her liking, Tejada said, "You have clearly thought all of this out. How do you propose I present this idea to Mr. Snowden?"

Maria smiled. "Oh, I'm leaving that part to you. I have faith that you will handle it with complete diplomacy."

His expression turned somber. "One thing does disturb me, however."

She knew what it was, but she asked, "What is that?"

"You suggested that I question Mr. Snowden's loyalty to me. What did you mean by that?"

Maria gave her best sigh. "It may be nothing. It was just something in his notes, from a meeting I wasn't privy to. You were mentioned—something about seeing that projected reserves were in place for a deal that had already been agreed on." Maria put up a hand, even though Tejada showed no signs of protesting. "I know these kinds of things go on, and quite without malice in most cases. My concern is that such information came my way. To be plain, I don't think I was supposed to see those notes."

Tejada put down his fork and wiped the corner of his mouth with a napkin. His eyes shone with the same concern he'd shown at the beginning of the meeting. "I know what you're referring to," he said. "And you're correct. That information was not for your eyes. I will assure you, though, that nothing underhanded is indicated there."

"I take you at your word."

"You are also correct that the matter shows carelessness on Snowden's part."

"Or simply overwork."

"And your solution is, rather than my calling him on it, you step in and take over some of the workload here in Barcelona to eliminate the possibility of similar mistakes in the future."

"You are correct."

Maria forced herself to slide a clam onto her appetizer plate but she had stopped eating. Stopped moving. Stopped breathing.

"You are either a very shrewd businesswoman, Maria, or a very ambitious one."

"Can't I be both?" Maria said, hating every word as it came out.

"You can. And I admire both." He raised his water glass and motioned for her to do the same. "To our future working relationship."

"There's one more thing," Maria said.

He waited, glass still lifted.

"I would like to keep Elena on as my assistant when I'm here."

"I apologize. Whom are you referring to?"

"Elena Soler. The assistant you had Carlos Molina hire for me. Which, by the way, I appreciate."

Tejada lowered the glass and shook his head. "I did not have Molina hire anyone, although I wish I had now. I would like to be deserving of your gratitude."

"Oh," Maria said. "My mistake then."

"If, however, you would like for me to retain *Señorita* Soler as your assistant, I will see to it. Then that grateful smile will be for me."

Maria smiled in response.

19

The flights from San Francisco to London and then to Barcelona were more grueling than a two-day stakeout. Winters emerged from the last plane bleary-eyed. His spine felt twisted like a question mark and his face was dotted with stubble. He was grateful that Sophia Conte wasn't meeting him at the airport. His breath alone would be enough to send her away.

Not only that—he was cranky. The little sleep he'd gotten was tormented by snatches of dream from the raid and images from the book he'd brought for the plane ride—Columbus' *Book of Prophecies*. It read like a nightmare.

By the time he got through customs, found a cab driver who spoke English, and located his hotel, he was ready to pinch off someone's head. Not the best frame of mind for meeting the woman who was supposed to help him solve the riddle of his ancestry.

Exhausted as Winters was lying in the hotel bed with the drapes drawn against the brilliant Barcelona sun, he stared, sleepless, at the stained ceiling. A four-star rating obviously meant something different here than it did in the States. He counted the drips from the bathroom faucet . . .

✦　✦　✦

The zip tie they used to secure his hands behind his back should have gone on smoothly. Whoever was applying it had the coordination of a drunk. The guy was either nervous or he didn't know what he was doing. Or both—and both could be used in Winters' favor.

They didn't blindfold him either, and that part worried him most because it only made sense if they were going to kill him anyway.

But why not do it now? Why lead him to another room in the basement? Why hurl him into a chair?

Winters continued to ask himself rational questions until the Russian who had held the gun to his head stepped forward and plunged his fist into Winters' face. Again. And again—each time sending bone-jarring pain through his head. There was a pause, long enough for him to think it was over—then once more the Russian punched a fist that was not just flesh but also brass straight into Winters' nose. He cried out in agony—a long, thin cry he didn't recognize as his own—followed by the piercing ring of his cell phone that interrupted the dream.

Winters fumbled for the phone on the nightstand, then found it at last and pressed a button to accept the call.

"*Bienvenidos, Señor* Winters," a female voice said. "How do you find our Barcelona so far?"

"Who is this?" he asked, still groggy and confused from the dream.

A short pause was followed by a stiffer version of the voice. "This is Sophia Conte. You *are* John Winters, yes?"

Winters bit off a curse and climbed out of bed. "Sorry, Sophia. I'm a little disoriented."

Did he just say that? He did *not* just say that.

"Ah, jet lag will do that, yes," she said. "I should have waited longer to call you, but I was eager to reach you."

"No, it's all right. Let me just get myself together here—"

Did he say *that*, too? And how was he planning to get himself together? There was no coffeepot in the room and the water drooling from the faucet was rust-brown so a face wash was out of the question.

"I have captured you at a bad time," she said.

Winters pushed at his closed eyes with his thumb and index finger. "I think the word you want is 'caught.'"

"I think the expression I want is 'Good night.'"

"What time is it?"

"Barely 10 a.m. But you need sleep. Call me in the morning—around eight?"

"No, really, I'm fine."

"No. Rest. We have a full day tomorrow."

"We do?"

"I have arranged for us to meet with a man who knows much more than I do about a link you have not explored yet."

"Okay." Winters blinked his eyes until he could actually see. He needed to salvage this conversation. "Sounds good. How about if I buy you breakfast?"

"That would be lovely. Where shall we meet?"

"How about—the hotel dining room?"

"Where are you staying?"

Winters told her and was met with a stony silence.

"Hello?" he said. "Are you still there?"

"Get some sleep, John. And first thing tomorrow, find a different hotel. I will e-mail you several suggestions. And in the meantime . . . do not drink the water and do not eat the food."

"That bad, huh?"

"Worse," she replied. "I am being kind."

Winters hung up feeling the same way he had the first time he asked a girl on a date and she turned him down because, she said, he couldn't afford to take her anyplace she wanted to go. Maybe Ben was right when he said Winters was cheap. Sounded like he couldn't afford this town.

"I'll worry about that tomorrow," he groaned. Right now sleep was all he wanted and he fell back on the bed. Let the dreams hit him. He was too wiped out to care.

It was they in Barcelona who controlled the finances, Diego—
it was they who resisted. They were afraid to know the truth,
and not only the truth about the means of reaching the East
by sailing west, which would disrupt their power. They were
terrified of the truth about us . . . and about themselves.

—Christopher Columbus

Thanks again for picking me up," Maria said. "I know it's a hassle to get in and out of Dulles, but you can see now why I didn't want to talk about this at the office."

Austin glared at her across the table. His brown hair seemed to be standing up even straighter than usual, and his eyes were narrowed to slits the way he looked when he was aggravated.

Maria couldn't really blame him. He had every right to dump her here, go back to Gump, Snowden and Meir, and turn in his resignation.

"It didn't occur to you to request that I go *with* you to Barcelona?" he snarled.

"Of course it occurred to me. I've been missing you since the moment we left."

"Oh, that's clear."

Maria shoved her half-eaten salad aside and glared at him. "Listen to me. First of all, if you came with me I wouldn't need Elena and that is the whole *point* in my going back."

"And second of all?"

"I need you here to find the best attorney for her and look into what happened that got her into this whole mess."

"On the firm's time."

"I haven't gotten to that part yet." Maria leaned closer and lowered her voice. "I want to pay you myself. On the side."

"You can't afford me."

"My grandmother left me some money—"

"You can't use your inheritance for this. I won't let you do that."

Maria gave him a look. "And you started not letting me do things when?"

"I meant I'm not taking any money from you. I'll do it for free, but on one condition."

"Anything—as long as it's legal."

"You have to promise me the Barcelona thing is only temporary."

"Of course it is. I'm going back *there* to bring Elena back *here.*"

"And what about this Tejada character?"

"What about him?"

"You don't see yourself getting hooked up with him? I mean involved."

"Not gonna happen," she said shaking her head. "I don't trust him. Not totally, anyway."

"What does that mean?"

"It means he's not some villain. He's just a successful businessman—"

"Over-the-top successful."

"—who may bend the occasional rule."

"I thought you didn't like people bending the rules."

"I don't. Which is why I'm not getting involved. As soon as you get things set up here, I'm bringing Elena back and I'm done in Spain."

"I don't see why you didn't just bring her with you now."

"Yes, you do. There's too much to do, including finding a place for her to stay. I can't harbor a fugitive, no matter who she is."

"I'm glad to see you draw the line somewhere."

"Austin—what is going on with you?"

"This just doesn't feel right to me. No—" he said, correcting himself. "It's worse than that. It feels dangerous."

"Well," Maria shrugged. "It kind of is. One of the reasons I'm going back is to see if I can find a way to take Molina down."

"No stinkin' way."

"It doesn't feel right to smuggle her out of there to face the music here while he gets off scot-free. He's been blackmailing her—and who knows how many others. I can't let him get away with it."

"Come on," Austin groaned. "Let somebody else deal with that."

"I intend to."

"Who?"

Maria smiled. "Emilio Tejada."

"And you're going to do that how?" Austin put both palms up. "Never mind. I don't want to know."

"Good, because I'm not sure yet. You want dessert?"

"No."

"Then ask for the check, will you?" She reached into her purse for her wallet. "Here's some cash. I'll be right back."

"Where are you going?"

"To the bathroom, Austin. And I'm sure I'll be safe."

"I'm afraid to let you out of my sight."

She hadn't been lying to him, Maria thought as she wove her way among the tables of the large dining room. She *had* missed Austin and if she could do this any differently she would. But that would only slow things down and it had been hard enough to leave Elena yesterday. The only thing holding Elena together at this point seemed to be Maria's promise that she would return within a week. But all the plans she'd made with Austin evaporated as she neared the restroom hallway.

From the corner of her eye she saw two men seated at a table to the far right. The guy facing her she recognized as Jake Schlesinger. His picture was all over Washington media. Him she wasn't worried about. But the figure with his back to her sent a chill down her spine. She would have known that square head and those menacing shoulders anywhere.

He was Carlos Molina.

What were the chances that he'd show up here—now?

Acting more on instinct than plan, Maria continued straight across to the hallway and ducked out of sight beyond the corner—hidden from view but close enough to hear the voices from Molina's table.

Maria pulled her cell phone from her purse, flipped the screen to Notes, and typed what she could hear. It was disjointed, but she'd try to figure it out later.

JS: Appreciate your help with that matter in Kenya—

CM: —return the favor . . . intercepted in Chechnya . . .

JS: . . . secure location, I assure you . . .

CM: (mutter, mutter, mutter)

"Is it full?"

Maria jerked her face up to see a woman standing nearby.

"The restroom," the woman explained. "Is it full?"

"I don't—"

"You're standing in the hall. I thought it was full." The woman gave her an annoyed look and pushed open the restroom door. Maria went back to the conversation but she'd clearly missed something. They were now talking about a suitcase and some agent named Jason Elliot.

JS: . . . out of your mind . . .

CM: . . . like you were in Copenhagen . . .

JS: . . . you assured me . . .

CM: You assured *me* . . . pictures.

Two women erupted from the restroom, voices blaring. By the time they'd carried the discussion out to the dining room, the voices from the table were silent. She glanced around the corner to check and saw Molina and Schlesinger standing, shaking hands.

Maria ducked into the bathroom and made for an empty stall, where she read the notes.

Molina had done Schlesinger some favor in Kenya and was now asking for payback. Something about whatever Schlesinger had intercepted in Chechnya, something that was now in a secure location. Whatever Molina was asking of him was insane, although apparently Schlesinger had done something crazy in Copenhagen that involved pictures. And, somehow, there was a suitcase and an agent involved.

None of it made any sense—unless Schlesinger was being blackmailed . . . just like Elena.

21

Tejada stood at the Ritz-Carlton penthouse window, watching the Atlantic lapping up on the Key Biscayne shore below. Catching a glimpse of his reflection he noticed he was scowling.

He prided himself on keeping his emotions in check, but Prevost could peck them out without even being in the same room. Or the same country, for that matter. He was still dallying in Brussels rather than meeting him here as Tejada had "suggested." And until he spoke to him in person, he'd have no news of his discussion with Koslov.

His phone swished a text. From Snowden. At least the trip here wasn't a complete waste of time.

He texted Snowden his room number. The knock on the door was immediate, and Tejada smiled to himself as Louis went to open it. He'd been standing right outside. Like Prevost, he sometimes groveled.

When Snowden had been supplied with bourbon and an armchair overlooking the ocean, Tejada said, "You can leave us, Louis. I'll ring you if we need anything."

Louis nodded and disappeared into a bedroom, discreet as always.

He turned now to Snowden, relaxing in the wicker armchair, eyes closed, glass resting on his knee.

"You are spent," Tejada said.

"It's a good kind of tired, as my mother used to say."

"You speak very little of your family."

"And I'd like to keep it that way." Snowden took a sip of his drink. "I have what I think you'll find to be good news."

Tejada eased onto the sofa and nodded him on.

"All the preliminary work has been completed with McCarthy. Think-tank position papers. Community organization. Public campaign. All in place."

"Good. And what about you?"

"What about me?"

"Are you in place?"

"You've lost me, Emilio."

Tejada swirled the bourbon. "You are following the plan, but is your heart in it?"

"Does it matter?"

"It does to Lord Abaddon."

Tejada saw a flash of fear in Snowden's eyes, though it quickly disappeared.

"My heart can be in implementing the plan without my having complete faith that it's going to happen. This isn't all under our control."

"Of course it is."

"The US Congress has never defaulted on its debt and I'm just not sure all our manipulation guarantees that it will this time either."

"We do not need an actual default," Tejada said. "We need only the threat of one."

"I hope you're right."

Tejada stood up. "Can I freshen your drink?"

"No. Thanks."

"I'm glad you brought up Congress." Tejada went to the bar and topped off his glass. "That is our next—and final—step. The matter needs to come to a vote."

"I know."

"It's time to—how do you always put it?—get the ball rolling on that." Tejada smiled. "You're sure you don't need another drink?"

✦   ✦   ✦

Maria tossed in the bed until the comforter was in a complete knot. She finally gave up on sleep at 5 a.m. Jet lag in this direction was supposed to make her want to sleep well, but there was too much in her head clamoring for attention for her to even doze off.

The worst of it was the conversation she'd overheard between Molina and Schlesinger. She'd been so sure about going back to Barcelona—she still was—but Molina now cut a far more menacing figure than merely a bully who would blackmail a young girl. That was bad enough, but if he had sufficient clout to strong-arm the director of the CIA, maybe she was getting in over her head.

Maria curled up on the windowsill cushions. The Adams Morgan neighborhood still slumbered, although a few lights were blinking on in the distance. At the moment she envied those people in other apartments who would soon be headed out to day jobs they could leave behind at five o'clock, jobs that didn't tug at them no matter where they were.

Maria knew when she went to law school that she wasn't signing up for forty-hour workweeks. The ten years of life with her mother hadn't been wasted on her. Many a night a babysitter or her dad tucked her in to bed because Mom was working on a case. But Maria chose corporate law specifically so she wouldn't have to deal with people like Carlos Molina. She'd wanted to have a career like her mother's, not like her father's.

And look who had ended up being killed.

Maria shook that off and went to the kitchen. If she wasn't going to sleep, she might as well make coffee—something a little thinner than the stuff she drank in Spain. As she filled the pot with cold water, she returned to the idea that had been niggling at the back of her brain all night.

Her father *did* have a career handling things like this. She didn't know if he was still out on paid leave. They hadn't talked since *Abuela*'s funeral and they'd only exchanged e-mails about the estate. But he'd take her call, she had no doubt of that.

She poured the water into the coffeemaker and grunted. And then what? A barrage of questions. A boatload of unsolicited advice. He'd probably send a covert ops team over to Barcelona to arrest Carlos Molina, right after he had her taken into protective custody. For the rest of her life.

Maria watched the French roast drip into the pot. Dad would take *overprotective father* to a whole new level, despite the fact that he'd shown progressively fewer visible signs of emotion toward her since her mother died. Not that she'd given him much of a chance in the last seven or eight years. Now it was hard to sort out who had first stopped making the effort to connect.

She looked at the digital clock on the coffeemaker. Time had passed, but it was still only 7 a.m. Four in San Francisco. She'd give it a few more hours and call. And until then, more coffee and the Internet. Maria wanted to find out the last time Jake Schlesinger was in Copenhagen.

Seeing Sophia Conte in person for the first time was a little like spotting a TV personality at a restaurant. They were always thinner, shorter, and less perfect than they appeared on the screen.

Only two of those applied, Winters decided as Sophia approached him outside of a restaurant called Dostrece. She was far more slender and definitely more petite than she'd looked on Skype. When she reached his side, hand outstretched, her head barely came to his shoulder.

As for imperfections, though, the screen had covered up the smoothness of her *café au lait* skin and the keen intelligence in her dark, deep-set eyes. Even the fuzzy halo of hair around her face seemed more on-purpose than the Internet had allowed. Winters suddenly felt like a gangly teenager again.

"A pleasure to meet you in person," she said. "Have you rested?"

"Yes," he lied.

Actually he'd spent the last twenty-two hours changing hotels, trying to get his cell phone to work, and fighting off nightmares. But then she would have no way of knowing that the bags beneath his eyes were a recent development. She'd just think it came from the jet lag.

"Shall we go in?" she asked. "I'm sure *Señor* Vespucci is waiting for us."

Before Winters had a chance to ask who *Señor* Vespucci was, Sophia stepped forward and led the way through the heavy glass door. She had mentioned they would be meeting someone but he didn't know the guy was joining them for breakfast.

Sophia greeted the wait staff as if they were family members at a reunion. Amid the cheek-kissing and the bantering in Spanish, Winters was introduced to a paunchy gentleman with a chin that melted into his neck.

"*Señor* Gilberto Vespucci, Mr. John Winters."

Sophia gracefully gestured to a corner table with a pot of coffee already on it. Winters, on the other hand, banged the table with his knee as he sat down and caught his foot in the tablecloth.

"I hope you don't mind," Sophia said as she perched next to him. "I have taken the liberty of ordering for us—in the interest of time." She turned to Vespucci. "I know you are a busy man, Gilberto."

"Time stops when I am with you, *mi tesoro*."

Winters pawed awkwardly at his napkin.

Sophia poured the coffee while simultaneously giving each of the men a three-sentence bio of the other. Winters was transfixed by the thickness of the coffee but he managed to get that *Señor* Vespucci was a well-known Columbus scholar.

"Before we can make the link between you and *Señor* Christopher," Sophia said to Winters, "we need to explore the Jewish aspect. "Gilberto has made that his life's work—"

"I'm sorry," Winters said, "did you say 'Jewish aspect'?"

They both looked at him as if he'd stumbled into the wrong classroom. Sophia was the first to recover. "Yes. Am I to assume you have not encountered this in your research?"

"I don't know." Winters shrugged. "What was I supposed to encounter?"

"It is easier to miss than you might think, Sophia," Vespucci said, burying his chin deeper into his neck. He pulled a pair of wire-rimmed glasses from the pocket of his jacket and placed them halfway up his wide nose. He peered through the lenses as if this was his first impetus to actually look at Winters. "Shall I start at the beginning?"

Sophia put her hand on his arm. "Can you spare the time?"

From what Winters could tell, he would probably clear his schedule for the next week if it meant a chance to "start at the beginning." He, on the other hand, was ready to cut to the chase. "Are you saying Christopher Columbus was Jewish?"

"There is a theory that says so," Sophia said.

Vespucci's thick eyebrows lifted. "It is far more than a theory, Sophia. There is hard evidence."

"Now you're speaking my language," Winters said. "Tell me what you're working with here."

Vespucci ticked the evidence off with a flick of his fingers. "One, he spoke Castilian Spanish, which was referred to in his time as the 'Yiddish of the Spanish Jews.' Two, on personal correspondence with his son he included a cryptic message written in Hebrew letters. Three, in his will, he left a bequest to provide a dowry for poor girls and also directed his executor to give money to a Jew who lived near the entrance to the Lisbon Jewish Quarter." Vespucci shrugged as if his point was clear without explanation, though he gave one. "That was Jewish custom, providing a dowry for an indigent girl. And four—and this is the most telling of all—his first voyage was financed by Jewish businessmen."

Vespucci sat back in his chair with a satisfied look. Winters didn't have the heart to tell him that it all sounded circumstantial to him. He could hear Anne saying, *Show me his bar mitzvah certificate and then we'll talk.*

Vespucci turned his attention to the *huevos Florentine* a waiter set before him. Sophie turned hers to Winters. "I apologize. I thought you knew about this."

Winters tried not to sound as irritated as he felt. "We never talked about this. But anyway, how does Columbus worrying about the Antichrist work if he was Jewish? Wouldn't he have to have been a Christian for that to even be an issue?"

"A good point!" Vespucci spattered yolk onto Winters' sleeve. "One of the purposes for his voyage was to find a place where Jews could live free of persecution."

"You remember what Spain was going through at that time," Sophia said.

Winters felt as if he could finally press the buzzer on *Jeopardy*. "The Inquisition."

"Yes!" Vespucci said. "More important, he was looking for a source of gold to fund the retaking of Jerusalem."

"That's where the end-of-time idea comes in," Sophia said. "He believed that for the Messiah to return, the Temple had to be liberated and restored."

"I did read that in the *Book of Prophecies*," Winters said. "But it still doesn't make sense, if he was a Christian. And he didn't say anything about being a Jew."

"Of course not!" Vespucci's face reddened indignantly. "Or he himself would have been on the rack."

Sophia put a calming hand on Vespucci's wrist as she turned to Winters. "Not only that, but my reading of the *Prophecies* tells me that he was a Jew by birth but was converted to Christianity."

That still didn't resolve Winters' dilemma. Anyone's reading of anything could tell her whatever she wanted to believe. They both seemed to be waiting for some kind of response—as if this should be a moment of great insight for him—but he didn't know what to say. Diplomacy had never been his strength. He'd always left that to Anne. "It would be ironic," he said finally, "if he was a Jew and yet wanted to have a hand in confronting the Antichrist."

Vespucci nodded and wiped his mouth on the napkin. "Christian or Jew," he said, loud enough that it brought one of Sophia's friends from the kitchen. "The fact remains, Columbus wanted to discover the Ark of the Covenant and restore it to Israel. You see . . ." He moved to the front of his chair, rendering its back legs helpless above the floor. "He didn't know he was going to discover what would eventually be called the Americas. He thought he was going to Asia. He thought someone had stolen the Ark and taken it to China. He didn't realize there was a huge landmass in the way and neither he nor any of the scholars of the time understood just how big that landmass really was." Vespucci looked Winters in the eye. "There is so much more I could tell you."

"Tell me this," Winters said. "How is anyone ever going to prove that this was what was going through Columbus' mind? Sophia told me that he wrote things purposely to send people off the track—"

"Would he lie to himself in his own journal?"

"You wouldn't think so but—journal?" Winters frowned. "What journal?"

Vespucci gave Sophia a stricken look. "He does not know about the journal, either?"

"As you've said, Gilberto, there is so much to tell." Sophia turned to Winters. "In his notes from the fourth voyage, Columbus wrote that many in Andalusia—that's the southern part of Spain—wished to take his discoveries from him but that he had received prophecies from Almighty God about his end, the end of the earth—"

"Right," Winters said. "That's in the *Book of Prophecies*."

"Not all of it, apparently. In those same notes he wrote that all of it—the conspiracies, the prophecies, the signs he saw in the heavens—had been set down in his most private journal."

"Have you seen it?" Winters asked.

"No one has seen it." Vespucci answered.

"Many scholars do not believe it ever existed," Sophia said.

"But it did," Vespucci insisted. "The Admiral of the Ocean Sea would not have said so in his personal writings if it were not so!"

The bulbous nose was scarlet and the veins along Vespucci's jawline seemed to pulse. Sophia reached over to him and ran a hand up and down his arm. "You and I know that, Gilberto," she said in a soothing tone. "Many faithful people know it too. We do not need to concern ourselves with the others."

Yeah, and it wasn't a good time for Winters to align himself with "the others," even though all of this seemed more like wishful conjecture than anything else. The question was, why did Sophia think he needed to know about this . . . theory?

"You have been a help to us," she said to Vespucci. "But we must allow you to return to your work."

Vespucci reluctantly agreed, good-byes were said, and Sophia escorted him to the door. Winters grabbed the opportunity to take care of the bill and pour himself another cup of coffee.

"Listen," he said when Sophia returned to the table, "I hope I didn't come across as a jerk."

"Your skepticism was clear to me," she said. "But I don't think Gilberto noticed it. He is so enraptured with the stories he seldom notices how anyone reacts to them."

"Good. I wouldn't want to offend him."

She didn't say anything. The woman was hard to read. "So," he said, "what was that all about? I mean, in terms of my genealogy?"

"Were any of your mother's relatives practicing Jews?"

Winters started to shake his head, but he reconsidered. "You know, I remember talk about my great-grandfather being Jewish, but he'd never admit it." He thought some more. "After he came to America he attended the Episcopal Church. And did so for the rest of his life. He's buried in the church cemetery." Winters shrugged. "Still, there was no reason for him not to own up to it if he was. He didn't live during the Inquisition."

"No, but there weren't that many generations from the Inquisition to your great-grandfather. There was a tradition that if you were Jewish and you converted to Christianity you needed to give every outward sign of that conversion you could so that no one would mistake you for someone who converted in word only and not from the heart."

"It was still that big a deal, even so many years after the Inquisition?"

Sophia grimaced. "Before the 1960s, Jews were as discriminated against here as blacks were in your country."

"You're not serious."

"If they were interested in fitting in, the last thing they wanted was to be labeled as Jews, and the easiest way to avoid that would have been to show a solid, incontrovertible conversion and to emphasize their Spanish heritage. What?"

Winters realized he'd been staring at her, mouth slightly open. "Sorry," he said. "Your English vocabulary is impressive. I don't know that I've ever used the word 'incontrovertible.' Maybe I should start."

"Are you mocking me, Mr. Winters?" she asked.

Winters went cold for a second before Sophia laughed—a sound he hadn't heard from her before.

"Now, back to the issue—"

"I do remember we'd be watching TV," Winters said, "and there would be something about discrimination against African Americans and Mom would say, 'We had nothing to do with that. We're Spanish.'"

"That is precisely what we're referring to here." Sophia's eyes went birdlike. "We must track down all these small hints to see if any of them lead us somewhere."

Winters had a sinking feeling in his chest. "Don't take this the wrong way," he said, "but aren't we grasping at straws?"

"Research is my area of expertise," she said, chin tilted up. "This is how it is done." She curled her fingers around her clutch bag and stood. "Come. We have miles to go."

"Where are we going?"

"To Alba de Tormes," she said. "Your hometown."

23

Tejada summoned every internal resource he had—the power of Abaddon, the pride of the office of CEO, and the reluctance to spend the rest of his life in prison—to keep himself from placing his hands around Philippe Prevost's pencil neck and shaking him.

Self-control achieved, he stepped from behind his desk, perched on its front edge, and said in a matter-of-fact tone, "Give me the bottom line. That is all I want to hear. Not how little the Russians trust me. Not how much influence they believe I have over you. Simply tell me—are they in or are they not?"

Prevost's face went deathly pale. "They are not."

"Summarize for me where that puts us."

Prevost was clearly rattled. "What you have not allowed me to explain—"

"*Summarize*," Tejada demanded.

"Okay," Prevost began in a halting voice. "The Russians . . . and the Americans . . . want to maintain the currency as it is. The Chinese want everything to switch to the yuan. The European Union and Great Britain would like to go along with us, but they are wary of the Russians."

"Then we have failed in this part of the plan."

Tejada was sure the small sag of relief in his nephew's shoulders came from Tejada's choice of pronoun. If Prevost had been any kind of man, he would have taken responsibility for the failure, but there was no time to call him on that now.

"I see only one thing to do," Prevost said.

"What?"

"That dramatic event you spoke of."

"Yes," Tejada sighed. "That's about all that's left."

"I don't suppose you're going to tell me what it is."

"No," Tejada said. "I don't suppose I am."

"What is my next step then?"

Tejada slid from his perch at the edge of the desk and moved around to the chair.

"I will contact you," he said, picking up a file from the desk.

"And in the meantime?"

Tejada didn't answer but kept his eyes focused on the file in his hand. He heard Prevost leave the room and a moment later, the door opened again. "We have nothing more to talk about," he said, his eyes still trained on the file.

"We have said nothing yet," a voice replied.

Tejada looked up to see Molina standing across the room. "I thought you were my nephew returning for a replay. Come in."

Molina crossed the office to the desk but didn't take a seat.

"You made contact in Washington?" Tejada asked, anticipating the reason for Molina's visit.

"I did," Molina replied.

"And?"

"The process has begun."

"Any resistance?"

"As expected, yes," he said. "But it has been handled."

Tejada didn't ask how. The less he knew the better, a philosophy he could never get across to Prevost. "They will wait for our signal, then," Tejada said instead.

"Yes."

Tejada folded his hands on the desk and examined his knuckles. "I had hoped to avoid this, Carlos. But it seems inevitable."

"Anything else?" Molina asked.

"Yes, in fact, there is." Tejada said. "You recall Snowden's associate, Maria Winters."

"Yes, sir."

"She will be returning soon to work with me on a few matters. I'd like for you to provide better office space for her and more than adequate living arrangements. Make sure she has everything she needs. And make sure you keep the Soler woman as her assistant."

Molina nodded. Tejada searched his face for a hint of reaction but found none.

"Do you have a problem with *Señorita* Winters?" he asked.

"May I speak freely?"

"When you are not speaking freely you are not speaking at all."

"She has an agenda."

"Who among us does not?" Tejada watched Molina's neck stiffen. "My apologies, Carlos. If you have a serious concern, I don't mean to make light of it."

"I would like permission to research her background and put her under surveillance."

Tejada forced his brow to remain smooth. "Only in terms of her work here," he said. "Her social life is off-limits."

"It's difficult to keep them separated."

"Find a way."

The air became electric with tension. Tejada didn't want to leave it that way. "I appreciate your concern," he said. "I know you have only my best interests and those of Catalonia at heart. All the more reason to keep your focus there, as you do so well."

Molina seemed to relax.

"And," Tejada continued, "since she seems to have an aversion to Louis, perhaps you should meet her at the airport. That will give you a chance to begin your 'surveillance.'"

Their eyes met. Tejada smiled. Molina did not.

24

Y ou lied to me," Austin blurted out.

Maria looked up from loading the dishwasher. "I never lied to you. How did I ever lie to you?"

"You told me you weren't staying in Barcelona permanently."

"I'm not."

"Then why are you taking all this stuff?"

Maria closed the dishwasher door and pushed the button. "What stuff are you talking about?"

"Two suitcases. A carry-on as big as the trunk of my car. *And* a briefcase so full it won't even zip."

"I'm not a guy, Austin," she said, crossing the living room. "I can't get everything I own into a sock."

Austin glared at the luggage parked by the front door. "I'm depressed and you haven't even left yet."

"And I'm *not* leaving right this minute so come here. I want to show you what I found." She motioned for him to join her at the counter where her laptop was still open.

"Aren't you taking that with you?"

"Yeah . . ."

"And it's going to fit in that briefcase?"

"Okay, stop it. Now look at this."

Austin parked in front of the computer and frowned. "Danish schoolgirls?"

"I found this hidden in—well, never mind—the gist of it is Schlesinger was at a Global Security Conference in Copenhagen. Apparently there was an issue with some parents insisting that their daughters were in his room."

"Were they?"

"According to the girls and their parents they were, but the whole thing got smoothed over."

"You're thinking this is what he and Molina were talking about?"

"Molina was on the roster of attendees."

"Why wouldn't he be? He's the head of security for Catalonia."

"But the fact that he mentioned it to Schlesinger—and mentioned having pictures—is pretty damning."

"Circumstantial at best, but yeah." Austin chewed thoughtfully at his lower lip. "So you kind of know what Molina is blackmailing him *with*, but you don't know what he's forcing him to *do*."

"Right. And that's not all Molina has on him. Something went down in Kenya, too, but I haven't been able to put that together. The point is, whatever Molina wants him to do is pretty big or he wouldn't need all this ammunition."

Austin hoisted himself from the stool and crossed to the living room, rubbing the back of his neck.

"What?" Maria said.

"This is scaring me."

"Come on, Austin. If I find out anything I'm not going to confront Molina with it."

"Not even to use it as leverage for Elena?"

"I told you, I'm just going to bring her back here so we can make this whole thing right."

"Then what *are* you going to do with it?" Austin strode back to her. "Swear to me you're not going to take it to Tejada. You don't know whether he's involved. Molina works for him and—"

"Would you chill? My best option is to take it to my father."

Austin's mouth fell open.

"I know. But it makes sense, right?"

"Don't you think you should tell him you're doing this in the first place?"

Maria piled her hair up and let it drop back to her shoulders. "I've been trying. His cell phone keeps going straight to voice mail."

"Did you call his office?"

"He's on some kind of leave."

"What—bereavement?" Austin put both hands up in that way he had. "Sorry. You can be snarky about him . . . I shouldn't be."

"It's okay." Maria twisted a curl. "Actually he told me he's being seen for depression."

Austin stared until she nodded. "I should follow up."

"Ya think?"

Maria glanced at the time on her phone. "I guess I could call his friend Taylor Donleavy. Dad used his phone to call me one time so I think it's in my contacts." She looked at Austin again. "But what do I say—'Has anybody checked my dad's place lately?'"

"You'll think of something. I'm gonna start loading the car. I should've started yesterday."

Maria wrinkled her nose at him and searched for Donleavy's number on her phone. She'd never met the guy, which made this weird. Her dad had mentioned him a few times—the only friend he'd talked about since he moved to California. Uncle Ben brought him up more than Dad did. The three of them had hung out together when Ben was visiting. He had a whole stand-up routine about Donleavy's geek quotient.

The phone rang several times before a voice mail greeting said, "Donleavy. Leave an encrypted message."

Yeah. He was a geek all right.

Maria couldn't decide what to say so she hung up. Maybe her father was back at work, doing something undercover and just wasn't bothering to check his messages.

She heard Austin fiddling with the doorknob and she drew her hand down her face to remove the worried look she was sure was there. Maybe then he'd believe her when she said Donleavy was going to get back to her. Otherwise, all that luggage was coming right back up the stairs.

25

Winters looked for something to grab on to and reached for the dashboard.

Sophia smiled at him. "Are you a nervous passenger, John?"

"I'm a terrified passenger. Did I miss the memo about us being entered in the Grand Prix?"

"That takes place in France."

Her laughter rose above the wind whipping through the windows. He was having to shout to be heard. Fortunately she'd been doing most of the talking as they crossed Spain and had filled him in on how she'd found his distant cousin Jacobo Colon through birth and death records going back from Winters' great-grandfather to previous generations.

"What's he like?" Winters shouted to her.

"I do not know."

"You couldn't gather anything from talking to him?"

"I have not spoken with him."

Sophia slowed the car as they crossed an ancient bridge over the Tormes River. Winters was finally able to speak rather than shout. "Nothing from his e-mail either?"

"I have not been in contact with *Señor* Colon at all. I discovered his address . . . which should not be far from here."

"He doesn't know we're coming?"

She shook her head and took a corner way too fast for Winters' comfort.

"What if we came all this way and he's not home?"

"He is eighty-five years old and lives in a long-term-care facility. I am certain he will be there and grateful for the company. Here most families take care of their own elderly so he must truly be alone."

Winters tried not to groan. Another old guy with theories and foggy memories. How much money had he spent on this trip?

Sophia abruptly pulled the vehicle to the side of the road and lowered her sunglasses to look at the long, low pink-stucco building with a rose-colored tile roof. "We have arrived."

Winters glanced to the right. "This is a long-term-care facility?"

"Yes, it is."

Winters guessed the word "care" might be an overstatement, but he kept that to himself. He was going to keep his own counsel this time. And then he'd be looking for that return flight home. Archer was never going to let him live this trip down.

The inside of the building didn't reflect the outside, at least not entirely. The floor of the wide central hallway was covered in much-washed clay tile and the walls were a butter-yellow stucco that had worn off in places to reveal patches of brick. Sunlight streamed from the rooms on the west side into the hall, giving it a playful, striped effect, and the woman who walked toward them was smiling. The gaps left by missing teeth would have detracted from her credibility if her English hadn't been crisp when she asked, "I can help you?"

While Sophia told her their business in rapid-fire Spanish, Winters pulled out his phone and checked for the umpteenth time to see if he had service. *Nada*. Not that he was expecting to hear from anyone, except maybe Ben, and even that was doubtful. He wanted to let

Maria know he was in Barcelona in case she was still there, although he didn't think that was possible either. She'd said she was just going for a short business trip.

"You will follow?"

Winters looked up to see Sophia already trailing the attendant into a room to his left. He caught up and felt himself nod appreciatively when he got there. Arched windows lined three walls and cream stucco bounced light from the other. Ceiling fans spun lazily overhead. Not a bad place to spend the end of your life.

Only three people were in the room. Two of undetermined gender napped on a couch at the far end. Another, a wiry old man with an impressive moustache, sat upright in a wheelchair near one of the windows, chortling over a book.

"*Señor* Colon!" the attendant shouted at him.

Winters jumped but the old man barely gave her a glance. Wonderful. He was either deaf as a post or senile. Uncle David heard better than this guy.

The woman rattled off something in Spanish of which Winters caught only the word "Columbus," and *Señor* Colon turned his gaze on Winters and Sophia. His eyes were an unexpected blue that gleamed as they surveyed Sophia. At least the old guy could still appreciate a good-looking woman. He closed his book, set it aside, and stroked the moustache.

More give-and-take in Spanish as chairs were pulled up to the wheelchair and the attendant laughed and made some kind of assurances to *Señor* Colon. He didn't take his eyes off Sophia as she perched in her light-as-a-sparrow fashion on the edge of one of the chairs and patted the other one for Winters. He sat, but he might as well have been invisible. The old man was clearly smitten.

"I have heard these stories, too," he said.

Winters startled.

"Your English is very good, *Señor* Colon," Sophia said.

"Please. Jacobo."

"Jacobo. I am Sophia. This is John."

Jacobo gave Winters a cursory glance and returned to the object of his affection. "My mother, she insist that I learn English as a boy. She wanted I should go to America but it never happened. I did not want to go anyway." He smiled at Sophia. "Too much beauty here, no?"

The old man could still flirt, Winters had to give him that.

"So you have heard the stories," Sophia said.

"Of our relation to Columbus? Yes."

"Are they true?" Winters asked.

"Yes. And no."

Winters sat back. It was going to be a long afternoon.

"True for me, no. True for you. "He shrugged his shoulders. "Maybe."

"Why not true for you, Jacobo?" Sophia said, her voice laced with sympathy.

Yeah. Definitely best to let her do the talking.

"I am related to *Señor* Christopher Columbus, but not in the line of direct descent. I am a relative very distant, not of the main branch."

"I'm sorry," Sophia said.

"I am not! Why do I want Americans knocking at my door who want to see me?" He looked at Winters for the first time—and burst into barroom laughter. "I only joke with you, my cousin! Come—let us drink together!"

The smiling attendant pulled a small table closer and deposited a tray on it. A pitcher of something cold with citrus curls floating in it was flanked by three glasses. Jacobo looked up at her. "You have used the sangria recipe, Anita."

She shook her head the way any good nurse would who refused to serve alcohol to her aged patient. Winters didn't have to speak Spanish to know what was going down. Uncle David and this guy were clearly related.

Sophia poured and asked Jacobo to go on.

"*My* family, it has a colorful history," he said, caressing his moustache.

Big surprise.

"We are related to a servant who took the name of Colon." Jacobo winked at no one in particular. "This woman, she had . . . *asunto amoroso* with her master." Jacobo let out a horselaugh again. "They had something hot on the side—a child was born—and there you have it—another Colon!"

Winters let himself grin. He was beginning to like this old character.

"Now you, *el primo*," he said, gesturing to Winters. "You are no son of a servant."

"How can you tell?" Winters asked.

"You have the . . ." He snapped his fingers and looked at Sophia.

"*El aura?*"

"Ah, *sí!*"

"You have the aura," she said to Winters.

"*Sí,* the air of the descendants of the third duke of Liria, Jacobo-Franscisco Eduardo Fitz-James Stuart y Colón."

"That's nice of you, Jacobo," Winters said, "but I don't think you can say—"

"You have not seen his portrait?"

"I saw his picture online—"

"You must see the portrait or—" He snapped his fingers again.

"Or a copy," Sophia offered.

He grinned at her. "You and me—we are the perfect team. Why don't you marry me?"

"You far outclass me," she said, without missing a beat. "I am not in the line of the Colons."

Jacobo faked a jealous glare at Winters and laughed again.

"In the stories you were told by the old ones," Sophia said, "did you ever hear of a secret journal that *Señor* Columbus kept?"

"Heard of it? I know where it is!"

Winters choked down a laugh. Sophia, however, kept a straight face. "And where is that?" she asked.

"He give it to a monk by the name of Gaspar Gorricio for the safety keeping. He lived in a monastery, the best place for the keeping of secrets." He gave Winters another wink. "This was common in that day with the important papers."

Sophia's face was no longer emotionless. Her eyes were keen on Jacobo. "What monastery was this monk connected with, Jacobo?"

"You haven't heard this story before?" Winters asked, glancing in her direction.

"This is the first time—"

"The monastery at Santa Maria de las Cuevas." Jacobo looked pleased that he'd been able to impress her. "In Seville."

Sophia nodded.

"But you will not find it there." Jacobo shook his head with more sadness than he felt, Winters was sure. "The monastery, it was closed long ago. It is now a place for history—"

"A historical site," Sophia said, her voice deflated.

Winters frowned. She was *buying* that whole thing?

"But"—Jacobo waited, one long bent finger up, until they both looked at him—"the trail to the journal, it begins there."

Winters couldn't handle it any longer. "If it was once there and the trail still leads to it, why hasn't anybody found it before now? Or maybe they have."

Jacobo's glare was genuine this time. "They have not, or you would have heard of it."

"That's true," Sophia agreed.

"And . . . only a direct descendant of *Señor* Columbus will be able to find it."

And Winters thought his mother was strange. It must run in the family. They were all nuts and he was beginning to feel that way himself. What was he even doing here?

But as long as he *was* there, okay, he'd play along. "So the journal knows if the person who's about to find it is a direct descendant of its original owner?"

Jacobo looked at Sophia in disgust. "He is *loco*, no?"

"Maybe," Sophia said, "but please, go on."

The old man turned to Winters and all but rolled the searing blue eyes. "No, the journal does not 'know.' It is an—" He snapped the fingers at Sophia again.

"Inanimate," Sophia said.

"Yes. An inanimate object. But the keepers of the journal have always known, through the generations. They have knowledge who will have the right to it." He shook his head ruefully. "All who have tried have failed."

"What do you mean?" Sophia said.

Winters watched her watch Jacobo, her eyes measuring his face. The old man was suddenly sober. No barroom laugh was forthcoming and he seemed to have forgotten his moustache.

"They have all died," he said in a somber tone.

"What?"

Jacobo kept his eyes on Sophia, who hadn't uttered a word. "Your friend, he is not only *loco*. He does not believe."

"He's a man of logic, Jacobo," Sophia said. "His work requires him to see only what is reasonable."

"I understand then," he said.

She smiled at him "What do you understand?"

"I understand why he needs you."

Winters stood up and extended his hand to the old man. "It's been a pleasure, Jacobo. Let's keep in touch now that we know we're related."

"Send me a Christmas greeting," Jacobo said. His voice was as dry as Winters' ever was.

Winters left Sophia to the prolonged good-byes and waited for her in front of the building. No doubt the old guy was trying to get her phone number.

When she joined him, her face was unreadable again, but her walk wasn't.

"You certainly have a way with people," she said coolly.

"I guess I should have humored the old guy."

"Or perhaps you should have believed him." Sophia's eyes flashed as she swept past him to the car. He hurried after her, only because he wouldn't put it past her to drive off without him.

He waited until they were on their way out of town before he said, "Are you telling me *you* believed him?"

"I believe he is passing down what he knows without embarrassment."

"Just because someone's passing down a family legend doesn't make it true. I heard all my life that George Washington chopped down a cherry tree and then caved to his old man, but I wouldn't swear it happened."

She looked at him blankly.

"You wouldn't know about that," he said. "But you get my point."

"Yes," she said. "And no."

At least the sparkle was back in her eyes. "Look, I don't mean to offend you, Sophia—"

"Then stop doing it."

"Tell me how I'm doing it."

"By discounting the spiritual aspect of this. I am not trying to press any of my religious beliefs on you, but I would appreciate your not belittling them."

"Were we talking about religious beliefs? I'm serious—did I miss something?"

"Do you have dinner plans?" she asked.

"I *know* I missed that."

"Do you have plans?"

"No."

"I know a place. If we are still speaking to each other when we arrive, I will buy our meal."

"And if we aren't?"

"I will take you to your hotel and we will say good-bye."

"I really did miss something." Winters gripped the dashboard. "But I'll agree to that on one condition."

"What is that?"

"You don't kill us before we get there."

She gave it a minute before she eased off the accelerator.

"Thank you," he said. "You wanted to say?"

"I wanted to say that I do not think we should discount everything

Jacobo said. There may be some merit to the possibility that the sacred keeping of the journal has been passed down through generations of monks and that they do have some way of recognizing a direct descendant." Sophia glanced at him. "And that way may very well be from the seeker's motives."

"I'm listening."

"Only someone with pure motives should have access to the journal. And who better than a person who has been given a sacred trust to be able to discern that?"

"What possible motives could there be?" Winters watched the tile roofs zip past. She hadn't slowed down much. "I suppose it could be worth a lot of money—but I'm not interested in selling it."

"What are you interested in?"

"I'm sorry?"

"Why are you on this search?"

My shrink said I needed a hobby? That wouldn't buy him dinner. And it wasn't true. But the *real* reason suddenly caught in his throat.

"My mother started this," he said. "She left me a letter asking me to continue the search. It meant something to her—I don't know what—but . . ." Winters spoke more slowly now, "she was like you. She saw something spiritual in it. She said God told her to do it."

"Do you believe that?"

"I believe she believed it," Winters said. "And I want to honor that."

They rode in silence for a few miles. By then the sun was turning the hills to silhouettes.

"Then I don't see that you have much choice but to pursue this," Sophia said finally. "If it leads nowhere, then you've lost nothing except a little time. But if it proves to be true, think what you will have done for your mother. And for all the rest of us."

"And my daughter, maybe?"

Sophia glanced at him with a questioning look but didn't ask. He'd never told her anything about himself, much less that he had a daughter. Instead she said, "If God did ask your mother to carry out this mission, there must have been a reason—a reason that still exists or she would not have handed it on to you."

Winters nodded. "Tell me—how far away is Seville?"

Sophia brought the car to a stop in front of a tiny, tile-topped building. "Four hours."

"Where are we now?"

She smiled at him. "Dinner."

26

Maria had way too much on her mind to sleep on the plane like she had on her first flight to Barcelona, despite the fact that she'd been mysteriously upgraded to first class, where the flight attendants all but rocked the passengers to sleep. Even though her Barcelona experience had started only a few weeks ago, she felt years older than when she began.

At the exit from customs she spotted Elena, just as they'd arranged. Maria grinned and waved but Elena's response was unenthusiastic.

Actually that was an understatement. Her eyes were wide with panic and her face pasty-white. It didn't take long to figure out why, either. Carlos Molina stood no more than six feet behind her.

The Austin voice in Maria's head told her to get back on the plane. A wiser voice told her to pretend not to see him. She went straight to Elena, dropped her bags, and gave her a brief hug, lips close to her ear. "Did you come with him?"

"I would rather be shot. I don't know why he's here. He's acting like he doesn't know me."

Maria could hear the terror in her voice and she squeezed tighter. "I'll handle him. Just grab my carry-ons and head for the door."

Elena did exactly as she said, though *fled* for the door would better describe her exit. When Maria turned to grab her suitcases she found Molina already had them.

The words *Scream and run because you're about to be kidnapped* entered her mind, but Maria inhaled and gave him a smile. "I wasn't expecting you, *Señor* Molina," she said. "It's a shame you came because I made other arrangements for pickup."

"*Señor* Tejada instructed me to come."

Then *Señor* Tejada was going to get a very large piece of her mind. "I'm happy to tell him you followed orders," Maria said. "Let me take those from you. I need to catch up with my assistant."

She made a grab for the handles of her roller bags but Molina deftly moved them aside.

"Seriously," she said. "Elena's getting a cab and I don't want to make them wait."

"Go, then," Molina said. "I will take your things to your apartment."

Maria stopped in mid-grab for one of her bags. "My apartment? No. I have a reservation at the—"

"*Señor* Tejada thought you would be more comfortable in the complex near Catalonia. Three bedrooms, two baths, full kitchen—"

"I'm not settling down here!" Maria reached up to scrape her fingers through her hair. Everything about this was wrong and she had to make it right, or Operation Save Elena was going to be over before it started.

"Tell you what," she continued. "I'll keep all my belongings with me until I've had a chance to speak with *Señor* Tejada. Then—"

"He has gone out of town for the day."

"Then I'll call him on his cell phone."

Molina gave the hint of a smirk and Maria immediately knew why. She didn't have Tejada's cell phone number. That was going on the list of things she would discuss with him first thing . . .

"All right," she conceded at last. "I'll go to the apartment, but Elena can take me. What's the address?"

Molina said nothing, either by word or expression. She truly wanted to smack him. But that would get Elena exactly where?

Maria forced a smile once more. "You know what, I get it. You have your orders and if you don't carry them out, it's not going to go well for you with *Señor* Tejada. I imagine he can be a pretty tough boss. Where else are you going to find a great gig like this, right?" She started toward the exit, still talking over her shoulder. "I'll let you take me and my things to the apartment. If *Señor* Tejada is out of town today I'll just use the time to get settled."

As she moved toward Elena to explain the new plan, she could only imagine what Molina's reaction must have been.

✦   ✦   ✦

Tejada rarely dreaded meeting with Abaddon. On the contrary, since the age of twelve he had savored his visits the way other boys enjoyed playing *fútbol* and practicing their budding machismo on young girls. From adolescence through his adult years, he had decided nothing without Lord Abaddon's personal counsel. His leadership among his friends, his strict, grueling education, the relationships with women that could never go far, his rise to power at Catalonia, all of it had transpired with the wisdom of his Master in his head if not in his physical ear. That had always been Tejada's joy, particularly after Abaddon began to groom him to take his seat when the day came that he could no longer lead the Brotherhood. And that day was almost here.

As Tejada's car made the final descent into El Masnou the joy and the savoring turned to dread. He was not bringing good news, and far worse, he was certain Abaddon already knew that.

The day was overcast and the sun gave no promise of appearing. Tejada found Abaddon seated on the balcony off his office. Despite the lack of light, he wore his gray hood pulled down over his forehead and sat in his straight-backed chair facing away from the windows. His greeting to Tejada, however, was strong and unusually friendly.

That drove Tejada's sense of uneasiness even deeper.

Their ritual greeting completed, Tejada reached for a cushion from a nearby chair to take his place on the floor, but Abaddon shook his head and pointed to the chair itself. Tejada lowered himself into it.

"I think we will see eye to eye today, Emilio," Abaddon said.

Tejada had no idea how to respond to that so he simply nodded.

"Has the attempt to pull all the leading nations together on a common currency been successful?"

"Not yet," Tejada replied.

"Do you believe the US debt default will be enough to force any of the reluctant nations to change their minds?"

"That was part of the original plan that you—"

"Do you believe it?"

"I did," Tejada said.

"But now you have doubts."

"I am not as certain as I once was. Though it has not come to a vote in the American Congress."

Abaddon's eyes rested on him. "But you would like to wait and see what happens there."

"I would." Tejada nodded. "But if you think it is pointless, there is no reason to continue."

Abaddon held up his hand. "It is not pointless. What you have set up will not go as planned, but it will serve its purpose." Abaddon lowered his hand and rested it in his lap. His eyes fixed on Tejada.

Though the plan was a long shot, Tejada had always hoped it would work and that events would not lead them to this point. And yet now, it seemed as though it always had been inevitable and so he asked, "Why, Lord Abaddon? Why put us through these paces if they were for naught?"

Abaddon leaned forward and lowered his voice. "Because there was no other way you would accept this, Emilio. You had to know there was no alternative. There is still a softness in you—a softness that has been the Achilles' heel of many before you. But the time is *now* and you must have only strength. No weakness at all."

His voice, thin and raspy until that moment, struck Tejada with a force that knocked him backward.

Abaddon leaned back in the chair. "Have you set things in motion?"

"Yes, Lord Abaddon."

"I will allow you to wait until one more task has been completed."

"What would you have me do?"

"It is not for you to do." Abaddon's voice was calm but he moved restlessly in his chair. "I want you to know about it nevertheless. We must make certain that when this thing is done and the Brotherhood has taken its rightful place—we must be sure that nothing exists to contaminate it."

"What could that possibly be? The line from the ancestors through you to me is pure."

"So I have always thought." The old eyes flashed. "But I sense the approach of someone else from our ancestral line."

Tejada arched an eyebrow in a questioning look.

"Yes." Abaddon nodded. "There are many secrets buried in the past, things even I do not fully know. Rumors of documents that have been hidden for centuries. These are the things that can destroy us if we do not discover them . . . before someone else does."

"And that is the task that must be completed? Destroying this person before he destroys us?"

"But perhaps not before he leads us to the secrets."

Tejada was incredulous. "Secrets *you* have not been able to uncover?"

"I will! Be sure of that!"

Abaddon leaned forward once more and erupted in spasmodic coughing. Tejada resisted the urge to reach for him or offer him water. As he waited for Abaddon to recover, his mind quickly reviewed what they had discussed.

This question of another heir had never come up before. This idea that someone else was in their line, someone who was not a member of the Brotherhood, someone who could "contaminate" the purity of a body that had spent centuries preparing to accomplish what Jacobo-Franscisco Eduardo Fitz-James Stuart y Colón, and Admiral Columbus before him, had believed in. To assemble a one-world government capable of marshaling resources and assets on a global scale.

"This task has been put in the hands of others." Abaddon said, finally. "But you, Emilio, must stay alert. Pay attention. The stakes are rising every day."

Tejada recognized his dismissal. Usually he wanted to linger in the presence of this man whose wisdom he lived on, but today he could not escape quickly enough.

27

Molina hadn't been exaggerating about the size and scope of the apartment Catalonia had provided for her. The spacious digs could have been advertised as a luxurious executive suite, complete with a Jacuzzi and a seemingly endless view of the coastline. The master bedroom featured a raised-platform bed and a fully equipped wet bar.

Maria looked the place over, then opted for one of the smaller bedrooms that didn't scream, *This was made for seduction!*

She wished the third bedroom could be Elena's, but when they'd finally connected that afternoon Elena insisted again that they keep everything as it was.

"It has to look like I'm just your assistant and nothing more," she'd said tearfully when they met for lunch. "Molina mustn't suspect that we're close enough for me to tell you anything personal."

Maria hadn't told Elena, but in the car driving from the airport to the apartment, Molina had spent more time watching them in the rearview mirror than he had paying attention to the traffic. That was just one of about five thousand reasons she'd leapt from the car when they arrived. Better to keep that to herself for now.

"Let's meet for coffee at seven thirty tomorrow," Maria had said.

"We'll walk over to Catalonia together. Meanwhile, I've already heard from Austin."

Elena's face brightened for the first time since Maria had arrived.

"He has a line on a good attorney. And my priest friend I was telling you about has a safe house for you until we can get you reconnected to the justice system."

Elena stared at the cheese croquettes that had grown cold on her plate. "Do you really think you can get me out of Spain without . . . him knowing?" She looked over at Maria. "He knows everything."

"I know people," Maria said. That part was true. Her father had connections. She reached across the table and squeezed Elena's hand. "They're going to help us." That part wasn't exactly true, at least not so far. No one else but Austin knew what she was trying to do.

Elena withdrew her hand. "I'm never going to be able to repay you for this."

"Who says you have to? Your freedom will be payment enough for me."

Their gazes met. The fear had all but dissolved from Elena's eyes.

Maria pictured those eyes now as she wandered from the bedroom through the finely appointed dining room she was never going to use and into the kitchen where she'd set up her laptop on the table. It was the only cozy room in the place and she needed cozy for what she was doing.

En route from Washington she had reviewed her notes from the Schlesinger-Molina conversation. What was she missing? Just before landing, she scrolled down below the bottom of the list—and there it was—Jason Elliot. An agent. For the CIA?

Maria sat at the computer and Googled his name. It was ridiculous, of course. The CIA wasn't going to publish a list of its agents.

She'd been lucky to find out what she had about Schlesinger. And even if she heard the name correctly from their conversation, wouldn't that name be an alias?

She shook her head. Her body screamed for sleep but she wanted to see what she could learn, now, while it was fresh on her mind. Maybe tomorrow she'd hear from her dad or Taylor Donleavy and she could ask them for help. Actually, if she didn't receive word from her father, she was going to call the Secret Service office in San Francisco. Even if he couldn't help her with this, she'd at least like to know he was alive.

In fact, maybe she should do that now.

As Maria picked up the phone, it rang in her hand. The sound of it startled her and she jumped, sending the phone tumbling across the counter. She retrieved it and took the call without bothering to check the caller's number.

"Maria Winters," she said in a businesslike tone.

"Maria."

She recognized Tejada's voice immediately.

Her first impulse was to snap at him. *Why in the world did you send Molina to meet me at the airport?* But something in the way he spoke made her ask simply, "Is everything okay?"

"I'm afraid not," Tejada replied. "May I speak with you privately?"

"Here? In the apartment?" Maria knew she wasn't making any sense but then, neither was he. Nine o'clock at night and he wanted to visit her? "What's going on?"

"I have some bad news I would rather bring to you in person."

"Then I'll meet you somewhere."

"Maria. Please," he insisted.

"Okay," she said reluctantly. "How soon will you be here?"

"I am just down the hallway."

The phone went dead and seconds later a light tap sounded on the door. Her heart sank as she slid from the kitchen stool, made her way to the door, and peered through the peephole. No Louis. No Molina. Just Tejada.

Maria opened the door and Tejada stepped inside. His face was grim and his pace determined as he made his way past her. He was as formal and reserved as ever, but there was something warm in it this time that had been missing before.

Maria folded her arms tight across her midriff as he faced her.

"You should sit down," he said.

"No," she said. "Just tell me." His eyes conveyed distress and he seemed to want to reach for her, but she took a step back. "Just tell me," she insisted. "Is it Snowden?"

"No," Tejada said. "It is *Señorita* Soler."

Maria frowned. "Elena?"

He nodded. "There was an accident. She was crossing the street this afternoon and apparently she didn't see the car—"

"She's hurt?"

"Maria," he said, lowering his voice. "Elena is dead."

The air went dead, too, and Maria turned away.

"I am truly sorry," Tejada continued. "I know you worked together. You were a team, yes?"

His voice was solid, deep, and filled with compassion. But Maria fought to make some sense of what still hung in the air. *Elena is dead.*

She drew in a deep breath. "How do you know this?" she asked.

"A news report," he replied. "I keep myself apprised of what is happening in the city, especially around Catalonia. It happened only a few blocks away, outside of Teresa Carles."

Where they'd had lunch. A chill ran through Maria's body. "What time?"

"Around three o'clock. The lunchtime traffic would have been heavy then."

"What about the driver? Did he say what happened?"

Tejada stared at her.

"What did he say?" she repeated.

"The driver did not stop," Tejada said.

"A hit-and-run?"

"The worst kind of cowardice. The Barcelona police are looking for the driver, of course, and I have initiated a full-scale investigation myself. Our employees cannot be run down in the street without justice being served."

"Who's in charge of your investigation?" Maria was surprised at the evenness of her voice.

"I have a team of people who handle such matters," Tejada explained. "Not that we have ever had anything nearly this tragic before."

Tejada stepped closer. "What can I do for you? You are far from home. None of your associates are here. I know you thought highly of her. What can I do to help you through this?"

Tell me you aren't behind it. That would help. Because he was right—she had no one here to turn to for comfort—and his arms looked so strong.

Maria shook her head. "I need to process this, that's all. We weren't close, but . . . she was *mowed down.* I need to wrap my mind around it." She glanced in his direction. "Alone."

"Will you call someone? Family?"

Who? Mom was gone. *Abuela* was gone. Her father was unreachable. Uncle Ben was useless. If Tejada would just go, she could call Austin.

"I'll be fine," she said. "Thank you for telling me yourself."

She waited for him to leave but he remained right where he'd been. And now his eyes expressed concern. "We have begun a search for Elena's family," he said. "But so far we have come up with nothing—no relatives, not even distant ones. Do you know whom we should contact?"

"We?" Maria asked.

"We have asked for her body to be turned over to us so that we can take care of arrangements, assuming no next of kin step forward."

The realization of Elena's circumstances swept over her. No one from her past knew where she was—or who she was now. "I didn't know her well enough to find out about her family," Maria replied. That was true. Elena's family in Madrid wouldn't know about her either. This person named Elena Soler did not exist for them. She was gone and there was no one to care.

No one except Maria.

"What kind of memorial service do you think Elena would want?" Tejada asked.

"I'll think about it," Maria answered. "But like I said, I just didn't know her that well."

"I understand. If you need anything, anything at all, please call me. This is my cell phone number." He placed a card on the glass-topped coffee table. "Do you need time off tomorrow?"

"No," Maria said. "I'll be alright."

Finally, he touched her lightly on the shoulder, turned toward the door, and made his way out. When she heard the elevator close, she ran to the door and turned the dead bolt. Because suddenly, she was terrified. The long, thin wail of a faraway siren drew nearer and nearer, more and more alarming until it was screaming into the room. Maria was on her knees on the floor before she realized it wasn't a siren at all, but her own mournful cries.

Those in Barcelona blocked me at every turn. But then my friend Gaspar Gorricio, who was well acquainted with the monarchy and many others, approached the king and queen on my behalf. Unable to deny his appeal, they agreed to fund two boats. The other I must procure myself, and so I turned to a group of Jewish investors living in Valladolid. Although not as wealthy as the men of Barcelona, they were nevertheless quite capable of funding my expedition.

Two of them, two members of this group whose names I shall not mention, were reluctant to participate and because of them the rest hesitated. In response, I asked to meet with those two separately and explain myself as to the meaning and purpose of this undertaking.

—Christopher Columbus

28

Locating the former Santa Maria de las Cuevas monastery wasn't difficult. Old Jacobo was right. It was a national historic site—complete with a tour Winters wanted to skip, but Sophia insisted they take.

The tour guide pointed vaguely to various books and artifacts and droned on about the Moors occupying Spain. And, just as with every other Catholic site he'd ever heard of, an image of the Virgin Mary had appeared to someone—this one in one of the many caves below. Hence the name, Saint Mary of the Caves.

According to their guide, the government seized the property during *La Desamortización* and it was later purchased by a man who was in the pottery business. The guide's face lit up when she invited them to visit the museum of tiles in an adjacent building. Winters silently vowed that if Sophia tried to drag him there, he would bolt for the border.

"That would be lovely," Sophia said.

Grrr. . . .

"But I have a question."

The tour guide sighed and waited impatiently.

"What happened to the monks?" Sophia asked.

The answer came in spurts. "Most went to monasteries elsewhere . . . became local priests . . . melded into society."

"Was there a library? Any records?"

A strange look came into the guide's eyes.

"They were taken to a church in Toledo," she replied. "*Santa Maria la Blanca.*"

Winters felt a trip to Toledo coming on, although he hoped it wasn't happening that day. It had already taken them over four hours to get to Seville.

"Thank you so much for your time," Sophia said. "May we look around?"

The guide looked pleased to have completed the tour, although she couldn't have been as happy as Winters.

"If you're going to look at tiles," he said to Sophia when the guide was gone, "I'll meet you at the—"

"We didn't come to see tiles," Sophia said. "But I have a feeling there's something else here."

She was already headed toward the entrance area. Winters followed but instead of leaving the building, she turned down a broad hallway, lined on either side with rooms that had been refurbished to look like fifteenth-century monks' quarters.

"It wasn't the Ritz-Carlton," Winters observed.

"I'm going to give you a quick history lesson," Sophia said as she continued quickly up the hallway. "You heard the guide talking about *La Desamortización.*"

"Uh-huh."

"That was a series of decrees issued by the prime minister, Juan Álvarez Mendizábal, who was also prime minister during the Carlist Rebellion—which started in the first half of the nineteenth century—about the time your family left here and went to America."

"Good to know, I guess."

"By Mendizábal's decrees, most of the monasteries in Spain were seized by the government and sold to private owners. That is how the tile factory came to be at this location.

"What about those caves she said we are on top of?"

"Those were used during the rebellion. For hiding."

Sophia stopped when they came to a stairway that plunged down into the darkness below the monastery. She looked at him with a mischievous smile. "What do you think?"

"About what?"

"You know," she said with a knowing look and a nod toward the stairway.

"You think that's where old Gaspar may have hi—"

"John," she whispered in a teasing way. "Are you afraid of the dark?"

"No," he said, glancing around the empty hallway. "But let me go first."

"I am glad to."

Winters led the way down the steps and soon found it wasn't as dark as it appeared from the top. At the base of the stairs, they followed the hallway past more reproductions of monk cells until they came to a doorway leading to yet another dank stairway. The entrance was blocked by a steel gate fastened with a heavy padlock. Winters held it in his hand and looked it over. He could easily pick it open with a paper clip or hairpin.

"Well," Sophia sighed. "It was a good idea."

"I can open it," Winters offered.

"I don't think you should," Sophia said. "Would this be a good time to tell you that I am claustrophobic?"

"Ha," Winters laughed. "Have I finally discovered something

that daunts you?" He grinned at her. "How did you like that word—'daunts'—pretty impressive?"

A voice behind them interrupted. "This area is off-limits to visitors."

Sophia jumped. Winters kept his cool as he turned to face a man wearing a security uniform.

"Sorry," Winters said. "We got a little lost. This place is like a labyrinth—"

"Allow me to guide you to the visitors' area," the guard offered.

Winters would have told the guy to get a grip, but he felt Sophia's hand curl around his arm. "Lead the way," he said with a smile.

They followed the guard back to the ground floor and over to the entrance. He gestured toward the doorway and Winters escorted Sophia outside to the parking lot.

"I suppose he just threw us out," Winters noted.

"That was unnerving," she replied.

"The guard?" Winters asked.

"The whole place," she said. "It disturbs me. We should leave at once."

"*Now* you're daunted," Winters teased.

"Yes," she replied. "Take me to the car."

"You want to go to Toledo next, right?" Winters asked as they made their way across the parking lot.

"You read my mind," Sophia said.

"Let's not do that tonight," Winters suggested in a kind voice. "How about I get us a couple of rooms, we have a nice dinner, and then head out in the morning?"

"I like the way you think, John Winters." She took his arm. "And over dinner, I would like you to tell me what it is you do in the United States."

"What do you mean?"

"I mean, what line of work makes you think you can pick a lock and stare down a security guard as if it is nothing?"

"What are you talking about?"

"You know." She took the car keys from her clutch bag. "And now it is time to tell me."

✦　✦　✦

Staying busy was the key to getting through this, Maria told herself. If she sat and thought too much, she conjured up images of sweet Elena's body flying through the air while hundreds of people watched. Hundreds of people who so far couldn't lead either the Barcelona police or the Catalonia investigative team to the killer.

The deliberate killer.

She had called her father's number for four straight hours and then resorted to Taylor Donleavy. He answered, finally, and it took fifteen minutes to fill him in on who she was and all that had happened. By then she was too wound up to stay in the apartment any longer so as she continued to talk, she made her way down to the street.

"Don't tell me to contact the police, Donleavy," she said. "I don't think I can trust anybody here right now."

"Wasn't going to," he replied. "Have you always been as paranoid as your old man?"

"I think I have reason to be," she replied.

"I guess you do."

"So, can you tell me what to do?"

"The first thing you need to do is buy a disposable phone. One with international access."

"Where can I get one?"

"Any electronics store . . ." Donleavy let his words trail off and started over with a tone that didn't sound like, *Anybody knows that.* "Find a store in a phone book, okay? And from now on, don't use your laptop for anything but work."

Maria knew that should be scaring her, but the fact that he was taking her seriously was reassuring.

"We have to make sure they don't know you're onto them," Donleavy continued. "And you'll need to check for bugs in your apartment *and* your office."

"Bugs?"

"We're not talking roaches here."

"What do they look like?"

"Maybe a small rectangle, no longer than your thumb. They can be stuck anywhere, so be thorough. And check the phone too."

"How do I do that?"

"Unscrew the cover off the mouthpiece if you can."

"I don't use the apartment phone."

"You don't have to. The right device can allow it to hear anything in the room, whether you use the phone for calls or not."

"I can't believe this is happening to me," Maria sighed.

"I know," he said in a sympathetic voice. "But it's important. You have to do it. Call me when you get the new cell and do your sweep."

"I'll call you," she said and she ended the call.

After talking to Donleavy, Maria felt more hopeful, although she never let her guard down. And there was no sleeping that first night.

So after the sun came up, she took a cab to the nearest electronics store and bought a phone, then she called Austin as she walked toward the office. He didn't answer but she left a simple message. "Nine-one-one, Austin. Nine-one-one."

She hadn't walked a block farther before he called her back. The moment she heard his voice, her eyes filled with tears.

"Are you all right?" he asked in a worried tone. "What's wrong?"

"Everything is wrong," she said. "Elena is dead."

"You're coming home," he responded. "Today. I'm making the arrangements."

"I can't," Maria said glancing over her shoulder. "Not right now."

"Why not?" Austin demanded. "It's too dangerous for you to be there now. Not that it wasn't before. Tell Tejada you're sick. Give me the story and I'll feed it to Snowden. Just get on the plane."

"Tejada's the one who told me about Elena. If I say I'm that grief-stricken he'll know something's up. I told him Elena and I weren't close."

"So you're convinced Tejada's in on it."

"No, actually I don't think he is."

"Good for him. But you have to get away from Molina."

"Or I have to expose him."

"Maria, no. Come on—you don't know how to do this without getting yourself killed."

"I'm going to find my father. He'll know what to do."

"So come home and find him. What's he going to do from San Francisco anyway?"

"I need you to do something for me."

"What?"

"I need you to Google the name Jason Elliot."

"There have to be a thousand people named Jason Elliot."

"I know, but see if you can find one who's into anything weird or shady. Maybe he's been arrested—anything like that."

"Why? Who is he?"

"Somebody Molina mentioned when talking to Schlesinger. He called him Agent Jason Elliot. I'm thinking that may have been a code name."

"So it's not going to do any good to look him up under that name."

"Just do it, please." By then she was at the Catalonia campus. "I have to go. If you find out anything, call me on this phone. Not my cell phone. And no e-mails to my computer."

"You're scaring me," he said.

"And don't say anything to Snowden, okay? I need to do some digging around to make sure he's not involved in this."

"Involved in what?"

"I don't know. I'll talk to you later."

He was still protesting when she hung up and tucked the phone into her pocket.

✦ ✦ ✦

Her new office was three times the size of the one she'd used when the Snowden team was there. So big, in fact, the oversized bouquet of irises on the desk looked lost in the space. As she dropped her briefcase beside the desk she studied the room. There were so many places a small rectangle could be hidden she didn't know where to start.

The one thing she did notice were the four divots in the carpet where a piece of furniture had been. Probably the desk she'd requested for Elena.

Okay, she couldn't go there. No time to break down in grief. Right now the name of the game was to stay busy.

Maria disregarded the large desktop computer and plugged in her laptop. She did turn on the flat-screen TV that took up most of one wall. Tejada said he kept up with local news and it wouldn't be a bad idea for her to do that too.

She turned to CNN, where they were covering a protest somewhere. Obviously not in Spain. She was about to do a channel search when the words at the bottom of the screen read, GRASSROOTS PROTEST AGAINST RAISING THE DEBT LIMIT. A well-coifed reporter was yelling into a microphone but she was still barely audible over the crowd of blue-collar workers waving signs and chanting.

"They're saying, 'The rich are getting richer and the poor are getting stuck with the bill!'" the reporter shouted. "They're calling out by name congressmen who have argued for spending cuts and then voted to increase the debt limit."

In the corner screen the in-studio anchorman asked, "Who's behind this, Selena? Have you been able to find out?"

"As far as we can tell it seems to have been fueled—and funded— by the Community Action Committee. And apparently well-funded, Brandon, because these protests have cropped up not only here in Birmingham but in Springfield, Missouri, Huntington, West Virginia, and as far away as Salem, Oregon. They're saying it's irresponsible to raise the debt limit."

Maria muted the television and went back to her work. Those protests seemed so far away from her life right now. It was important. She knew that. But nobody was being killed over it.

She turned to the stack of files on the desk—the work that was going to keep her mind occupied until Austin called. And until the San Francisco Secret Service opened.

The stack seemed manageable, but the handwritten note on top took her by surprise.

Maria,

None of this is urgent. Take some time away today if you need to.
My home is open to you if you would like to retreat there.

Tejada

Her phone vibrated. "Yes?" she said, answering the call.

"I'll talk, you just listen," Austin said. "A Jason Elliot was found dead a couple of days ago in rural Maryland. Out in the middle of nowhere. Apparently a hit-and-run. I am making you a plane reservation for tonight."

"Hold off on that, would you?" Maria replied. "I'll leave soon but I'm not quite ready for that yet."

"Maria—"

"I'll let you know, promise, 'kay?"

She hung up before she could hear more and tucked the phone back into her pocket. After fifteen seconds of listening to her heart beat in her ears, she stuffed her laptop back in her briefcase and took it with her as she walked out of her office.

"I'm Maria Winters," she said to one of the secretaries.

"I know—"

"I'm going to be working off-site today. If *Señor* Tejada needs me, he can reach me on my cell phone."

The woman seemed nonplussed. She nodded and jotted down a note to that effect. Maria tried not to bolt as she left the building.

She walked for what seemed like miles until she located the library—Biblioteca Sofia Barat. As she hoped, the library had public computers and she sat at one in a back corner. Before she logged on, she fished the temporary phone out of her pocket and consulted her own cell for Snowden's number. It was time to find out what he knew.

He answered on the first ring, though he seemed to have to shout over background noise.

"Bill Snowden," he said.

"It's Maria," she said. "I need to talk to you—"

"I didn't recognize the number. Listen, Maria, it's going to have to wait. I'm about to go into a meeting."

"I just need to ask you—"

Maria heard a female voice say, "Your table is ready, Mr. Stafford."

"Gotta go," he said. "I'll get back to you."

"It's urgent," she stressed.

But he was gone. Loneliness descended like a shroud.

"Don't go down with this, Maria." She could hear her mother saying—about science projects that had gone awry and friends who had shunned her and teachers who didn't appreciate her endless questions. She'd even said it the very day she died, when Maria dissolved into tears because Mom couldn't be there to see her win the math prize.

"Don't go down with this, Maria. There will be other times."

Maria swallowed hard and turned to the computer. She would check the Jason Elliot story herself. But something about her phone call with Snowden bothered her. It wasn't like him to have business meetings in crowded public places. It smacked of Molina and Schlesinger.

She went to Google and typed in *Stafford Washington DC.* Several names came up, but only one stood out—Michael Stafford. Financial lobbyist.

And a fairly influential one from what Maria could tell. He represented the interests of high-end financial enterprises, most of which Maria recognized. She grunted to herself as she scanned the list. These were the people those folks on CNN were protesting against.

That 1 percent of the population who controlled 99 percent of the wealth. Nice guy, this Michael Stafford. He had even lobbied for the interests of foreign corporations, including Belgium Continental.

Maria caught her breath. And Catalonia Financial.

She sat back. Okay, that wasn't a shock, really. Why wouldn't Snowden be meeting with someone who was connected with Catalonia? There was probably something about it in those files on her desk.

But if that was the case, Snowden would've said something to her while he had her on the phone. She had expected resistance from him after she knew Tejada had told him she was coming back to Barcelona, but there had been none. Now she wondered why.

She spent the rest of her allotted time on the library computer digging further into information about Michael Stafford. The only thing that jumped out at her was his previous record of activity every time debt limit debates came up in Congress, and that grabbed her attention merely because of the news report she'd seen that morning.

The screen went black, signaling that she'd used up her time, and Maria pushed back from the computer. None of it made any sense, and it probably had nothing to do with Elena—or Jason Elliot. She wanted to put Austin on this, too, but after the phone call to Snowden, she wasn't sure he was safe either.

Donleavy was probably right—she was getting paranoid. She took a circuitous route back to Catalonia all the while forcing herself not to look over her shoulder.

29

Tejada was observing the sunset from his home on the hill when Carlos Molina knocked at the open doorway behind him. Tejada was grateful for the interruption. All day long he'd thought of nothing but Maria, and now he imagined he heard Abaddon warning against temptation.

The Master was right. As always. But this was not a temptation of the kind his lord had in mind. He didn't want to be in bed with Maria. He just wanted her company.

"Carlos," Tejada said, "what brings you here?" He tried to keep his voice even. "News of the Soler investigation, I hope?"

Molina shook his head. "Something else. I think you should see this."

Tejada followed him into the study, where Molina had his laptop. "This came up today," Molina said, "from a source Lord Abaddon set up some years ago. The source was told to report any unusual activity to us."

"Unusual activity? Where?"

"A museum in Seville. Former monastery. They said once you saw this you would know what it was."

Tejada was mystified but he gave Molina a nod. "Let's have a look at it then."

Molina clicked on a series of still photos taken by a low-tech camera. The images were grainy, but Tejada could see that they were of a man about his age and a woman probably in her thirties. The man's face was turned away from the camera, though he had a distinctive build with sturdy shoulders, narrow hips, and muscular arms. A physique a man his age would have to work at—something Tejada knew only too well.

"First of all, who is the woman?" Tejada asked. "And second, why is this important?"

"We are running her image through several facial-recognition programs," Molina replied. "I was told by the guard who supplied these that these two were 'poking their noses where they don't belong.'"

Tejada was amused at Molina's stilted rendition. "What is it that they shouldn't be 'poking into'?"

Molina looked over at Tejada. "There are many secrets buried in the past . . ." he said, as if he were reciting a childhood lesson, "things that can destroy us if we do not discover them . . . before someone else does.'"

Tejada recognized those words immediately. They were Abaddon's words. Had he said them to Molina? A man who knew nothing of their meaning? And were these two people the "someone else" Abaddon had foreseen?

"Find out who they are," Tejada said. "Put someone on them right away."

"Surveillance only?"

Tejada shook his head. "If they uncover any documents, the documents are to be seized."

"And these two?"

Tejada glared at him as if to say Molina knew better than to ask that question.

✦ ✦ ✦

"Did you ever protect the president?" Sophia asked.

Winters' turned away from the scene that whipped past them en route to Toledo and grinned at Sophia. They'd been driving in silence for an hour and she plucked that out of the blue?

"No," he said. "You don't want that duty. No disrespect to the presidential office, but it's a lot like babysitting. Besides, I'm not tall enough for it."

Sophia tilted her head. "Forgive me. I am afraid that what I know of the Secret Service has come from watching American movies."

"That's probably all anybody needs to know."

"Am I to assume that is all you plan to tell me about your work?"

"It's all I *can* tell you."

"I understand."

Winters liked that about her. That willingness to let it drop was why he'd told her as much as he had the night before. That and the fact that Sophia Conte looked even more intriguing by candlelight than she did when the sun was shining across her face the way it was now.

"I certainly feel safe now," she teased. "I have a trained profes-sional with me."

"But you're still not going into any caves with me."

"Maybe," she grinned. "One day."

Winters turned away to look out the window once more.

"Did I say something wrong, John?" she asked, suddenly concerned.

"No," he sighed. "You didn't say anything wrong. I just haven't told you the whole story."

"Is it a story I need to hear?"

"You mean you wonder if you hear it whether you might want to drop me off at the nearest bus station?"

"Maybe."

Winters' voice took a distracted tone. "I think you should have that choice. Then you can decide how safe you feel."

"Something happened," she said.

It wasn't a question. It never was with her.

"I was on a raid that went bad."

"Were you hurt?"

"Just my pride more than anything else."

She was quiet until they'd passed through Talavera de la Reina. "If you choose to tell me the story," she said, "tell the truth."

"You sure you're not a psychiatrist?" Winters held up a hand. "No, if you were a therapist you would ask me if I always mask my pain with jokes."

"I do not have to ask that," she said.

"Because you know the answer," Winters said. And suddenly he couldn't think of a punch line. "I was captured," he continued.

"In the raid."

"Yes."

"And that was not your fault."

"No one ever said it was." Winters glanced over at her. "That wasn't what drove me to the edge."

"I would think being captured would be enough. But then, I am not you."

"I'm not sure I'm me either," Winters said. "How much farther to Toledo?"

"We are nearly there, my friend." She looked inexplicably shy. "Was that presumptuous of me?"

"What?"

"To call you my friend."

"No," Winters said. "It makes me feel safer."

Half an hour later they had arrived in Toledo and found the large stone church on a back street. Sophia had called ahead to arrange a "tour" with the priest. Winters couldn't wait to see how old this guy was. At the rate they were going he was sure to be ninety if he was a day.

But the cassocked man who met them was fifty at the most, with graying tonsure and a strong chin. His brown eyes looked hungry for company.

"Father Ramone Padilla," he said in perfect English. "You have come to see the records from the monastery."

"We have, Father," Sophia responded.

"Then let us walk and talk." He led them into the church, talking as much with his hands as his mouth. "The records were moved here when the monastery closed. They were here for many hundreds of years."

"Were?" Winters said.

He waited for Sophia to squeeze his arm. Yep, there it was.

"Most of them merely sat on a shelf in the church office before anyone thought to do anything to protect them. As you can imagine, they deteriorated noticeably during that time."

Great.

They passed through a musty sanctuary and up the steps to the altar. Both Father Ramone and Sophia paused there and bowed silently before continuing to a door off to the side. Winters followed after them.

"We had a room constructed several years ago so we could control the environment for the records and perhaps extend their life a little longer." He pushed the door open and stepped aside, allowing Winters and Sophia to enter. It was clearly temperature-controlled, but the musty smell was still strong. Winters thought, if history had an odor, this was it.

"The records are here," Padilla said, pointing to a row of plastic containers. "All I ask is that you use these."

He produced two pairs of rubber gloves but it didn't appear many people came through here asking about the lives of long-dead monks. Speaking of which . . .

"Do you know if there's anything in here about a monk named Gaspar Gorricio?"

The look in Padillo's eyes hardened. "I thought you were genuine genealogical researchers looking for relatives, not plunderers of the treasures of Spain."

Sophia spoke up. "*Señor* Winters is very likely a direct descendant of Christopher Columbus—"

"A story I have heard many times before."

"From tourists?" Sophia asked as if she felt his pain.

"No," Padillo said, standing straighter. "From bullies bent on taking what should be left alone."

"Bullies, Father?" Sophia asked.

The reverend looked embarrassed. "They tried to strong-arm me but I refused to let them handle the records. After that, I put all references to Gaspar Gorricio in the safe."

Winters followed Padillo's gaze to a framed print of a decidedly Spanish Jesus on the wall.

"I understand, Father," Sophia said. "We are sorry to have taken your time." She smiled at him. "Thank you for keeping our national treasures safe."

She nodded Winters toward the door and he went, with one last glance at the kindly portrait.

"Wait." Padillo sighed. "I have reacted poorly. It is obvious your hearts are sincere."

"They are," Sophia assured.

"Please," he said. "Sit down."

He turned his back to them and removed the print from the wall. Winters watched Padillo unlock the hidden safe and retrieve an object.

Padillo placed the plastic container and the two pairs of gloves reverently on the table and went to the window, leaving them to explore the disintegrating pieces of yellowed paper. Winters thought the priest might be praying until he realized he was sending a text message.

Winters wasn't much help with the contents of the box. The old, yellowed documents all were written in a mixture of Spanish and Latin, languages he knew little about. Consequently, Sophia did the sorting and reviewing. When she found something that seemed important she read it aloud to him in English so he could write it down. An hour later, he had gathered a disjointed list of dates and events.

Gorricio took a trip to Madrid late in 1492.

He made a trip to Valladolid early in the spring of 1506.

Columbus died in Valladolid. Gorricio had visited him two months before his death.

In June of 1506, right after Columbus died, Gorricio traveled to a monastery near Santa Cruz de la Serós. San Juan de la Peña.

"Which is where?" Winters asked.

"In the mountains near the French border," Sophia replied. "A long way from Seville."

"How far from here?"

"Six hours northeast," Padilla said from the window.

Winters had all but forgotten he was there.

While Sophia wrote a check for the parish as an expression of their gratitude for being allowed to see the records, Winters wandered from the church and stood in the afternoon sunlight, gazing at an ornate pink building across the street that seemed to ramble haphazardly down the block.

There was no question they would go to San Juan la Peña. They'd come this far, so why not go all the way? But the chances of finding the journal now seemed about as good as Winters' winning the lottery, and the thought of that was disappointing on several levels.

He was about to enumerate them in his mind when he had an uncanny realization, something he hadn't experienced in a while. Lonnie Smith used to call it his "spider sense." That inexplicable—and very accurate—sense that he was being watched.

Moving nonchalantly, Winters let his gaze drift over the church-yard, out to the street, and up the wall of the building on the other side. At first he saw nothing unusual, but after a moment he caught a glimpse of someone standing at a third-floor window. Just a glimpse—and then they were gone.

Winters glanced back at the church. Sophia stood in the doorway talking with Father Padillo. He could go in pursuit and let Sophia think he was a basket case, or he could leave it alone.

Before he could decide, Sophia moved away from the door and started toward him. "Father Padillo says there is a nice little inn just a few blocks east," she said when she reached him.

"You know what?" Winters said. "I need some think time, and I think best when I'm driving. You mind if we go up the road a ways? Find something there?"

"Are you asking if you can drive my car?" she said, eyes dancing.

"I am," he said. "I ran out of tranquilizers."

Her brow furrowed.

"Bad joke," Winters said. "How 'bout those keys?" he said, holding out his hand.

"You are incorrigible, Agent Winters," she said.

30

Waiting for people to return her calls was becoming Maria's new career.

Her father was clearly not listening to his messages.

Taylor Donleavy's geekiness must have replaced social skills.

Snowden's meeting must still be going on.

And obviously James Rebhorn of the San Francisco Secret Service office was far too busy to let an agent's daughter know that her father was still alive.

The one person who did call her was Austin, although he had little to offer except to beg her to come home.

Maria was on the phone with him again the next morning as she took another convoluted route from her apartment to Catalonia. A longer journey than usual, it gave them plenty of time to talk.

"I'm getting paranoid," she told him as she passed through the iron entryway into La Boqueria.

"It's only paranoia if people *aren't* out to get you," Austin said. "But listen, I learned something."

"What?"

"These protests that are going on about the debt limit."

"Yeah?"

"The organization sponsoring them has ties to Catalonia Financial. And every Congressman who's pushing to keep the ceiling where it is can be linked to Catalonia, too—mostly through campaign contributions."

Maria dawdled at the fruit market examining an orange but seeing only Austin's long face. "Why does Catalonia care about our debt limit? I mean, I know the American economy affects the entire world, but I don't see this company struggling to stay afloat."

"I don't know but I don't like it. Oh, and that hit-and-run—the Jason Elliot thing?"

"Uh-huh."

"Turns out he was thrown out of a vehicle and then run over. At least that's what the media is saying." Maria heard him sigh. "I know it doesn't do me any good to ask you to come home, but at least be careful. Where are you right now?"

"About a mile from the office."

"Okay, call me every two hours. Otherwise I'm reporting you missing."

"Now who's paranoid?" Maria said.

Austin hung up and Maria dropped the phone in her pocket. It was hard not to look around to make sure nobody had seen her do it, which was why the car that was idling in the alley across the street caught her eye. She hadn't told Austin this wasn't the best neighborhood—and definitely not the kind where you parked your pricey sedan.

Maria glanced at the car's reflection in the window of a shop. Someone was sitting in the driver's seat and although she could see only the top of the head, the square shape was all too familiar.

Maria feigned delight at the macabre masks in the shop window as she stepped inside. She silently cursed the bell on the door, but when she peered through the glass, the square head was still facing forward. Even when a man in tattered khakis and a long T-shirt climbed in on the passenger side.

"I can help?" a woman asked behind her.

"I was just admiring your window display," Maria said, eyes still on the pair in the car.

The shopkeeper scowled. Maria took her law firm phone from the briefcase and smiled. "Would you mind if I took a picture of it?" she asked, gesturing toward the display. "It's beautiful. I'd like to send it to my friend. "

The woman responded with a *These American tourists!* expression and turned away shaking her head.

Maria opened the camera app on her phone, aimed it out the window, and waited. She could feel perspiration beading on her back. Just as the shopkeeper bustled toward her again, the man in khaki pants emerged from the car. Maria snapped pictures until he disappeared around the corner. By then Molina and the sedan had sped down the alley raising a cloud of dust.

Maria turned to the shopkeeper and smiled. "I'll take one of those cat faces," she said, pointing.

She was just stuffing the purchase into her briefcase—and wondering what on earth she was going to do with it—when the phone rang. The call was from a San Francisco number.

"Dad?" she said.

"No, Maria," a male voice replied. "It's Taylor Donleavy."

✦ ✦ ✦

Winters and Sophia arrived at the monastery a little before noon. The crumbling, white stone seemed to glow in the sunlight. Either that or sleep deprivation was getting to Winters. He'd had another night of bad dreams, this time twisted around Anne and planes flying into buildings, but not the Twin Towers—the churches and monasteries of the Spanish countryside.

The real questions before them now, of course, were whether the elusive journal was here and whether anyone would even let them see it.

Once again Sophia had called ahead, but the abbot who marched across the ancient pavers to greet them was not yet part of her fan club. He nodded vaguely at her, before he directed his remarks straight to John. "You are *Señor* Winters?"

Just enough English to get by.

"I am. And this is—"

"We do not allow women on the premises."

Winters bristled. "You could have mentioned that on the phone."

"He did," Sophia said. "I am happy to wait out here."

"No," John said. "Look, Father—"

"Brother."

Winters didn't care if he was somebody's sister, but he put on his game face. "I apologize, Brother. I understand you have rules, but Ms. Conte is a scholar and my translator."

Sophia, meanwhile, was gazing in fascination at the rock formation the monastery was built into. Her dark eyes seemed to be soaking in every crack, as if it might tell her a tale of its past.

The abbot said something to her in Spanish, to which she answered simply, "*Sí.*" He looked as if he were pondering the meaning of life before he said, "Good then. I will make the exception." He offered his hand to Winters. "I am José Gris."

"Pleasure," Winters said, glad to have the issue resolved.

Sophia, on the other hand, seemed unfazed as Brother José led them inside the monastery. Light from the many candle sconces lining the walls gleamed on the ancient floors. Winters thought it had probably looked exactly the same for five centuries.

John was beginning to suspect Brother José was the only one living there when a hooded monk passed silently behind them. Winters saw him only because he was keeping his eyes, ears, and nose attuned to everything. The dreams weren't the only thing that had kept him awake. The more he mentally reviewed the figure in the window across from the church in Toledo the more sure he was that they had been watched.

Then there was the death trap of a compact car with one bumper askew that had followed them for fifty kilometers before they stopped for the night. He'd memorized the license number when it passed them but he didn't know what he could do with it. There was no Donleavy there to track it down for him.

Winters watched the other monk hurry down the steps, to what appeared to be a struggling vegetable garden.

"You grow all your own food?" Winters asked.

José merely nodded his head.

As they were ushered into a cool room with a row of narrow, arched windows, Winters saw that the monk's disposition toward Sophia had improved. What was it with her? She wasn't even charming him with a smile, just listening intently as he chattered away in Spanish. Still, he seemed taken by her.

Then she asked, "How will you know if *Señor* Winters is worthy of seeing the journal?"

Winters stopped with his hand on the heavy, wooden chair he was about to pull out from the equally heavy table where José was motioning for them to sit. "The journal is here?" he asked.

"It is." Sophia's eyes were bright, but they held a warning. "Brother José tells me others have traced it here but no one has been allowed access to it."

"Because they can't prove they are a direct descendant?" Winters said.

"No." The monk shook his head. "Because they cannot prove their hearts."

So old Jacobo had been right, Winters thought.

Brother José gestured for John to sit next to Sophia, which he did, but he was uneasy about what would follow. He didn't know how he was supposed to prove his heart to this man who would obviously take a bullet rather than let the journal fall into the wrong hands.

"I must ask you some questions," Brother José said. "The answers will tell me everything."

Sophia squeezed his knee, but Winters didn't need the warning. He'd faced tougher opponents than Brother José.

"*Señor* Columbus," Brother José said. "Does he seem *un hombre loco* to you?"

"Do I think he was a crazy person?" Winters said. "No more so than I am to come here looking for my connection to him. I think he had a vision and he thought it came from God and he followed it."

"If I show you the journal, what will you do with it?"

"I don't intend to do anything with it," Winters replied. "It doesn't belong to me. It belongs here." He moved to the edge of the chair and spread his hands on the table. "Look, my mother started looking for our link to Columbus because she said God told her to. I promised my mother I would continue the search. I owe her that and maybe God is telling me to as well—I don't know. I'm here and I want to follow through." He shrugged. "Once I've looked at it, I don't know what will happen. I'll probably go home. But I'm sure not planning to take it out of here with me. I only want to look at it."

Winters paused for breath and realized Sophia had been simultaneously translating while he waxed eloquent. He had no idea where any of it had come from.

"I think you must see it," Brother José said with a nod. He scraped the heavy chair back from the table, crossed the room, and made his way to a door on the far side. He pulled it open and disappeared on the opposite side.

"John," Sophia whispered, "do you realize what this means?"

"Do you?"

The hand she put on his was clammy. "We are about to see something no one else but these monks has seen since Gaspar Gorricio brought it here over five hundred years ago."

"And I'm not even Catholic."

"You're not a practicing Jew either."

Winters looked warily at the door. "You think these guys believe that theory? Would they be this protective of Columbus' stuff if he was Jewish instead of Christian?"

"I think they're just following the orders of Brother Gaspar."

"You think Gaspar knew Columbus was Jewish?"

Sophia straightened in her chair. "I think you're about to find out."

The door creaked open and Brother José entered wearing cotton gloves and carrying a glass case about the size of a box of chocolates. Inside it was a wooden box, burnished with age.

Brother José set it on the table between John and Sophia, just within their reach. He handed each of them a pair of gloves. "Use these to touch it," José said. "Otherwise, the oil from your skin will damage the pages."

He took a key from the folds of his coarsely spun robe and unlocked the glass case. Winters saw his fingers tremble inside the clumsy gloves and found himself holding his breath as the monk lifted out the wooden box.

Sophia gasped audibly as he set it on the table before them.

"*Sí,*" José said.

"You see the inscription," Sophia said, pointing. "Across the top."

Winters studied the letters scrawled into the wood. "Is that Latin?"

"Yes. It says 'Gaspar Gorricio.'" She slid on the gloves. "May I?" she asked the monk.

His nod was almost indiscernible.

Carefully and reverently, Sophia traced the letters with her index finger. "This is very old," she observed.

"Very old indeed," the abbot said. "It has been here since Gorricio brought it in 1506."

Winters was willing to stop right there. It was worth the whole trip to see the joy on Sophia's face.

"I will warn you," the monk said. "The papers are frail."

Winters was sure he meant *fragile* and that turned out to be an understatement.

Brother José removed the rough-hewn lid from the box and lifted out a small book. The leather cords that had once held it together were rotted through and the heavy brown cover with its raised letters began to fall away in the monk's hands. Brother José laid it between them, and it splayed open. A small, browned corner chipped off and floated to the tabletop.

Sophia pored over the pages, gloved hands in her lap except to turn the leaves. Soft murmurs came from her throat.

"It's in Spanish, of course," Winters said.

"Castilian Spanish," she said. "Once I get used to it, the reading will go faster. This I know so far." She hovered a finger over the paper and read, "'God made me the messenger of the new heaven and the new earth of which He spoke in the Apocalypse of Saint John. Having spoken of it also through the mouth of Isaiah, He showed me the spot to find it. We are rapidly nearing the end of the age.'"

"He thought the new heaven and earth were the New World. Right?"

"Listen to this. 'This is the Divine providence that has guided me and will furnish Isabel and Ferdinand with the gold and silver for the re-conquest of Jerusalem . . . Jerusalem and Mount Zion are to be rebuilt by the hands of Christians as God has declared by the mouths of His prophets.'"

Winters didn't know whether to say it in front of the abbot, but he would bring it up with Sophia later—if Columbus was Jewish, he certainly wasn't anti-Christian. It was like the two religions were supposed to coexist. Interesting thinking for a guy in the midst of the Inquisition.

"'The year has come in the succession of ages when the oceans will lose the bonds by which we have been confined. And immense lands hitherto unknown and unseen shall lie revealed.'"

Winters found himself nodding. They could say Columbus was certifiable, but Winters had never known a mentally ill person who could write like that. He wanted to sit right there and listen to Sophia read the whole thing.

Despite his apparent trust in the two of them, the monk was getting jittery. He rubbed his hands together in the unwieldy gloves and glanced uneasily toward the door more than once.

"Do you have a photocopier?" Winters asked.

The monk looked scandalized.

"Perhaps you would let me photograph the pages?" Sophia asked.

"No flash," Brother José cautioned.

"Of course not."

"And the photos will be only for your own use?"

Winters nodded. "I have to consider that promise," Sophia said, to his surprise. "I cannot make it lightly."

Winters could only stare at her . . . until it dawned on him. She was a Columbus scholar and this was the discovery of a lifetime. She would want to share what she knew. For Sophia, not being able to share it was worse than not knowing it at all.

"Take the photos for *me*," Winters said. "You can decide later whether you want to study them."

Sophia searched his face and slowly smiled. What he loved about the moment was that she didn't seem surprised.

Winters put on the second pair of gloves—as too-small for him as they were too-big for Sophia—and stood on her left side. "I'll turn and you snap," he said. "And Brother José, you pray."

"What am I praying?" José asked, eyes smiling.

"That I figure out what I'm supposed to do with all this."

"God will show you," the monk said and closed his eyes.

A few pages into the process, Sophia looked up at John. "I'm having trouble not reading it all right now."

"I promise I'll share. Keep going."

She held his eyes the way she had hold of his arm—warm, soft, and unmoving. If she didn't look away soon, he was going to kiss her.

But just then, movement to the left caught his eye and seconds later, the door to the room banged open. A brown-robed figure filled the doorway, his face barely visible beneath the hood.

José rounded the table and placed himself between the errant monk and the journal. "Please leave, Brother," he said. "This is private business."

"Over there," the man ordered. "Against the wall."

"I beg your pardon—"

His words were cut off by the smack of something hard against his cheek and he fell sideways. Winters shoved Sophia under the table—and watched the pages of the journal scatter like confetti.

31

With a gun in his left hand, the robed man swiped his right arm across the two facedown leaves of the journal still on the table. Winters automatically reached for his own gun and silently cursed its absence. Not only that, he couldn't get to the guy with the heavy chair between them.

Gun still clumsily in one hand, the pseudo-monk stuffed the pages into his robe. Pain shot up Winters' leg as he kicked the chair into him, sending the man staggering backward. As he struggled to regain his balance, the gun came free and slid across the floor, out of reach for both of them.

Surprisingly, the man abandoned his gun and instead lunged toward the doorway. Winters started after him, but he checked himself and stopped, hand on the wall. He could grab the gun and take him down, but he had no authority to do that. And who knew how many thugs in monk robes he had with him?

Winters sprang to the window, calling over his shoulder, "Are you all right, Brother?"

"*Estoy furioso!*"

Winters interpreted that as an angry yes. He saw the robed man jump from the cloister wall. Moments later, the familiar banged-up compact car appeared on the road in the distance. Winters turned to

Sophia, who peered at him from beneath the table, her hands clasped to her chest.

"Did I hurt you?" Winters said.

"No. But could I hand these to you?"

Winters squatted.

"I got everything that fell," she said. Sophia unfolded her arms to reveal the pages of the journal.

He took the pages from her and helped her to her feet.

Brother José was now beside him, face ashen. His cheek was already starting to swell.

"He took what was left on the table," he said, "after you pushed the rest onto the floor."

"I'm sorry," Winters said. "I just reacted."

"No." He lapsed into Spanish that Sophia, now on her feet, quickly translated. "He says if you hadn't done that, all of it would be lost."

"How much did we save?" Winters asked.

"Everything except what we had already photographed, I think."

"You must leave."

They both looked at the monk.

"When he finds he does not have it all, he will be back."

"We can finish the photographs—"

"No," Winters said to Sophia. "He's right. We need to get out of here. What about you, Brother?"

"I will call the police."

"Good plan." Winters took Sophia's elbow and steered her toward the door. "Brother José, you've been a prince."

"No!" The monk's voice was shrill. "You must take *la revista* with you! Please!"

"What—"

"If not, the police will take it—as evidence—"

"So lock it up again. Hide it," Winters said.

"But then he would have to lie," Sophia explained. "We can keep it until it's safe to bring it back."

"Which is going to be when?" Winters tried to edge her toward the door again but she grabbed the back of a chair and set her face.

"When the police find this thief," she said. "Then we can return it."

Please." The monk's lips were blue. "You must take it away." He grabbed the box from the table and thrust it into Winters' hands. "I am begging you."

Sophia let the pieces of the journal fall into the box and slid the lid from the table. Winters tucked it under his arm and with his other hand guided Sophia toward the door. "Call the police," he said to the monk. "Now."

"You have my number, Brother José," Sophia called as Winters pushed her out the door.

"*Vaya con Dios,*" Brother José said.

Once they were out the door, all trace of Sophia's stubbornness disappeared and she ran for the car, reaching it ahead of Winters.

"Here," he said, handing her the box. "You hold this, I'll drive."

"I can—"

"You're gonna have to trust me."

She didn't need to ask why. Winters had barely backed the car out of the gravel driveway when the heap driven by the thief squealed out from a side road ahead of them and stopped in the middle of the street.

"Hold on, Sophia."

Winters took a hard right and skirted him. The car swayed and righted itself as Winters fishtailed into the side street. It would take only a matter of seconds for the guy to turn his car around, seconds Winters had to use to his advantage. He scanned both sides of the road and found a short alley that ran behind a row of squatty houses.

"Get down!" he barked at Sophia. She started to look behind them but Winters pushed her head forward. "Get *down.*"

The engine whined as he whipped the car into the alley, praying that no kid chose that moment to chase after his soccer ball. The alley dead-ended but Winters slid sideways over a gravel driveway, got the car back under control, and headed across an open field that spanned the distance to the next street, where a busy intersection would provide some cover.

Winters tried to maintain control as the car bounced across the field. A particularly heavy bump brought a cry from Sophia. "Sorry!" he said. He glanced in the side mirror and saw the compact swerving on the driveway. "Get ready to stop."

He jammed his foot on the brake and watched in the rearview as a barrier of red dust rose up behind them, thick as San Francisco fog. Gunning the engine again, he jumped the curb at the edge of the lot and, to a cavalcade of honking horns, joined the traffic in the intersection. He winced as tires screamed behind them but he didn't stop.

One more look in the mirror told him what he needed to know. The intersection was a snarl of confusion the thief would have a hard time getting through. Winters pressed the gas pedal to the floor and they headed for the far side of town.

When they were safely away, Winters slowed the car to the speed limit and placed his hand on Sophia's shoulder. "You can get up now," he said.

Sophia lifted her head from between her knees and looked at him through a maze of hair.

"Did I mention that I was claustrophobic?" she said with a smile.

✦ ✦ ✦

Leaving the monastery, they drove north until dusk. If the thief were going to catch up with them, he would have done so by then and Sophia knew of a small inn off the beaten path in Navarre. She looked a little frayed around the edges so Winters agreed to pull in.

From the conversation with the owner, Winters gathered there was only one room available. "I am too afraid to stay by myself tonight anyway," she said to Winters as she took the key. "I know you will be a gentleman."

Winters brought the luggage from the car and followed Sophia upstairs to the room. While he put their things in place, she went downstairs to find out about dinner. A few minutes later she returned with two plates of food. "This is all I could talk him into giving us," she said. "The kitchen has already closed."

"I'm sure we'll make do just fine," Winters replied.

They sat on the floor at the foot of the bed, their backs propped against the bed frame, and ate. Winters was too hungry to ask what it was and too tired to care. What he really wanted was to read the rest of the pages from the journal, but just then, eating seemed more important.

As they finished their meal, he glanced over at her. "I think we should get you back to Barcelona first thing in the morning."

"What about the journal?"

"I don't know yet. You can photograph the rest of it tonight, so the trip won't be a total waste for you."

"Huh," she said.

"What does 'huh' mean?"

"It means even though you regularly speak before you think and with your cultural bumbling, you have rarely offended me. Until just now."

Winters frowned. "What did I say?"

"The trip would be a total waste if I did not take information from the journal back with me? Is that what you think?" Her eyes were sharp with something he couldn't quite discern. "Well?" she asked insistently.

"Look," Winters said, setting his plate aside. "This thing took a different turn this afternoon. It's dangerous now. This isn't what you agreed to."

"I think I can decide that for myself."

"No," Winters said. "You can't. I'm not going to be responsible for you being hurt because I'm carrying a Columbus artifact around with me."

"Then we make a deal."

"Uh-uh," he said with a shake of his head. "No deals."

"If I am hurt I will take full responsibility."

"It doesn't work that way."

"Is that a Secret Service rule?"

"No. It's my rule."

"We'll see about that."

Sophia pushed herself up from the floor and set her plate on a table near the window, then she reached for her iPad. "We have Wi-Fi," she said as she propped against a pillow on the bed.

At least she was still speaking to him. "Listen, Sophia." Winters was still seated on the floor. "I know how quickly this can go south—"

"Oh!" she exclaimed.

Winters turned to look in her direction. "You okay?"

"John . . . no!"

He scrambled to his feet and came to her side. She handed him the iPad. "I went to the newsfeed," she said, pointing. "Look!"

Winters scanned the screen and saw a picture of the San Juan de la Peña monastery. Below it were the words *"Monje Asesinado."*

"What is this?"

Sophia closed her eyes. "Just scroll down the page," she said, gesturing with her hand. "I don't want to see it again but you need to look."

Winters moved the cursor down the page and cringed as more images appeared. The back of a crushed skull. A bloody rock. The lifeless face . . . of Brother José Gris.

"That's awful," Winters groaned.

"He was murdered!" Sophia blurted. She drew her knees to her chest and clutched them with both hands. "Who would do such a thing?"

"What does this say?" Winters asked, pointing to the screen.

"Scroll past the pictures," she said, "and hand it to me."

Winters gave her the iPad and her eyes skimmed over the article. "They think the murder was part of a theft," she said. "Something valuable was stolen from the monastery. One of the other monks reports seeing a couple flee the scene. A man and a woman." Her eyes widened. "John, they think *we* did it."

"Okay," he said, reaching for her. "Come here, it's okay."

She dropped the iPad and fell into his arms.

32

Tejada ran a finger across the archival plastic that encased the pages.

"This is all Rivera was able to come away with," Molina said. "He didn't anticipate the man—"

"We pay him to anticipate," Tejada replied. "This couple. They're the two at the museum in Seville?"

"I compared the description Rivera gave me with the photographs. They match."

"What do we know about them?"

"The woman is Sophia Conte. She lives here in Barcelona. Historian. Genealogist. Divorced."

"You've searched her home."

"Yes," Molina nodded. "Nothing suspicious."

"And the man?"

"No ID on him yet. Almost impossible without a face."

"I've come to trust that nothing is impossible with you, Carlos. Where are they now?"

"Rivera lost them."

Tejada's eyes darkened. "Then lose him."

"Done."

"Notify me when you pick up their trail."

"What do you want me to do with that?" Molina said, pointing to the pages in Tejada's hand.

"I will take care of them," Tejada responded.

When Molina was gone, Tejada collapsed in the chair behind the desk and and scanned the pages again. What were these ancient puzzle pieces he had before him? He didn't know, but he was certain they were the very thing Abaddon was talking about. And whatever they were, the rest must be found and destroyed.

As for the people who now possessed them, Abaddon would demand they be destroyed as well. There was no question about that, and in the past he wouldn't have given it a second thought. But now, things seemed different and eliminating these two was no longer a casual matter. *How is this any different from the others,* he wondered. *And when did he start caring?*

"*Señor* Tejada?" a voice said from the office intercom.

Tejada reached to the left and pressed a button on the phone. "Yes?"

"*Señorita* Winters to see you?"

Tejada opened the desk drawer and swept the pages inside. "Send her in," he said and he pushed the drawer closed.

A moment later, the door opened and Maria appeared.

"I hope I'm not disturbing you," she said.

"Not at all." Tejada rose to his feet. "How are you?"

"Better," she said. "I've been thinking about—"

"Please, sit down." He gestured toward a chair in front of the desk. "Would you care for something? Water, perhaps? Or coffee?"

"No, thank you," Maria said as she took a seat. "I can't stay long." Her usual smile was missing. "I've been thinking about what you said . . . about Elena's remains and a memorial. I wondered, since there's no family, if the best thing to do might be to have her cremated."

"Of course." Tejada nodded. "I will take care of that at once."

"Okay. Thank you." She gripped the edge of the armrest of the chair.

Tejada seemed to notice. "Is something else troubling you?"

"Where are you with the investigation?"

"I'm afraid I've heard nothing more. I can contact the team right now if you—"

"No." She held up her hand in a dismissive gesture. "I suppose we may never know for sure what happened. Whether it was an accident or not."

Tejada leaned forward and propped his elbows on the desktop. "Why would we consider that it was something other than an accident?"

"I don't know," she said as she shrugged. "I'm probably overreacting." She looked at him a moment, then continued. "Anyway, the two reports you asked for are being proofread right now. You should have them in the morning." She stood and put out her hand.

He stared at it a moment before he realized she wanted him to shake it.

"You've been very kind to me," she said.

Tejada rose and took her hand in his. "Why does this sound like good-bye?"

"It's not," she said, looking him in the eye. "In fact, I wondered if your offer to let me use your home as a retreat was still open."

Tejada was stunned and unaccumstomed to being caught completely off guard. "Of course," he said, recovering quickly. "Please call me when you're ready and I will send a car for you."

"I think I can find my way," she replied, then she turned toward the door and was gone.

After she left, Tejada moved to the window and stared out at the campus below, thinking of what had just transpired.

Did Abaddon know the temptation he faced after all?

Did he know that Tejada was capable of falling in love?

"But if he knows," Tejada whispered to himself, "Maria will be in serious danger." He ran his hand over his face. "And there is nothing I can do to save her."

✦ ✦ ✦

Maria took a cab back from Catalonia and waited on the sidewalk until it drove away. As it disappeared around the next corner, she took the phone from her jacket pocket and called Donleavy in San Francisco. She listened to it ring as she hurried up the brightly lit sidewalk.

"It's me," she said when Donleavy answered.

"Did you plant the bugs?"

"Yeah," she replied. "But I had to put them under the armrest of a chair."

"A chair?" Donleavy wasn't pleased. "I told you to put it some-place where it wouldn't be found."

"I did the best I could do," Maria retorted. "He didn't give me much choice. He steered me to a chair near the desk."

"What about the desk?"

"The chair was too far away. It would have been too obvious to stick one under the desk."

"Okay," he said, much calmer than before. "We'll have to work with it. What about the house?"

"I'm going there tomorrow."

"Go ahead and use your laptop to activate the one in his office. I sent you the program—"

"I got it." She stepped into the doorway of a closed shop. "You still haven't heard from my dad?"

"No," he replied sharply. "And it's ticking me off. He's supposed to stay in touch with me."

"Yeah, there's a lot of that going around. Listen, thanks for getting back to me—and helping me with this."

"Your old man is probably going to kill me."

"Then don't tell him."

"Well, you know that's not happening."

"Right now, all that matters is that I get something on—"

Donleavy cut her off. "Don't say his name out loud."

"Sorry."

"The first piece of condemning evidence that comes through, you're outta there. That was our deal, right?"

"Believe me, I don't want to stay here any longer than I have to."

"Okay. If you hear from your dad, tell him to call me. I have some information for him."

"Are you sure he's here in Spain? I mean, it just doesn't make sense that he wouldn't let me know—although I guess he'd assume I've gone home by now. You think he's in trouble?"

"No, I think he's just being a jerk."

"Well, there's that."

"Hang in there," he said.

"Yeah."

Maria ended the call and returned the phone to her pocket, then started back toward the apartment complex. There was a bug to activate and more Internet searches to complete. That would keep her busy until tomorrow.

And tomorrow was as far ahead as she could think.

Winters stood at the end of the bed and watched Sophia stir in her sleep. Light was just beginning to filter through the thin shade. It was time for her to wake up. They couldn't stay much longer, but he hadn't wanted to leave so early that they aroused the suspicions of the innkeeper. He had already shown too much interest when Winters had gone down for coffee without Sophia. Not being able to speak Basque had paid off.

Winters put Sophia's cup on the nightstand but still didn't wake her. It had taken nearly two hours last night to reassure her that they had not caused Brother José's death. After that she had slept only fitfully, while Winters sat in the uncomfortable chair, trying to determine their next move.

Sophia had won on one point. He would not take her back to Barcelona. Until he knew who was after the journal she would be safer with him. Father Padillo could probably give them a clue, but Winters didn't want to drag him into it.

The trouble seemed to have started at the museum with the overly-aggressive guard. In Toledo, they were watched from the building across from the church. And the car that followed them apparently belonged to the killer.

But this was more than just one guy determined to get his hands on the journal. Several people were involved. Even a network. And what were they going to do with it? What was so important about it that they were willing to kill for it?

Experience told Winters the only logical answer was money. And even that didn't quite fit. He wondered just how much this journal could be worth.

Certainly the whole journal was worth more than just a part of it. And Winters now had most of it. But that wasn't what had kept him up all night.

It had been no surprise to the attacker that he and Sophia were in the room at the monastery with the journal. He must have been the "monk" who went digging in the garden when Winters and Sophia arrived. Which meant he'd known they were coming and the likelihood they'd be allowed to see the journal.

But how? Who knew they were on this quest besides old Vespucci, the even older Jacobo, and Father Padillo? All of them were protective of the journal, so why would they tell anyone? Unless they were coerced.

"Do you have a plan, Agent Winters?" Sophia asked from her place on the bed.

Winters looked up to see her propped against the pillow, coffee cup in hand. "No," he replied. "I'm afraid I do not."

"Good," she said, "because I do."

"Okay. Let's hear it."

"'Hear' is the important word." She paused to take a sip of coffee. "You must hear me out before you tell me it cannot be done."

"Not the best way to start this conversation," Winters said. "But go ahead."

Her eyes took on their familiar brightness. "What I read in the journal last night, before we saw the news about the monk . . ."

"Yeah?"

"You remember the group of Jewish businessmen who financed *Señor* Columbus?"

"Right."

"When he returned from his first voyage he met with them and then he met separately with—and this is exactly the way he wrote it—'with Simon Vega, my kinsman.'"

"Wait—he was related to one of the Jewish guys?" Winters' eyes were wide with surprise. "So he *was* Jewish."

Sophia nodded eagerly. "That is the first straightforward admission he makes. Then he goes on about a discussion they had—he and Vega—about the blood moon he saw the night they first landed, and he says that Simon Vega told him they were in the midst of a lunar tetrad, a series of eclipses, coinciding with the Passover and the Feast of Tabernacles." She gestured toward the journal they'd left on the dresser. "According to what he wrote, Vega sent him to a rabbi—a Moses ben Jacob Cordovero in Cordoba—and *he* told him about Jacob ben Isaac, who prophesied in 2 BC that after the destruction of Jerusalem and a fifteen-hundred-year period of persecution, a new land would rise from the sea." She smiled at Winters. "It would rise in the year of the blood moon."

Winters could have listened to her talk about this all day, but he wasn't sure they had even an hour. "I'm lovin' this," he said. "But we have to be thinking about getting out of here. So far I'm not hearing a plan."

"I am coming to that," Sophia said. "Just hear me out." She took another sip of coffee and continued. "In the journal, he says that an evil one will rise to power when the four levels converge—"

Winters looked puzzled. "What four levels?"

"A series of four consecutive lunar eclipses occurring on the Jewish holidays of Passover and the Feast of the Tabernacles. He said that at that time, the righteous one will defeat the evil one who opposes the fulfillment of the prophecy about a land rising up from the sea."

"Okay, I get that," Winters said. "Opposition arose to Columbus' efforts to discover the New World—that land—because he was this 'righteous one.'"

Sophia nodded. "I think that is what he is saying."

"Huh," Winters grunted. "The man had an ego the size of Montana. Did he think the group in Barcelona—the ones who resisted him—did he think they were the Antichrist?"

"I do not know. That was all he wrote except for some symbols at the end that I cannot decipher."

Winters moved from the chair and took a seat at the edge of the bed beside her. "This is all great," he said, "but we need to figure out where to go next and what to do with the journal before pseudo-monk in the junk car tracks us down."

"I think I have the answer to both of those problems," she said. "I had to give you the background first."

"Sophia—"

"We must go to Jerusalem," she interrupted.

Winters' chin dropped. "You mean *now?*"

"Yes."

"I don't—"

"I have a friend there."

"Of course you do, but—"

"His name is Jacob Hirsch. He is a professor at Hebrew University. His specialty is the history of Judaism."

"I'm not following you, Sophia."

She placed a hand on his arm. "We can find shelter with Jacob and we can turn the journal over to him for safekeeping. Now that I've been able to think it through, I realize it belongs to the Jewish people, John. It is part of their heritage, not ours."

It made a bizarre kind of sense, but Winters still shook his head. "I've taken you as far as I can on this," he said. "It's too dangerous. There are too many unknowns."

"I told you last night that I will not hold you responsible for my safety."

"And I told *you* it doesn't work that way. I won't watch another woman I care about be destroyed by some terrorist with a fanatical religious agenda. I won't do it!"

Sophia's eyes were wide, as well they should be. He had just shouted into her face something he'd never said to another human being. But she didn't step back and instead said quietly, "No, John, you did not tell me that."

Winters turned away but she tugged at his arm.

"Tell me," she said. "Tell me what happened to your wife."

"It doesn't have anything to do with this."

"I think it has everything to do with it. And I think if you do not let it out, you will be in more danger than I will ever be."

Winters forced a grin. "That's it," he said. "You've been lying to me all this time. You *are* a psychiatrist."

"Do not do that," she said. "Do not make a joke of it. Not this time."

He pulled away from her and stumbled to the door—where he stopped. He could run away. Or he could face the thing that was tearing him up inside.

Winters looked back at her. "My wife died in the 9/11 attacks," he said. "In New York." Sophia didn't flinch. He kept going. "She was in the second tower, trapped above the crash site. I kept my old flip phone—the one she left the message on."

"From the tower? That day?"

"Yeah."

"You have kept a piece of her."

Tears filled his eyes and ran down his cheeks. "A voice message," he said shaking his head. "That's all I have left of her."

He placed his arm on the door and pressed his forehead against it. This was a bad idea, digging this up now—no matter how compassionate Sophia might be. It felt as raw as it did back then, as torturous as it was the day she died. That's why he'd buried it deep inside.

"I am sorry, John," Sophia said softly.

"Me, too," he replied.

He pulled himself from the door, ready to get Sophia out of there before he lost her too. But when he turned to face her he saw she was weeping too.

"How did you survive?"

"I had a daughter to raise," he explained. "That's how I survived. That and not thinking about it."

"Except for her phone message."

"Yeah. There's that. I listen to it every September eleventh, just to hear her voice."

"Do you want to tell me what she—"

"She said, 'I'm sure you've heard the news.' She was trying to sound so calm, but I could hear in her voice how scared she was. The plane had hit a number of floors below them and they'd tried to go down the stairs but the heat and smoke were too much." Winters' own voice broke. "She was still—I mean, she was sitting there at her desk, hoping firefighters could get the fire out and they could get down—and she was saying, 'Maybe you should get Maria from school so she doesn't hear about this from someone else.'"

"Maria is your daughter."

Winters nodded. "She was ten then."

"Your wife's last thoughts were of her."

Winters tried to smile. "No, her last thoughts were that she'd forgotten to take something out of the freezer for dinner so we were going to have to eat out again. She said she was sorry about that."

Sophia pressed her hand to her mouth and wept even harder.

"We'd been talking about money the night before and I was going on about how much we were spending in restaurants. The next morning I was sitting at our dining room table without her and wishing we had eaten out every night."

Sophia pulled her fingers from her lips. "Guilt is such a painful part of grief."

"My office was in the same building, but I was out in the field that day." He looked at Sophia. "Why did she die and not me?" Winters clenched his fists. "That's why I don't talk about this . . . because I can't stand it."

"If you had both died, what would have happened to your daughter?"

"She might have been better off living with my mother. I botched the whole thing after Anne was gone. I'm not much of a father." Winters bent his head toward Sophia. "I really can't go there. My daughter—I can't—"

"You do not have to. But thank you."

"For dragging you through my stuff?"

"For trusting me with your grief."

"My grief," Winters said. "This all happened fourteen years ago— you'd think I'd be over it by now."

"No," Sophia said. "Some things go so deep they become a part of who you are. I know this." She put her arms around his shoulders and pulled him close. "But that is for another time."

Winters pulled away and looked her in the eye. ""That's the thing. I want there to *be* another time, which is why I'm going to get you to a safe place and then figure out what to do with the journal."

"Well, my safe place is with Jacob Hirsch. In Jerusalem."

Winters sighed. "I don't think you can use 'safe' and 'Jerusalem' in the same sentence."

She just looked at him.

"And if we start calling up airlines, making plane reservations, using credit cards, and going through customs we'll—"

"I can make that simple."

"How?"

"I have a friend."

He smiled and shook his head. "Why am I not surprised?"

"He works for a company. They make frequent trips to Jerusalem in the company's cargo plane. I know he will take us, without entanglements."

Winters looked skeptical. "We're going to stow away on a cargo plane? This is just too risky, Sophia."

"It is not as risky as sitting here arguing. Let me ask you this again, Agent Winters. Do you have a better plan?"

"I don't know. I just—"

"As I thought," she said as she reached for the phone. "I'll make some calls."

34

As Donleavy instructed, Maria activated the bug in Tejada's office, then spent the next several hours listening to conversations from the office. Finally, though, she pulled the earbud from her ear in frustration. Why hadn't she worked on her Spanish when Snowden first told her she was coming to Barcelona? And why did it surprise her that Tejada and everyone else who came into his office never spoke English?

She turned off the laptop and tucked it into her briefcase. The one thing she'd been able to translate was that Molina was meeting someone for dinner at Restaurante Barceloneta. Seemed like a great place for her to eat too.

Just off the waterfront, the Barceloneta was a typical beach café with an odd assortment of tables and chairs with fishnets and glass buoys hanging on the walls for decoration. Windows along the back wall overlooked the water and afforded a view of the coastline. Maria had been there once for lunch with Elena on a Saturday afternoon when it was crowded with camera-toting tourists and sunbathers brushing sand from their skin. The food made up for the lack of ambience.

At night, however, it felt sinister. The interior lighting was dimmed and the men—there didn't seem to be any women—were unsavory characters.

As Maria lingered near the hostess station letting her eyes adjust to the light, she noticed Molina was not there. That didn't surprise her. She couldn't imagine him trolling a place like this.

The hostess asked her in Spanish if she would like a table. Maria had practiced saying *I'm waiting for a friend,* though from the condescending smile on the woman's face, she knew she'd mangled it somehow. The woman apparently understood enough to lead Maria to a table several rows from the windows, which was perfect. She was out of sight from the doorway but had a view of the entire room.

A man at the bar seemed to size her up, so she concentrated on the menu. She was reading the shrimp options for the fifth time when she caught sight of the hostess leading Molina to a table in the opposite corner.

Please sit with your back to me, Maria thought to herself. If he didn't, she would have to pretend she'd come to check out the guys at the bar and they were only slightly less revolting than he was.

But Molina didn't sit down at all. He stood talking to an olive-skinned man who had apparently been waiting for him. Maria slipped her smartphone from her bag and turned off the camera flash. The man looked up as he listened to Molina and Maria quickly snapped his picture.

They talked a while longer, then the man at the table stood and followed Molina toward the kitchen. Okay, *that* was weird. So weird, in fact, that Maria dropped her phone in her bag and left the table. The leech at the bar muttered something in Spanish as she passed by, but the leering look told her she didn't really want to know what he said. She ignored him and caught the hostess' attention to ask for a cab.

✦ ✦ ✦

When Tejada's cell phone rang, he glanced at the screen to check the number, then forced himself not to answer. He took a drag from his cigar and exhaled smoke in a long, winding curl above his head. All day he had denied to himself that he was waiting for Maria's call, despite the fact that every time the phone rang he looked eagerly at the screen, hoping to see the number he had memorized. Now that she was reaching out, he wouldn't answer. He couldn't. Not after Molina had brought him the news Tejada would give his life not to know.

Molina was good at what he did and so was his staff. Working around the clock, they had located Sophia Conte via her cell phone signal, but by the time they reached her location, she was boarding a private cargo plane at Pamplona Airport with the same man who'd accompanied her to the museum. Too late to stop the flight, they had determined the destination—Jerusalem—and they were able to photograph the man's face.

"We have an ID for him," Molina had said. "His name is John Winters. He's an agent with the American Secret Service."

"Winters," Tejada said slowly. "Not—"

"Yes," Molina nodded. "The same."

"Husband?"

"Father."

Tejada felt as if he had been kicked in the stomach. Moments later, however, that sense of betrayal turned to anger. "Why are we just now learning of this?"

Molina had an indignant look, which made Tejada even angrier. "Was she not vetted before she came here?"

"Your friend Mr. Snowden assured us he had done all of that with his employees."

Now, after Tejada had sent Molina to make arrangements, after hours thinking of what to do next, he could only blow smoke from the cigar and watch it fade away.

Did Maria come back to Barcelona to further her ambitions with Snowden's law firm? Or was that a cover? Was she working for her father? Spying on Tejada? Gathering information?

About what?

Tejada snuffed out the cigar in the marble ashtray that sat near his elbow.

The US Secret Service was part of Homeland Security. What would they want with antique Spanish documents? Tejada didn't know what those documents were and at this point he was averse to going to Abaddon with that question. Abaddon knew too much already.

Tejada glanced at the cell phone screen and saw that Maria had left a message. He had invited her to come to use his home as a place of retreat, then reiterated that invitation just yesterday. The call just then was probably to arrange that, and if he refused her now she would be suspicious . . . unless she was not involved with her father. Unless it was a mere coincidence that he was in Spain, wreaking havoc on its artifacts at the same time his daughter was wreaking havoc on Tejada's heart. The heart he was supposed to keep only for the Brotherhood. For the plan. For Abaddon.

Tejada laid the phone in his lap and closed his eyes. He needed to pull himself together. Handle this the way he would any other situation. Gather intelligence. Analyze it. Take the necessary action, whatever that might be.

Only this time, he wouldn't use Molina. This time he would have to do it himself.

Finally, he picked up the phone and tapped Maria's number.

Winters didn't expect to sleep that night, but the absence of rest the two nights before and the several-steps-lower-than-coach accommodations on the cargo plane had left him too wiped out to do anything *but* sleep. He and Sophia arrived at the hotel south of Jerusalem's city center at 3 a.m. Even though he gave her the bed and he crashed on the floor, he got five solid dreamless hours. Which meant his head was clearer and this whole idea seemed more absurd than ever before.

On the other hand, Sophia, who was up and ready, seemed visibly calmer than when they'd left Pamplona Airport. Though her eyes shone, she moved without hurry.

Yeah, Winters thought, nothing said "safe" like Palestinian terrorists and car bombs. "I need coffee," he groaned.

"Jacob will have something wonderful for us," she said. "He is sending his driver to pick us up."

"A college professor can afford a driver? What do they pay them over here?"

"It is a necessity for Dr. Hirsch. He is unable to drive—he has a condition that causes seizures."

✦ ✦ ✦

Professor Hirsch's home was in the Abu Tor neighborhood, which Winters knew to be relatively safe. Still he kept his eye on the surrounding vehicles and checked the rooftops of the buildings they passed. It wasn't as though something suspicious would necessarily stand out—everything looked dangerous to him.

Hirsch met them at the door with a German shepherd at his side. He and the dog, who was introduced as Aasim, had similar handsome features—long noses and warm, discerning eyes.

"*Shalom*," he said. "Come inside."

He led the way to a high-ceilinged sitting area where, as Sophia predicted, he had a tray waiting for them—coffee and a bakery item that Sophia informed him was *challah*. Winters had no appetite. The sooner he could make sure Sophia would be safe here, the sooner he could get back to Spain and find out what was going on. The thought of leaving her at all took away even his desire for coffee.

When the driver—who apparently doubled as a houseboy—took away the tray, Winters stood by the arched window and surveyed the safety features of the house. He quickly determined that other than the German shepherd, there weren't many.

Meanwhile, Sophia and Hirsch leaned their heads together over the journal.

"Ah, the blood moon eclipses," Hirsch said. "That term means more when tied to our festivals." He looked reverently at the journal that lay open on the table. "The fact that he mentions it in his private writings is further evidence of what so many of my colleagues and I believe."

"That he was indeed Jewish," Sophia said.

Winters turned to face them. "Maybe you can clear something up for me, Professor," he said.

"I hope I can."

"Columbus says in the prophecies that there had to be one final crusade to recapture the Holy Land before Jesus would return, and one of the reasons for his first voyage was to find enough gold to finance that crusade."

Hirsch gave him an approving nod.

"But if he was a Jew, why facilitate Jesus' return?"

"Excellent question," Hirsch noted. "We believe that may have been a cover for his real purpose. Or he saw himself as racially a Jew, but spiritually a believer in Christianity." His eyes fell on the journal again. "Hopefully further study of these writings will tell us more."

"Then we've brought them to the right place." Winters moved from the window to sit on the edge of the couch, close to Hirsch and Sophia. "I'm concerned about your safety, yours and Sophia's. These people who are after the journal—whoever they are—they're desperate enough to kill for it."

Sophia petted Aasim's head. "No one knows we're here. And as soon as Jacob has culled whatever he can from this, he will see that the journals are put in the right hands."

"Hands more capable than those of our poor departed monk," Hirsch said.

"I'm sure that sooner or later these people would have stormed in there and found the journal anyway."

"No," she said. "We led that man there. If they'd known the journal was there, they would have taken it long ago."

"Let us not borrow trouble from yesterday," Hirsch said. "I am interested in the signature here, at the end." He gestured toward journal.

Winters looked longingly at the door, but there was no cutting off Hirsch without insulting both him and Sophia. He suppressed a groan and nodded.

"You see here," Hirsch said, pointing to the symbols arranged in a triangle with dots and letters. "This is a formation often found on gravestones in Jewish cemeteries. Columbus ordered his heirs to use that same signature in perpetuity."

"What does it mean?" Sophia asked.

"It is a symbol for the Kaddish—a prayer of blessing and thanksgiving often said at funerals." He looked over at Sophia. "Would you like to hear it?"

"Of course," she replied graciously.

Hirsch stood, spread his arms apart, palms turned upward, and looked to the ceiling, then began in a low rich voice. "May the great name of God be exalted and sanctified, throughout the world, which He has created according to His will. May His kingship be established in your lifetime and in your days, and in the lifetime of the entire household of Israel, swiftly and in the near future; and say, Amen."

Sophia murmured an amen. Winters was about to do the same when Hirsch continued. "May His great name be blessed, forever and ever. Blessed, praised, glorified, exalted, extolled, honored, elevated, and lauded be the name of the Holy One. Blessed is He above and beyond any blessings and hymns, praises and consolations which are uttered in the world; and say, Amen."

Winters murmured it this time.

"May there be abundant peace from heaven, and life upon us and upon all Israel; and say, Amen."

Winters breathed the final amen.

Hirsch lowered his arms and rested his hands at his sides, as if the blessing had taken all of his energy. "By telling his heirs to use that signature forever, with those symbols," he said, "Columbus was in effect instructing them to pray that blessing over him and his descendants."

Sophia held a finger over a page in the journal. "What about these 'four levels,' Jacob? What is this about?"

"It's referring to the basic notion of Kabbalah, which teaches that there are four levels of reality—the obvious, the allegorical, the imaginative, and the inner esoteric meaning. In this case, it would indicate the lunar eclipse, solar eclipse, and the two Jewish festivals of Passover and Sukkot. When all four of those occur in order, an evil one will rise to power."

Sophia pulled out her iPad to take notes.

"I won't give you a crash course in Kabbalah," Hirsch said. "But in essence it is based on the belief that nothing is as it appears on the surface. There are always four meanings behind everything, with the obvious being the least important and the esoteric the most important." He nodded toward the journal. "What Columbus says he was told by Cordovero is just this kind of reasoning. However—"

"John does not like 'however,'" Sophia said, interrupting.

"Let's hear it anyway," Winters said.

Hirsch cleared his throat. "I find it hard to believe that Moses Cordovero told him this—about the rise of the evil one and the righteous one vanquishing him forever—as the truth. If he *did* put it the way it's written here, he did so only because he didn't fully trust Columbus."

Winters wondered why anyone would.

"If Columbus was Jewish," Hirsch continued, "and it seems obvious now that he was, he was only half Jew. His mother was Jewish but his father was Christian. Jewish business leaders might have dealt with him for commercial reasons, but on religious and philosophical issues they would have been far more circumspect."

"Are you saying—the journal really isn't that valuable?" Winters asked. "I mean, in terms of truth?"

Hirsch shook his head. "What he wrote here is accurate down to the part about the tetrads." He pointed again to the journal. "The tetrad he experienced while on his first voyage was, in fact, the first tetrad following the destruction of the Temple."

"Truly, Jacob?" Sophia questioned.

"Truly," Hirsch replied. "The evil one doesn't arise to oppose the fulfillment on the first tetrad. That is the part that Columbus has wrong. The evil one arises when the four levels converge—after the fourth tetrad."

"So . . . did the other tetrads actually occur?" Winters asked.

"Oh, yes," Hirsch replied. "We've had three so far. All of them associated with the Passover and the Feast of the Tabernacles. The first occurred between 1493 and 1494, just as Columbus was making his discoveries. It announced the first part of the prophecy—a time of tears and tribulation for the Jews. These dates are well known. You can find them on NASA's website."

"Then," Sophia said, "the 'time of tears and tribulation' would be the Spanish Inquisition, correct?"

"I think so. But the tetrad merely releases the thing announced in the prophecy. It's a point of beginning."

"Well, yeah," Winters agreed. "Since the persecution of the Jews definitely didn't end there."

"Correct," Hirsch said quietly. "It did not." He scratched absently between his dog's ears.

Winters suddenly wished the conversation would end. A shiver was working its way up his spine.

"And the second tetrad?" Sophia asked, oblivious to Winters' discomfort.

"That one happened between 1949 and 1950. Right after the founding of the Jewish state of Israel."

"Which part of the prophecy was that?"

"The close of the prior age and the beginning of a time of blessing and triumph," Hirsch explained. "For the following twenty years Israel prospered beyond all expectations."

"And the third age?"

"Between 1967 and 1968. That tetrad coincided with the Six-Day War, which marked the complete restoration of Jerusalem to the Jewish people. Until then Arabs still controlled East Jerusalem."

Winters was afraid to ask the obvious next question. "What about the fourth tetrad?"

Hirsch looked directly at him. "That one was set to occur between 2014 and 2015."

"And what is that supposed to mean?"

"It will announce the end of the age."

Winters tried not to roll his eyes. "Forgive me, Professor, but how many times have we heard people predicting the end of the world?"

"Not the end of the world," Hirsch corrected. "It will note the time when the end will begin." He moved to the edge of the chair. "Remember, tetrads announce the beginning of something. In the past they have ushered in an era, but the dawning of those earlier ages were not cataclysmic events."

Sophia put a hand on Hirsch's arm. "So, Jacob, the set of four would have been completed sometime between 2014 and 2015. What does that mean?"

"It means, my dear, that the age of the end will have arrived."

"Everything will be in place?"

"Everything necessary for the end to begin, but the dawn of the age will not be that ending point."

Sophia gently turned the pages of the journal. "This signature," she said, pointing to the page, "could it be a key to who the Antichrist is today?"

"I don't think so," Hirsch responded. "Signatures are personal. This has the feel of something between Columbus and his descendants. An inside communication." Hirsch smiled. "I wouldn't be surprised if his sons knew precisely what it meant. Maybe a message that reached back into their family history."

Sophia glanced at Winters with a knowing look. "And into yours, John."

Hirsch gestured toward the journal. "But I still think the prophecy of Jacob ben Isaac is the most important part of what he has written here. And it can be correctly understood only by properly applying the principles of Kabbalah." He looked at Winters and Sophia in turn. "Think of it this way. The prophecy is an encoded message. Kabbalah is the key."

Winters grinned. "The Columbus Code."

"Excellent," Hirsch said. "You take my meaning perfectly." He leaned toward Winters. "Deciphering the message of that prophecy will be a lifelong task for you."

"For me?" Winters seemed surprised. "No, Professor, I'm leaving that part to you."

"The journal was not put into my hands, but yours," Hirsch said. "Beginning with your mother and carried out by all the people who led you to it." He nodded to Sophia. "I am sure you've told him that the kind of information that was given to him by Vespucci and old Jacobo and our unfortunate monk is not easily passed, especially to 'foreigners.'"

"I have tried, Jacob," she said. "I have tried."

"I don't think so." Winters backpedaled. "You're talking about deciphering this code and figuring out who is the evil one, the person opposed to the fulfillment of the prophecy."

"I am," Hirsch said, nodding once more. "I believe that the two are tied together. Find one and you will find the other." He continued even though Winters was shaking his head and already backing toward the door. "I would begin with this group of businessmen in Barcelona, the ones who opposed Columbus."

"That was over five hundred years ago."

"Then seek out organizations that have been around that long."

"Come on—"

"Spain is not the United States," Sophia explained. "Our history goes back more than two centuries."

Fine, Winters wanted to say. *Let somebody in Spain figure it out.* But Aasim was suddenly on his feet. He circled Hirsch's chair and then placed his paw on his knee. "Will you excuse us?" he said and followed Aasim out of the room.

When the door closed behind them, Winters came to Sophia's side, a troubled look on his face. "I don't see him being able to protect you."

"He is in worse condition than the last time I saw him. I see other signs of failure." Her eyes were wet. "I cannot be responsible for another man's death. This was a mistake, John. I am sorry."

"No, you're right. And I can't leave you here." Winters looked away, thinking.

The more Hirsch had talked about an Antichrist, the higher the sense of dread Winters felt. He'd never thought about it much—perhaps Episcopalians didn't—but the attachment to the troubled history of the Jews and the power this journal seemed to have . . . it was too concrete to ignore now. And as over-the-top as all this prophecy stuff sounded, the fact remained that someone desperately wanted the journal. They needed a plan—preferably one that kept Sophia *and* the journal safe. But if staying with Hirsch wasn't going to work for Sophia, it wasn't going to protect the journal either. As much as he wanted to be rid of it, leaving it here was no longer an option.

"All right," he said, turning back to her. "Let's have the driver take us back to the hotel. We'll regroup there."

"I'll tell Jacob," she said. "And John?"

"Yes."

"I think we must take the journal with us."

"Yes," he agreed. "I think you're right."

✦ ✦ ✦

Hirsch protested their departure but Winters was sure he saw relief on his tired face. As they made their way back toward the center of the city, Sophia looked over at him. "Jacob is a good man," she said quietly.

"Yeah," Winters replied. "He seems okay. How do you know him?"

He meant it as a casual question, but he felt Sophia stiffen in the seat beside him. "Am I poking in where I don't belong?" he said.

"No," she said. "I poked into your life."

"Yeah." Winters grinned at her. "But if you don't want to answer, you don't have to."

"I think you should know." She glanced out the window. "Jacob and I did postgraduate work together at Stanford University in California. You know it?"

"Yeah," Winters said. "I know it. Impressive school."

"Yes," she nodded. "The education was excellent. My personal choices were not."

Winters couldn't imagine her making a bad choice but he nodded her on.

"I met and married an American. A very charming man. Handsome. Smart."

"But manipulative, unfaithful—"

"I will save you the list," she said, looking at him again. "He was abusive. In every way."

Winters twisted in the seat. "Did you call the cops? Get protection?"

"No. I called Jacob Hirsch. I was in a trap with my husband. Jacob knew people and he helped me escape back to Spain."

"This guy never came after you?"

Sophia shook her head. "He died not long after I left."

"You don't think Jacob's 'people'—"

"No, no, no," Sophia responded. "Nothing like that. We were living apart by then but still were married. A woman my husband was seeing found out that he had a wife and . . . she killed him. Shot him in cold blood."

"Will you think I'm a jerk if I say he deserved it?"

"I thought that a few times myself." Sophia attempted a smile, but the pain was obvious. "I told you that because when I first saw you on Skype, I almost said that I could not work with you."

"Don't tell me I look like this loser."

"No." Her hand touched his arm. "He became to me the ugliest man alive. You are far from that. I was simply afraid to trust an American man ever again, even in a business arrangement." Sophia looked down at her hand still on his sleeve. "But you have shown me that I was wrong. Not all Americans are like that."

Winters even leaned toward her, eyes already beginning to close as he leaned in to kiss her. But at the last possible moment something caught his eyes. He glanced out the front windshield in time to see a white van swerve in front of them. Their driver slammed on the brakes to avoid hitting it and the car screeched to a halt in the center of an intersection. Seconds later, a faded black BMW squealed to a halt behind them.

Winters banged his fist against the door lock button and shouted to Sophia, "Do exactly what I tell you."

"Why? John, what's happening?"

"Exactly what we were afraid of."

36

In less time than seemed possible, men from the van and BMW were at the car. One opened the driver's door and placed the muzzle of a pistol to the driver's head. Two shots rang out, and Sophia screamed. Blood spat across the windshield and Hirsch's young driver lurched forward against the steering wheel. The car horn blared in response.

At the same time, a second gunman jerked on the handle of the door next to Winters. Finding it locked, he shouted to the others for help. A moment later, the window on Winters' side cracked into a mosaic of glass.

But before the gunman could break through with the butt of his gun, Winters reached across Sophia and shoved open the door on the opposite side. "Run," he said. "Run as fast and as far as you can." And he shoved her toward the open doorway.

With Sophia on her way, Winters reached for the door lock and flipped it off, then lunged toward the door with all his might shoving it back against the gunman. The force of the collision sent the man backward and he stumbled to the pavement.

As Winters climbed out from the backseat, the man who shot the driver came around the open door. By then, the first man was off the pavement and both of them grappled for Winters to wrestle him under control. Winters struck the one nearest him with a fist to the side of the face and felt the jaw crush beneath the force of his blow. As the first one writhed in pain, the second brought his pistol around to end the fight once and for all. Winters threw an elbow to his gut and the man doubled over, gasping for breath. Winters pounded him on the jaw, too, and the pistol clattered to the street. Winters reached for it, scooped it up with one hand, and ran toward the opposite side of the street in the direction Sophia had gone.

✦ ✦ ✦

Maria spent more time in front of the mirror than usual that morning. Not because the setup in this guest bath—one of many in Tejada's mansion—was beyond luxurious, but because she wanted to hide the fact that she hadn't slept one moment in the sumptuous bed. All through the night she lay awake, certain that at any moment Molina would burst into the room holding the listening device she'd stuck to the underside of the bar in Tejada's study the evening before.

Did guys like Molina make regular sweeps to make sure Tejada wasn't being bugged? Why hadn't she asked Donleavy that question?

Maria leaned closer to the mirror and dabbed concealer at the dark circles beneath her eyes. Makeup wasn't going to help her with the next step, which was to stay long enough to convince Tejada that she was revived by her twelve hours in his home and was ready to face the world again. She wanted to go back to her apartment, set up her laptop, and listen for incriminating conversations.

She padded back into the bedroom and checked her briefcase for the thousandth time. If she could have carried it around the house with her she would have, but that was sure to raise Tejada's suspicions.

Assured that her laptop was still in place, Maria slid the briefcase under the bed and checked the gold Chelsea clock on the bedside table. She should stay until midafternoon, then she had to leave. Suddenly there was a sense of sadness to that. Despite her nervousness over planting the bug, her evening with Tejada had been . . . lovely.

He had been more of a gentleman than any guy she'd ever dated. The fact that he was twenty years older might account for some of that, but still . . . he was polite without being stiff and charming without seeming phony.

Their conversation had been surprisingly genuine too. Over a light dinner on the east portico and later in his study—which she had requested to see—he'd asked her questions about her family, her education, her rise at Gump, Snowden and Meir—all with a keen interest that gave no hint he was really waiting his turn to expound on himself as most men did. She'd been guarded, especially when he gently probed about her parents, but she'd told him more than she did most people.

"I blamed my father for my mother's death," Maria had said as they stood on the balcony overlooking the Barcelona lights. "It was stupid. I wanted her to come to my school that day because I was presenting a science project and getting an award. How big can it be in fifth grade, right?"

"It was big to you," Tejada noted.

"She said she couldn't—she had an important case and she needed to be at work." Maria brushed back the hair the breeze swept into her face. "That was always the way it was with her—the cases came before me. I guess at ten you have no concept of the importance of work."

"But you had a concept of the importance of family."

"It wasn't like we didn't have a family life, though." Maria gave him a wry look. "I was just being a brat."

"I can't imagine it."

"*Really*."

"All right." His smile was wide. "Perhaps I can."

"My father volunteered to go with me that day."

"Now, your father," Tejada said. "What did he do?"

"He worked for the government," Maria said—and hurried on with the story, though she suddenly doubted the wisdom of telling it. Things always got hairy when anyone questioned her about her father's work. "I told him, no, that he should tell Mom she needed to go with me. I wanted him to be on my side."

"Was he?"

"They usually didn't take sides. That was the problem that day. I knew I wasn't going to win and I was mad at both of them."

"And now?"

"It haunted me that my last words to her were angry. I know I was just being a kid, but sometimes I would give anything to take it back."

"And your father?"

"Like I said, I blamed him—for years, until I was old enough to realize that he was doing the right thing that day. But by then, we were miles apart."

She'd stopped there. It had always been hard to talk to anyone, except *Abuela*, about her father's emotional distance after 9/11. But she'd never even admitted to *Abuela* that she felt he didn't love her as much after her mother died, that maybe he'd only put up with her before because Mom wanted her. She wasn't going to tell Tejada that, either—even though he was looking at her with fathomless compassion.

But beyond that, something seemed not quite right with the conversation. Tejada had been listening, but perhaps too hard and too attentively, as if searching for hidden meaning in her words. Maybe she was being paranoid again. She had, after all, bugged the man's office and his home. Maybe it was just his natural intensity that made her feel as if she'd told him more than she realized.

All the more reason to get out of here soon, she thought now. That and the fact that, as much as it set her off balance, she liked the light in his eyes when he looked at her. That couldn't happen right now. Not as long as there was the smallest chance that Tejada knew what Molina was into. If he didn't, maybe they could revisit this sometime. If he did, she had to run as fast as she could and not look back.

When Maria reached the breakfast room, Tejada was nowhere in sight, but the food was there and ready. Eggs Benedict. Mozzarella cheese and tomatoes. Steaming croissants oozing with butter. A sweet-looking woman who spoke in delightfully broken English told her to get started, that *Señor* Tejada would be there soon.

As Maria took a seat at the table, the woman gestured to a television in the corner. "You would like to turn it off?"

"No," Maria replied. "You can leave it on."

While she waited for Tejada, Maria poured herself a cup of tea and focused on the news.

On the screen she saw images from Jerusalem and the announcer droned on about an incident that occurred overnight. Another issue in Jerusalem. Wasn't there always trouble there of one sort or another? What was it this time?

"Two tourists were attacked early this morning in Old City Jerusalem," the anchorwoman said. She seemed about as interested in the story as Maria. "While their names remain unknown, witnesses reported the victims were a man and a woman. Both victims escaped the attack but authorities have not been able to locate them. We turn now to our CNN correspondent in Jerusalem."

The screen shifted to a Jerusalem street clogged with traffic and pedestrians. Three vehicles sat in the middle of an intersection. A young man's body was draped over the steering wheel of the larger car. Maria grimaced at the sight of it. Why did they show that?

"The intended victims still have not been located," the young Israeli reporter was saying, "nor have the perpetrators, although witnesses said all three assailants were reportedly injured. A Jordanian group called the Army of the Mahdi, which is known to target Western tourists, has released a statement claiming responsibility and demanding that Israel lift the Gaza embargo."

"Why Western tourists?" the anchorwoman asked.

"They are apparently playing it as an attempt to drive a wedge between Israel and the US."

Suddenly, the screen went black. "This is not appropriate for such a beautiful morning," a voice said from across the room.

Maria turned to see Tejada standing behind her, holding the television remote in his hand. His voice was less inviting than it had been the night before and his face was expressionless, as if he were about to transact business. Maria felt a tightening in her chest.

"You slept well, I hope?" Tejada said.

"Yes," she replied. "You look worried. Is something wrong?"

Tejada had a surprised look. "You are a perceptive woman, Maria. One of the many things I like about you." He rested his hand lightly on her shoulder. "I have to attend to some business, but for only an hour at most. You'll stay, won't you, until I return?"

"I think I should go." *Go to the apartment, where I can hear what goes down in that office.*

"Please," he said. "Stay. We should talk some more." He lifted his hand from her shoulder and gently brushed it against her cheek. "One hour. And then we have much to talk about."

Maria nodded reluctantly, but the foreboding sense of uneasiness she'd felt that morning grew deeper.

37

Winters switched off the television in disgust and tossed the remote on the bed. With the other hand he pulled Sophia closer to him. She had almost stopped shaking, but the silent tears still ran down her cheeks.

"That group they were talking about just now," she said finally. "Are they the ones who are after us?"

"I doubt it," Winters replied. "The guys who came after us were *not* Jordanian. Someone fed that story to the police or the reporters as a cover story."

"Why?"

"To keep anyone from finding the real reason they were after us."

"Which is?"

"Who knows?"

She pulled away from him. "I think *you* know why."

"I don't know."

"But you have a theory."

"A guess."

"And what do you guess?"

Winters looked beyond her. "I don't know why they want us, but they fed that story to the authorities so they could continue looking for us."

"Unimpeded by the police."

Winters nodded.

"John?"

"Yeah?"

"I am truly frightened."

"I know," he said and pulled her into his arms.

She sobbed until she fell asleep.

As much as Winters wanted to stay there—to kiss the tears away from her cheeks and stroke her face—he had to make a plan.

He gently extricated himself from Sophia and folded the bedspread over her, then dug his cell phone from his pocket. As he feared, he still had no service. Sophia's bag lay open on the dresser and her phone was visible through the top flap. He picked it up and dialed the number he knew by heart.

Donleavy answered on the first ring. "Maria?"

Maria? "No," Winters said. "It's me."

"John?" Donleavy lowered his voice. "Where the—where have you been?"

"Why were you asking about Maria?"

"I thought it was her. This is a Barcelona number."

"Why would she be calling you?"

"Because she's looking for you. I ask again, where *are* you?"

"Why is she looking for me? Is she in trouble?"

Silence. "Donleavy," Winters said tersely.

"I'm here." Donleavy sighed. "She's not in trouble. She just needs your help."

"With what?"

"You want to give me a chance?"

Winters closed his eyes. "Sorry, man. Talk to me."

"Maria's back in Barcelona, doing more legal work with Catalonia Financial. Actually," he corrected, "with Emilio Tejada, the CEO. And before you go off on why she didn't let you know she was in Spain again, she's been trying. We both have."

"I haven't had phone service since I got over here."

"Because you're a cheap—"

"Back to Maria," Winters interrupted. "Why does she need my help?"

"A girl she was working with had an 'accident,'" Donleavy began slowly. "She was in some trouble over the—"

"Maria? I thought you said—"

"Not Maria," Donleavy snapped. "The girl. This other girl. She was in trouble. Somebody was blackmailing her and Maria was trying to help her. But that's a whole other story."

"So, the girl's death. It wasn't an accident."

"No—and Maria's pretty sure she knows who set it up."

"Did you tell her to call the Barcelona cops?"

"Tejada—the Catalonia CEO—practically owns the city."

"So, he was behind it?"

"Him or one of his employees. Head of security for the company. A guy by the name of Molina."

Winters ran his hand through his hair. "She's going after people like *that?*"

"Look," Donleavy said, "I've been helping her. She promised me she wouldn't do anything stupid. As soon as she has some solid evidence, she's going home. That's our deal."

Winters moved to the bathroom, closed the door, and sat on the toilet seat. "Well, thank you. I think. Should I ask how she's gathering this evidence?"

"No. You should tell me why you haven't gotten back to me about the laptop deal."

"Because I forgot about it."

"You forgot. What the heck is going on with you?"

"That's why I called." Winters peeked through the crack in the door. Sophia was sleeping soundly again. "I'm gonna give you the short version, and then I need your help."

"Hey, rescuing the Winters' family is my new career."

Winters summarized what had happened from the museum visit to the attack on the way back from Hirsch's. Taylor was uncharacteristically quiet as he talked.

"You still with me?" Winters asked.

"Yeah. But let me ask you this. Is there anybody who *isn't* after you?"

"I need to focus on the ones trying to kill us."

"Right. What do you need?"

"I need a safe house for Sophia and then I need information so I can find out who's doing this."

"I don't know about a safe house. You're persona non grata around here right now. But I might be able to help you with the other. Give me half an hour and I'll get back to you."

"Thanks, buddy. I owe ya."

"Don't mention it."

"Hey, and Donleavy."

"Yeah?"

"When you hear from my daughter, have her call me on this phone, okay?"

"I'm expecting her to check in anytime," Donleavy said. "And listen, we still have to deal with this other thing."

"One thing at a time," Winters said. "Right now the name of the game is keeping Sophia alive."

✦ ✦ ✦

By late that afternoon Tejada still hadn't returned to the house and Maria was frazzled from pretending for the benefit of the staff that she was "retreating." It was time to go back to her apartment and she was gathering her things from the bedroom when a knock sounded at the door. The maid had been trying to ply her with lunch, tea, and wine all day and Maria was ready to pay her to leave her alone. "I don't need anything, thank you," she called out.

But the thought occurred to her that the woman could be useful. She crossed the room hurriedly and said through the closed door, "Would you call a taxi for me, *por favor*?"

"Maria," a male voice replied, "it's me."

Tejada sounded solemn, if not grim, and the pressure in her chest made it almost impossible to breathe. He'd found the bug and traced it to her. She knew it. Molina was onto her and had reported to him. She was going to be dragged into the street and run over by Louis.

"Maria?"

Okay—she was freaking out.

She tossed her hair back and opened the door. Tejada stood with one hand high on the doorjamb and the other poised to knock again. He had a serious expression but he wasn't angry and he seemed to be studying her intently.

Desperate. That was how he seemed. But it was not a word she would ever have used to describe him before and it was the only thing that kept her from ducking under his arm and fleeing.

"Something's wrong," Maria said. "How can I help?"

"By staying. Please do not go."

"I can stay for a little while, if you need me."

"Dinner is being prepared. I would like to share it with you, in a private room where we can speak freely."

"I suggest your study," Maria said. "It is my favorite room in your house."

If the request seemed odd to him, he didn't so much as flinch. "Shall we go there now?"

Maria nodded and picked up the briefcase she had set at her feet. Tejada glanced at it. "I'd like to keep it with me in case I need any of my files when we're talking."

"You will not need it," he said.

But as he offered her his arm, she shifted the case to her other hand and carried it with her anyway.

✦ ✦ ✦

A supper of *escalivada*, chicken with raisins and pine nuts, and *crema catalana* arrived in the study shortly after Tejada and Maria entered. Servants rolled it into the room on a table already set for them. When the servants were gone, Tejada leaned back in the chair, steepled his fingers beneath his chin in a contemplative pose, and studied her face once more. She was so sure this had been a bad idea she almost bolted. And yet there was something about that look that made leaving as impossible as staying.

"You are a bright woman," Tejada said after a moment.

"Thank you," Maria replied. "But why doesn't that sound like a good thing right now?"

"You see?" A smile danced through his eyes. "I can hide nothing from you. What troubles me is whether you can hide things from me."

"I haven't told you absolutely everything about myself," Maria said carefully. "But I don't consider that 'hiding.'"

"Nor do I. In fact, I savor the process of discovery."

Tejada pushed his untouched plate aside, placed his elbows on the table, and rested his chin in his hands. It was a vulnerable position for anyone but it looked almost submissive on Tejada, and Maria had to force herself not to reach across the table and cup his face. What was happening to her?

"This is difficult," he said.

"Just say it, Tejada."

"I have feelings for you," he said. The words hung between them. "And I must know if you share those feelings, Maria. It is important that I know."

Important? That seemed far from the right word. *Vital* fit better— as if something far beyond her depended on it. When she didn't respond immediately, he leaned back in the chair once more. "And I suppose your silence is my answer," he said.

Maria frowned. "Come *on*, Tejada," she lamented. "You can't just say that to me out of nowhere and not give me a minute."

He rose from the table and moved to the window, where he stared out on the city below.

"Really?" Maria stood and tossed the napkin on the table. "You're not even going to give me a chance to answer?" She started across the room toward him "Because if you have that much pride, then you can—"

Maria stopped in midsentence as Tejada turned to face her. He slipped his arms around her waist, squeezed her close, and pressed his lips to hers, firm and full. And by then, she didn't want to resist.

After a moment, he leaned away from her just enough to ask, "What would you say, Maria, if I gave you a chance? Would you say you have no feelings for me?"

"I would not say no," Maria replied.

Tejada smiled and pulled her close once more.

38

I have intel," Donleavy said. "You sure this is a secure line?"

Winters wasn't sure of anything at this point, but he said yes, just to keep the conversation moving. Sophia was in the shower, which gave him limited time. She'd been upset when she awakened but a phone call from Hirsch had calmed her. Apparently he still "knew people" and had arranged for both of them to leave the next morning from a private airport near Masada. From there Sophia would go to a house she sometimes used for spiritual retreats, not far from Málaga. *If* they made it to the plane without trouble from—whom? That, he hoped, was what Donleavy was about to tell him.

"What did you find out?" Winters asked.

"Satellite images are a beautiful thing. The satellite is positioned in a geosynchronous orbit that keeps it permanently in place over the Middle East."

"Donleavy."

"Right. I also have files from satellites that circle the globe once every twenty-four hours but in orbits that brought them over the region at the time you two were attacked."

Winters tightened his jaw. "Bottom line, pal, we're running out of time."

"Okay, I got an image of the three cars and then frames of the other two cars leaving the scene. They went into the neighborhood of Sheikh Jarrah and pulled into a house behind Saint John of Jerusalem Eye Hospital." Donleavy gave a heavy sigh. "If I give you the address, you're gonna go there, aren't you?"

"I haven't lost it completely, Donleavy. Can you tell me anything about the guys who attacked us?"

"Couldn't get faces—we're not that good yet—but I did get some intel on the house. It's owned by a corporation called Belgium Continental."

"Belgium. That doesn't make any sense."

An uneasy silence.

"What?" Winters asked.

"This is probably nothing. Probably a coincidence."

"What is?"

"Belgium Continental was recently acquired by Catalonia Financial."

"Why is that name familiar?"

"Because it's the conglomerate Maria is working with right now. But don't flip out." Donleavy talked faster. "It's a huge corporation with business interests all over the world. It might not have anything to do with Maria. She hasn't told them who you are—"

"She doesn't have to. When was the last time you heard from her?"

"Yesterday morning. But something else makes me think this doesn't have anything to do with Maria."

"I'm hanging up," Winters said. "I have to call her."

"You don't have her number. She's using a burn phone. Listen to me."

Winters wasn't sure he could. His pulse pounded in his ears.

"This thing with your laptop," Donleavy said. "Somebody did tamper with it. Whoever it was loaded a program onto it called Eye of Horus—it's used in industrial espionage and domestic surveillance. It takes control of the built-in camera and microphone to monitor your activity."

"You are not serious."

"They—whoever they are—got four months' worth of audio and video files, along with mirror images of all e-mails. The good news is that whoever infiltrated your laptop wasn't able to corrupt your phone, although they could overhear the calls you made on it when you were near your laptop. I can explain how—"

"How did they get the program on there? I either had my laptop with me or it was secured at home."

"Evidently somebody got into your place—probably the same person in the e-mails. Now that I'm thinking about it, S.A.M. was probably you."

"I don't get the connection. Besides, who do I know besides you who could pull that off? I don't have that many friends who are geeks."

"You don't have that many friends period." Donleavy snickered. "And it doesn't take a computer genius to do something like this. Remember those e-mails I told you about—the ones that said 'all you have to do is insert a flash drive into the USB port.' I checked your activity logs. That's how they did it."

"All right." Winters felt anxiety rising in his gut. The shower was off, which meant any minute Sophia would come out of the bathroom. "What did they use all that stuff for? Do you know?"

"Oh, yeah. It was the Russians, man."

"The Russians."

"They probably didn't plant the program directly. They don't work that way. But with the information collected from your laptop, they knew we were coming that day."

Winters' mind spun. "Why didn't they just leave?"

"Money was on the line. The day we went over there, they were already running the transaction program. If they had just shut it down and hit the road, they would not have had time to complete the transactions. That would have left a lot of money on the table."

"They took me hostage so they could stay there until the transactions were complete?"

"Yeah."

Winters listened for sounds from the bathroom. The water was running in the sink. "I just need to know who was behind it," he whispered into the phone. "And I need to know if there's a connection between that and what's happening here."

"I'm still working on that. Both of these are pretty elaborate schemes. Someone else had to be involved besides the thugs who attacked you and Sophia, and whoever hacked into your laptop wasn't working alone."

"Okay. You'll keep working on it?"

"You know it. And listen, I'll take care of Maria. You take care of yourself and Sophia."

"Deal," Winters said. But as he hung up, he wasn't sure how he was going to hold up his end of it.

"You should rest," a voice said from behind him.

Winters turned to face Sophia, who stood in the bathroom doorway wearing the same clothes she'd worn earlier, yet looking as fresh as she had the first moment he'd laid eyes on her. "Really, John," she said insistently. "We have hours until we leave. Lie down. I am fine now."

He shook his head. "I wouldn't be able to sleep. And we need to talk through what's going to happen next."

She had a quizzical look. "Is there something that you are not telling me?"

There were many things he wasn't telling her, but none of it seemed to matter. These would be their last hours together and he wasn't about to sleep them away. He rose from the chair where he'd been sitting and crossed the room toward her.

✦ ✦ ✦

As Tejada leaned against the armrest of the couch and watched the sunrise through the window, he was struck with a sadness he had not known he could feel. But then the night had brought him one new emotion after another until he could neither speak nor sleep.

"You're awake early," Maria whispered.

He reached with his arm and folded her to himself. "I've been here since you abandoned me," he said into her hair.

"Abandoned you? We talked until three in the morning. I gave you my dessert *and* fifteen inches of the couch. What more did you want?"

Tejada tilted her face up to his. "There was a great deal more that I wanted from you."

"But you didn't ask."

"What would you have said?"

"I would have said no."

"That is why I did not ask."

"Are you sure you're for real?" she asked playfully.

Tejada pulled her against his chest and ran his fingers through her hair—hair he had wanted to touch since the day she marched into his office and demanded that he remove his bodyguard. He didn't want to see fear in her eyes. He couldn't bear to see that replace the affection that had warmed them as they told each other of their childhoods—their longings—their quirks. Like two normal people who had every right to fall in love.

Maria wriggled free to look at him. "Did I say something wrong?"

He shook his head.

"I mean, you've treated me with respect and I appreciate that about you."

The problem wasn't with what she said, but with the things he now knew to be fact. Whether she was working for her father or not—and there was no evidence that she had even been in touch with him since before she first came to Spain—he had had to risk having that one night, that one chance to experience what his commitment to the Brotherhood and Abaddon couldn't give. But now it was over and there could be no others.

"You look so sad, Tejada," Maria said.

"I am. I must leave—on business—and that means I will not be with you. And that—makes—me—sad." He punctuated each pause with a kiss, although the last one fell on smiling lips.

"And I must go back to my apartment today," she said. "Because I have things to do to get ready for the week."

"Do them here. I will not leave until tomorrow."

"I've run out of clothes."

"I will buy you new ones." He stopped, because she stiffened in his arms. "I have said something wrong."

"Not wrong for you," she said. "Just wrong for me. We said we would take this slowly. Remember?"

He kissed her forehead to avoid having to look into her doubting eyes. It had to stop here. Before Tejada swept her away from Spain and all he had dedicated his life to.

"I will have a car ready for you," he said. "But take your time. Enjoy a swim—have breakfast with me. Please."

"Breakfast," she said. "And then I'll go."

She turned but he caught her arm. "Once more," he whispered. He gathered her up and kissed her, then she turned again in a swirl of hair.

But the righteous one will oppose him and vanquish our enemies forever.

—Christopher Columbus

39

The car that Jacob Hirsch had arranged to meet Winters and Sophia at the Málaga airport wound through the Alpujarras to an ancient town on the southern slopes of Spain's highest mountain, Mulhacén. By midmorning the sun was blazing bright and hot. Sophia pulled her sunglasses from her bag and put them on. She looked even more beautiful, more mysterious than before.

Winters looked away from her. He couldn't keep doing this. He had to start steeling himself to walk away from her.

"John?"

He closed his eyes and pretended not to hear her. Until she put that warm hand on his arm. No matter how terrified she had been in the last twenty-four hours, she had always been warm. "Yeah?" he said.

She put her fingers to his chin and nudged his face toward her. "I want to know that you will be safe."

He wanted to lie to her but he knew she wouldn't buy it. "I can't guarantee it," he said. "Not unless we find out who these people are. Then I'll know what I'm working with."

"They are Russians," she said.

His eyes widened, but she shook her head at him. "You did not think I would be listening?"

Winters rubbed his forehead. "I should have known, I guess. And no, I'm not sure the Russians are the ones behind this. Those guys didn't look Russian to me—"

"What did they do to you?"

"Sophia—"

"I have to know how to pray for you." Her eyes were misty. "I am not a fool, John. I know when you leave me at Casa Aloe I may never see you again. But at least let me pray for you."

"Hey," he said. "Come on—of course you can pray for me."

"Then how?"

Winters groped for something, anything that would take the fear from her face. "I'd like to know who got into my house and hacked into my laptop," he said. "That'll get us on the track of at least one of the groups of the people who want to . . . That much would help."

Sophia slipped her hand in his. "You can probably think that out yourself, Agent Winters. I have seen you do it before." She gave him a wan smile. "You need only to be asked the right questions."

"So start asking," he said.

"Perhaps this person was not an intruder," she said. "He could have been someone you allowed into your home. Do you have a housekeeper?"

"You're kidding, right?"

"People who repair things."

"The place is in a state of total *dis*repair."

"Anyone who has come to visit since—how long?"

"Four months. I don't do much entertaining," he said drily. "Donleavy comes over every couple of weeks for beer and pizza. He was there more often when my brother, Ben, was in town. Probably to keep me from killing him." Winters pressed her hands. "I'm kidding.

The kid drives me nuts, but I'd never actually do him in—" He noticed the look on her face. "Sophia, what?"

She moved her hand from his and turned away. Winters reached for her and leaned close. "Hey. Say it. What's wrong?"

"No," she said. "If it is to be said, you have to be the one."

He stared at her a moment before the realization dawned on him. His first impulse was to tell her she was out of her mind. Except that he couldn't.

Ben had been at the house.

Ben could be talked into anything if he thought it meant a chance to have the life of intrigue he thought Winters had. If someone told him it was a test for getting into the Secret Service, he would have sold Winters to the Russians without a second thought. He wanted to be a Secret Agent Man.

"SAM," he said. "Secret Agent Man."

Sophia looked puzzled. "I'm sorry?"

"SAM. Secret Agent Man. That's what my brother, Ben, used to call me. I need to borrow that phone again."

"I'm sorry," she said as she pressed it into his hand. "But it seemed obvious when you were talking. He was the only one unaccounted for."

"We don't know for sure it was him," Winters said. But even as the words left his mouth he knew. He knew.

✦ ✦ ✦

Maria kept her expression serene and her eyes hidden behind sunglasses until she was inside the apartment—at which point she leaned against the door, slid to the floor, and sobbed.

She had promised Austin she would be careful. She'd sworn to Taylor Donleavy that she would protect herself from Carlos Molina. But she hadn't guarded her heart and now Emilio Tejada wanted to take it from her.

If she was honest, she wanted to give it to him. Ignore the possibility that he knew what Molina had done to Elena—that he was aware of Molina's secret dealings with the CIA and his suspicious meetings with men in alleys and restaurant kitchens. Aware of them . . . or behind them.

Maria crawled to the couch and sank her face in the cushions. How could that possibly be, after what she'd felt with him last night? But there was no way she could ever suggest to him that Carlos Molina couldn't be trusted. Or tell him that she hadn't trusted *him*.

Because she was afraid to be right.

Even now, she was terrified to listen to what might have transpired in Tejada's office yesterday, or in his study after she'd left. The study where she had let herself dream for a few hours that loving Tejada could be a possibility.

Maria stared across the room at the briefcase that held the laptop that held the answers. If she erased it all, called Austin, and told him to make her a plane reservation, maybe she could go home and get back to her life.

Except for Elena.

Maria had promised her that justice would be done. This wasn't the way she'd imagined it when she made that vow—but now it was the only way.

Reluctantly, she retrieved the briefcase and set up the computer on the kitchen table. While it came on, she made a cup of tea, then slipped in the earbuds and clicked on the eavesdropping program.

Just as before, the banter between Tejada and Molina was

in Spanish—though this time that was less a frustration than a relief. Maybe it would be better if she never knew whether Tejada was involved . . .

Suddenly the voices stopped and all she heard was static. Loud static. Maria yanked out one earbud, but before she could pull the other one loose the line cleared and Molina's voice came through, growling in English.

"Farsoun's attack was unsuccessful."

"Completely?" Tejada said. His voice was taut but controlled.

"He and the Conte woman are still at large."

Maria sank into the chair and pressed the earbud back in. She had no idea who they were talking about. *They finally speak English,* she thought, *just to go on about people who have nothing to do with Elena.* She'd give it five minutes.

"And they still have possession of the documents?" Tejada asked.

"They do," Molina answered. "It might help us track them if I knew what these documents are."

A pause ensued for so long Maria checked to make sure she was still connected. When Tejada finally spoke, she could hear the reservation in his voice. The thought that she knew him that well stabbed at her.

"They have stolen the personal journal kept by Christopher Columbus," Tejada said.

"And this is important to us how?"

For once Maria was thinking along the same line as Molina. What was with everyone and the sudden interest in Christopher Columbus? First Uncle David, then *Abuela,* and now Tejada. Maria took a sip of tea. She might as well get comfortable if they were going to entertain her.

"It could reveal the plan to those who should not see it," Tejada said. Each word was measured and precise. "You know what that means for us. My orders still stand. You must personally locate Agent Winters and the Conte woman and do what you have to do to get that journal."

The teacup fell from Maria's hands and shattered on the floor.

"Whatever it takes," Molina repeated.

"But hear me on this." Tejada's voice dropped, as if he were whispering into her face. "Bring Maria to me."

40

With that, Maria yanked the earbuds from her ears and threw them aside. She stared down at the shards of the cup and thought of what she'd just heard. Tejada was after her father. Her father. Winters. Agent Winters. Her father was with a woman. The Conte woman—whoever she was.

Her father and this woman had an ancient document that Molina would kill for. Something about Columbus.

Tejada was going to deal with Maria himself, but somehow that seemed less urgent than the need to alert her father—who had apparently managed to survive one attack already. She had to tell him before Tejada knew that she knew.

Maria reached for her phone to call him when she realized—Tejada and Molina had been talking in Spanish for hours. They only switched to English when they began talking about her father. And that was after she heard the loud static.

"They knew," she gasped.

Tejada and Molina had carried on that conversation in English because Tejada knew she would be listening. One of them had found the bug.

Heart slamming in her chest, Maria went for her phone again. Her fingers were already sweating as she tapped Donleavy's number.

The call went to voice mail after two rings and Maria didn't leave a message.

As she flipped through the contacts list for her dad's number, she heard a sound at the door. Then the handle wiggled ever so slightly. Someone was unlocking it. She had no doubt it was Molina. Maria stuffed the phone inside her bra and leapt across the room to the door. The dead bolt was set but she had not put the security bar against the door. She slid it into place and looked around frantically as if a plan would present itself from some corner of the room. She needed to get out of the apartment or she didn't stand a chance. No plan stepped forward, so she went with what came into her head.

Maria pulled an umbrella out of the stand by the door and hurled it toward the French door that opened to the balcony. She heard it smack against the glass as she slipped into the closet a few steps from the front door. Forcing herself not to breathe, Maria flattened against the back wall and pulled the door almost closed. Through the crack she watched the business end of a pistol enter the room first.

Molina stepped forward and, just as she'd hoped, headed straight toward the balcony exit. Still not breathing, Maria slid from the closet and scooted out the front door he had left open. No doubt, he already knew what she'd done and he meant to kill her.

She reached the elevator and banged on the call button. Miraculously the doors opened. Maria reached inside, punched *Uno* on the control panel, and threw herself toward the stairs. She heard the elevator close again just as she yanked open the door to the stairway and hurried down the metal steps. It would be only seconds before Molina realized what had happened and started after her. The only thing she had going for her was speed—and a head start.

Just as she reached the second-floor landing Maria heard the trouncing of footfalls above. She pulled open the heavy door and let it bang against the wall. While it slowly closed Maria crept down the final flight and waited by the ground-floor exit. She once more willed herself not to breathe and stood as still as possible. *Please, please, please,* she said in her mind. *Go through that door. Please, please, please.*

The footsteps pounded overhead and Maria squeezed her eyes closed, her mind spinning. Then she heard the door bang open on the second floor and, without waiting to see if he was playing her, Maria bolted from the shadows and into the blazing sunlight near the back of the building. She knew this spot well. Although the maid had insisted more than once that she would take out the trash, Maria had always come to the Dumpster herself, just to feel as though she had some kind of control—even if it was just over her garbage. Now she squeezed between it and the alley wall and waited until she saw Molina crawl past in that hearse of a car that was supposed to take her to Tejada.

When it appeared that Molina wasn't coming back, she took the alley at a dead run. Away from all things Catalonia.

✦ ✦ ✦

An error message said, "The voice mailbox is full." Winters cut her off with a jab of his finger.

"Still no answer?" Sophia asked from the kitchen, where she was brewing after-dinner coffee.

Winters shook his head. "I can't even leave a message now. Mailbox is full. Not that my brother has paid any attention to the four I already left him." He dropped the cell phone into his shirt pocket as he moved toward the kitchen. "I finally have service and it does me no good." He took Sophia's hand and brought it to his cheek. "Look, Sophia, I have to—"

"I know," she said.

"Of course you do. You always do. But how about letting me say it?"

Sophia closed her eyes and rested her forehead against his chest just as his phone rang. Perfect timing. Maybe he'd been better off without cell service.

"It's probably Donleavy," he said. "I can put him off for a minute."

But Sophia motioned for him to answer it and Winters took the phone from his pocket.

"Hey," Winters said, without checking the number.

"Dad?" Maria gasped. "Is it you?"

"Maria?" He had never known his daughter to be hysterical, but her voice was teetering on the edge.

"It's me," she said. "Dad, I'm in trouble—and so are you."

He could actually understand her now and his anxiety level was at an all-time high.

"Are you safe?" he said.

"For the moment, but they won't stop until they find me—and you."

"Who are 'they'?"

"Tejada's people. Emilio Tejada. I don't think he'll let them kill me—yet—but they'll do anything to get that journal or whatever it is you have."

Winters pushed the name "Tejada" aside to come back to later. "Where are you?" he asked.

"Put her on speakerphone," Sophia whispered. Winters pressed the button.

"Who's with you?" Maria's voice ratcheted up a notch.

"Sophia Conte," she said.

"He's after you too. Carlos Molina. He works for Emilio Tejada. He's looking for both of you. You have to get to a safe place."

"We're *in* a safe place," Winters said, fighting to keep his emotions under control. "You need to be here with us. Tell us where you are."

"Daddy, I'm scared."

Winters felt a lump in his throat. "I know, honey. Just give me your location and I'll come for you."

"No! It's too dangerous."

Sophia put her mouth close to the phone and spoke in the voice that had more than once talked Winters back from the edge. "He will not come himself, Maria. I will send a car for you. The driver will know the password—*refugio seguro.*"

"There *is* no 'safe haven' from these people."

Winters grabbed the phone from Sophia. "Maria Anne—you tell me where you are and you tell me now," he demanded.

It took him a moment to realize that the gurgling sound on the phone was Maria's. "Oh, Daddy," she said. "You haven't called me that since I was . . . ten."

"Where are you?" he insisted.

"I hitchhiked as far as Cartagena."

"You are only four hours from us, Maria," Sophia said. "Are you in a protected area?"

"I'm down on Los Nietos Beach. I can just keep walking."

Winters tried not to dwell on the fact that she was wandering on an isolated beach alone at eight o'clock at night. "Okay," he said. "Stay in that vicinity as long as you can. When the driver gets to Cartagena he'll call and tell you where to meet him."

"What about you?" she said. "Dad, you don't know what these people are capable of."

"Oh, yeah, I do," Winters said. "But handling the bad guys is what I do. You remember that?"

"I remember that," she said.

"How much juice do you have left on your phone?"

"Fifty percent."

"Turn it off for the next three-and-a-half hours. That way we know the driver can get through to you."

Sophia spoke up. "If you don't hear from him by midnight, go to the lighthouse and wait there."

"I'll see you in about eight hours," Winters said. "Don't be late or you're grounded," he teased.

"Oh, please, yes," she replied. "Somebody ground me."

When Maria hung up, Winters turned to the window that looked down over the now-darkened village. "She hitchhiked four hundred miles."

"Yes, she did," Sophia said. She slid her arm around his waist. "She is your child, after all."

41

Tejada stared through the one-way glass that gave him hidden access to activity in the Security Operations Center below. Through a reflection in the window, he saw an image of Molina standing behind him.

"I can't understand Farsoun's inability to capture Agent Winters," he said with disgust. "He was an incompetent idiot."

"Farsoun has been eliminated," Molina assured.

"But Winters hasn't. And now you have been unable to bring his daughter to me. I do not understand that either. I should have gone after her myself."

"She had help from her father," Molina replied. "She had to, or she never would have escaped from that apartment."

"You have to fix this," Tejada said with contempt.

"I have a plan in place."

Tejada nodded toward the large video screens that occupied the wall of the op center. A bevy of analysts stared up at the larger-than-life pictures he was seeing—one of the Conte woman, petite but poised. One of Maria, caught by Molina's camera as she exited a restaurant with her thick hair tossed by the sea breeze and her brown eyes intelligent and shimmering. And a the third of the fortyish man he'd seen in the previous photos—the man who was aging well despite a peppering of gray in his hair.

"This is your plan?" Tejada asked. "Another manhunt?"

"An expanded one," Molina said.

Tejada heard the resentment in his voice. "Go ahead," he said. "Explain it to me."

"We have been creating a plausible version of the facts to support our search effort."

Tejada shrugged. "Mere notice that we at Catalonia need to apprehend suspects should be enough to motivate the Barcelona police."

"We need cooperation at higher levels of government, perhaps even internationally before we're through, and they are going to require an explanation."

"And what is that 'explanation'?"

Molina went to the door and put his hand on the knob. "You are about to see. This is why I asked you to come here."

Tejada nodded, still watching only Molina's reflection in the glass. Molina seemed to be waiting for more and when nothing came, he jerked open the door and disappeared. Tejada knew he had angered him, but he no longer cared. He wanted this done, or he would suffer Abaddon's wrath.

Below, Molina moved among the analysts bent over their laptops to take his place at a microphone on the main operator's console. The microphone was for Tejada's benefit. Molina's unamplified voice could be heard for several city blocks if necessary. Without preamble, he launched into the "explanation."

"Yesterday morning, Maria Winters, the woman you see here, tried to murder *Señor* Tejada in his home."

Tejada couldn't hear the gasps from the staff but he could see the expressions on their faces. Under other circumstances, he would have found it laughable.

"Apparently she was aided in that effort by her father, John Winters, the man pictured here," he said, gesturing to a screen on the wall. "Winters is a United States Secret Service agent. He is armed and well trained. It is not clear whether the plot to kill *Señor* Tejada was his, hers, or both, or whether the Secret Service itself is involved. As for Sophia Conte—the other woman pictured here—she is John Winters' partner and do not be deceived by her size. She has proven herself dangerous on more than one occasion."

Molina glanced around the room as if he would shoot on sight anyone who wasn't paying attention. Apparently satisfied, he went on. "What is certain is that Maria Winters did attempt to kill our CEO and her father helped her escape."

Tejada sniffed. That last part was clearly an attempt to relieve Molina of responsibility for her escape. Somehow it seemed like more of a lie than the rest of the fabrication.

"Fortunately, *Señor* Tejada was not injured, but we know Maria and her father will not stop until they've succeeded. They must be apprehended."

An overeager analyst spoke up. "The police have been alerted, as have all airport and rail security personnel—"

"Listen to me." Molina didn't raise his voice but the menacing tone was clear. "We have resources here at Catalonia that the government does not have. Apply those resources and find these people. I don't care *how* you do it. Just do it."

Heads bent back to the computers and fingers flew across the keyboards. As the analysts went to work, Molina looked up at Tejada through the window and gave him a nod.

Tejada tapped the glass and watched Molina march from the op center. When he entered the room again, he had lost all control of his anger. "I should have killed her the minute I discovered who her father was," he ranted. "Then you—and I—would not be in this position." He stepped to the window and inserted himself between Tejada and the glass. "I may do it yet."

"You will not. If you find the girl you will bring her to me—unharmed."

The corner of Molina's lip curled up. "Are those Lord Abaddon's orders?"

Tejada tried to keep his emotions in check but the smile on Molina's face told him he had failed. "Go," Tejada snapped. "And do not come back until Winters is dead and I have the journal in my hands."

Molina didn't wait for further dismissal. He stalked toward the door, jerked it open, and slammed it closed behind him as he left.

Tejada stood at the window, lost in thought. Molina was right. The orders he'd given were not Abaddon's. They were his own, and if he wanted to survive this ordeal, he needed to renew his vow to the Master and get back to the plan. Seeing Maria had been a serious mistake, one he had known he was making from the moment he first spoke to her. And now they were both in trouble. He hoped she'd understood his warning to her and that she would get away as quickly as possible. At the same time, he was desperate for her to be returned to him. But if she was, could he bring himself to do what life in the Brotherhood required, or would he turn his back on everything they offered and join her for a life on the run?

42

The darkest hour, Winters decided, really was the one just before dawn. Since the instant Maria had called to say she was safely in the backseat of the car Sophia had sent for her, he had sat in a chair in front of the window, never taking his eyes off the street below. Sophia had begged him to get some sleep and she had eventually dozed on the couch. But he'd kept the vigil, praying for the sunrise. As the clock inched toward four he rose from the chair and paced, the questions deepening with every step.

How did Maria get so involved with Emilio Tejada? What happened that he was now threatening her life? She'd said something about Tejada wanting the journal. He was obviously behind the attempts to take it from them, but why the intrigue? Why murder? Why not just ask for it?

Could it actually be a coincidence that his daughter was working for a man who had some reason to keep him from having the Columbus papers? What were the chances?

And how did all of this tie in with Ben and the Russian situation? Or did it?

The only thing Winters knew for sure was that his feisty, stubborn, fearless daughter was terrified and not just for herself, but for him. He'd seen what Tejada could do. Brother José was one example.

The attack in Jerusalem was another. But Maria didn't know about either of those and yet she said, "You don't know what these people are capable of." She must have seen as much if not worse, which would account for the tremor in her voice—something he hadn't heard since she was very young.

The only other thing Winters knew for sure was that he had to protect her. He had to get his head out of his own issues and make sure she wasn't touched. It wasn't about him anymore. Or Christopher Columbus.

Headlights flashed against a white wall below, then two shafts shot through the darkness. In the distance he saw the car making its way up the winding road. Winters was out the door before it even reached the driveway and before it came to a complete stop the back door swung open—and then his daughter was in his arms.

"I love you, Daddy," Maria sobbed, her face against his chest.

"And I love you," he replied.

✦ ✦ ✦

Left to his own devices, Winters would have conducted a full inter-rogation the moment he got Maria into the house, but Sophia took over at that point—in the seamless way that no longer surprised Winters at all. She drew a bath for Maria, then prepared breakfast and had them all gathered at a table in a nook off the living room by the time the sun crested the mountains to the east. As they sat together, enjoying the food and each other's company, Winters found it hard to comprehend how he was going to function without Sophia at his side.

After a bath and breakfast, Maria began to open up and the more she talked about Tejada and the situation with Catalonia, the more Winters realized what he would have to do.

Maria appeared to be leaving out nothing as she presented them with what she'd experienced since Winters last saw her after his mother's funeral. As she talked, the flash came back into her eyes and her voice lost that ten-year-old's frightened tremor.

Only once did he blurt out, "You realize you could have been killed, don't you?" That was when Maria showed them a picture she'd taken in a bar where she knew Molina was meeting someone.

"This is one of the men who attacked us in Jerusalem," he said, pointing to the photograph.

"Molina must have sent him to do that." Maria shook her head. "He was probably setting it up right there, with me barely six feet away."

Winters opened his mouth to speak but Sophia said, "That is disconcerting, yes?"

"Beyond." Maria leaned forward. "I'm thinking about the conversation Tejada and Molina had, the one I heard in my apartment. They referred to a man named Farsoun and they said his attack on you was unsuccessful."

"Thank the Lord," Sophia murmured.

"Is he just somebody Tejada hired?"

"There's only one way to find out," Winters said. "Ask him."

The terror sprang to Maria's eyes again. "Dad—"

"Relax, kiddo." He fished his phone from his pocket. "I know people. And after I talk to Donleavy . . ." He let the name hang in the air until Maria's eyes met his.

"I couldn't get in touch with you," Maria said. "I tried—"

"I know." Winters smiled. "You did the right thing. He's the one I have a problem with. Planting *bugs?*"

"If I hadn't listened in on those conversations," Maria defended, "I wouldn't have known Molina was coming after us. I wouldn't have been able to warn you."

"The conversation you heard was in English, yes?" Sophia asked.

Maria nodded. "I think Tejada wanted me to hear it, but I don't understand why."

"That is easy, Maria," Sophia said. Winters watched her eyes soften. "He was warning you."

"Why would he do that?" Winters said.

Maria didn't answer. She didn't have to.

43

Tejada hadn't slept in forty-eight hours and his head buzzed as Molina entered his office. If Molina noticed the shadow of stubble or the bags beneath his eyes, he showed no sign of it. He launched straight into what he'd apparently come for. "We have tracked the woman as far as Cartagena."

Tejada's pulse quickened but he said, "Which woman?"

"Your woman."

Tejada chose not to take the bait. "How?"

"We tapped in to law enforcement surveillance cameras. We found video of her getting into a produce delivery truck behind Mercado de La Boqueria. By the time we located the driver she was no longer with him, but he told us where he left her."

"You paid him," Tejada said.

Molina smirked. "*He* paid. In a manner of speaking."

"Must every piece of information come from your fists?" Tejada held up his palm to stop the protest he knew was coming. "Go on," he insisted. "Where is she now?"

"My people are going over what surveillance video there is near Los Nietos Beach. That is where she was last seen. There are only glimpses here and there, but we will locate her."

"That is all you have?"

"For now."

This was the moment when Molina always waited for Tejada's dismissal—a kind of blessing from the leader of the Brotherhood and a tacit act of fealty in return from Molina, but he turned now without hesitation and strode to the door. His arrogant posture . . . his innuendo . . . the smirk . . . the nonchalant use of violence as the first response.

"Wait," Tejada called.

Molina took a few more steps before he stopped, and even then he only looked at Tejada over his shoulder.

"See that the plane is ready to leave in an hour. I am going to Cartagena."

Molina's eyes took on a knowing gleam. "Whatever you say."

As he went once more for the door, Tejada understood why Molina applied his fists to the people he regarded with contempt. His own were clenched at his sides.

Just then, an all-too-familiar voice whined from the doorway.

"The door was open," Philippe Prevost said.

Tejada waved him in and motioned to the chair in front of his desk. Prevost did as directed and flopped into a chair. His cheeks had grown gaunt since the last time they talked and he looked as tired as Tejada felt.

"I have done everything I can do," Prevost began.

"Not a reassuring way to start the conversation," Tejada said.

"Well," Prevost sighed. "It's not all bad news. There is some good."

"No need to be defensive," Tejada said, wearily. "Tell me."

"The measure in the US Congress to increase their government's borrowing limit has failed."

"It did not just fail," Tejada said, his voice crisp. "It collapsed—and that is precisely what we wanted. The federal government can no longer finance its operations through borrowed money." Tejada felt himself warming to the subject. It was good to fix his mind on something besides Maria.

"Japan is already in chaos," Prevost continued.

"And I have instructed our traders to get out of the Japanese market so it will continue to fall. What about China?"

"I told Peng to sell some of their US paper in Paris this morning, quickly. China will support any measures to move control of the world's transactions away from the United States." Prevost smiled. "Peng could hardly contain his excitement. China will support our global currency."

"And Germany?"

"Their leaders have met with the European Union. All are in."

Tejada had a questioning look. "Then why have you come to me looking like death, Philippe?"

"The Russians," he sighed.

"I thought you had a meeting with Koslov."

"I did." Prevost shifted in the chair. The whining, Tejada knew, was about to commence. "I cannot trust him, Emilio. He says Russia is preparing to revalue its oil reserves from dollars to euros, but I hesitated to tell him the EU supports us because I am not certain he is telling me the truth. Koslov says everyone is overreacting to the American situation—that the markets will right themselves when the US makes its first debt payment next week. I explained to him that the US won't be able to meet all of its commitments without credit, but he went on about its three trillion dollars in revenue, its army, etcetera. And we know about their credit-card-fraud operations in the US. They don't want any more eyebrows raised about that." Prevost's voice fairly screeched. "Even when I told him the dollar has already lost half its value and is still dropping, he was not convinced—"

Tejada cut him off. "Bottom line, Philippe."

Prevost's miserable gaze fell to the floor. "Koslov said no to our one-currency plan. I did everything I could—"

"Enough," Tejada snarled. The room fell silent and he stared across the desk at his nephew.

After a few minutes, Prevost finally said, "So what is next?"

"We give it another day of trading," Tejada replied. "Let the dollar drop further. Then you go back to Koslov."

Prevost looked as if he would rather be shot, but Tejada's withering glare was enough to make him do anything. Finally, he mumbled his agreement to the meeting and skittered from the office.

When Prevost was gone, Tejada leaned back in the chair and closed his eyes. In spite of the way things appeared, all wasn't lost. Not really. There was only Russia to persuade and that could be accomplished. He would have to coach Philippe, but he could do that too. Things could be salvaged. All was not lost.

Then the phone rang and he knew by the sound of the ringtone it was Abaddon's line. He didn't even have to pick it up to hear the Master's words. "Come to me. At once."

44

Sophia insisted that Maria go to a bedroom and at least try to sleep for a few hours. Winters knew she was right, but it was all he could do not to post himself outside her door. Of course, he didn't have a weapon, beyond a cast-iron skillet and some kitchen knives. But they were not completely defenseless. They had information and right then, that was what they needed.

While Maria rested, Winters used the time to chart out everything that had happened and the things Maria had told them. A time line, he'd learned, was an important tool for viewing events. It was like putting together a jigsaw puzzle with several significant pieces missing—pieces he needed if he was going to get into the heads of Tejada and Molina. He had to know how they thought, what drove them, or he couldn't protect Maria or Sophia . . . or himself.

Twenty minutes into the task, Winters tossed the pen on the table and folded his hands behind his head. He could contact the Service, but he had to have more to give them than this puzzle with its gaping holes. He'd also been away from therapy with Julia Archer longer than he'd expected to be, so who knew what kind of reception he'd get if he called Rebhorn?

Winters pushed his chair back and stood for a view of the chart from a different angle.

"How can I help?" Sophia set a steamy mug in front of him and glanced over the chart.

"You can tell me why Catalonia Financial cares about the journal," he said. "If they consider it the property of Spain or whatever, why not just ask us for it? Why all the subterfuge?" He scratched his head. "Usually when people in power are this desperate for something, it's because it threatens their power. But the journal is over five hundred years old."

Sophia looked over at him. "Will it do me any good to remind you of the prophecy of the tetrad?"

"You're talking about some Barcelona group being the Antichrist."

She nodded, still meeting his gaze.

"Catalonia Financial is a multibillion-dollar conglomerate, not a 'brotherhood.'"

"I'm not so sure about that, Dad."

Winters turned to see Maria crossing the room bundled in a pale blue terry-cloth robe, her hair pulled into a bun at the crown of her head. She looked so much like Anne he almost gasped. And just as her mother's so often had been, her eyes were bright with an idea she just had to tell.

"Coffee, Maria?" Sophia asked.

"Please." Maria came around the table to stand next to Winters.

He glanced at her. "What aren't you sure of?"

"That the board at Catalonia isn't a brotherhood. You should hear the chant they recite at the start of their meetings."

Sophia abandoned the coffee. "Do you remember any of it?"

"You would think I would—I heard it enough times, but it was in Spanish. Something about '*Con los antiguos . . .* and for the future something-something.'" Maria tightened the belt on the robe.

"I know it ended with '*nuestras fortunas con el maestro*' because I thought that sounded like a dish they served at Los Caracoles."

"'*Con los antiguos*' is 'with the ancients,'" Sophia said. "So 'with the ancients and for the future of'—we don't know. And then 'our fortunes to the Master.'"

"What master?" Winters frowned.

Maria shrugged. "I have no idea, but whoever it is, they practically worship him. They spoke the whole thing together and all of them had matching rings. Tejada wore his all the time."

Winters looked at Sophia. "Is that some kind of Spanish business custom?"

"Not that I am aware of."

"But this isn't just any business." Maria poured her own coffee and took a seat at the table. "They're all about their history, or at least Tejada is. He showed me pictures of his ancestors—Sebastian Somebody was one of them—he told me that Catalonia goes back to 1382."

Sophia squeezed Winters' fingers. Maria looked from one of them to the other. "What?" she said. "Does that mean something?"

"It could," Sophia replied.

Winters let go of her hand and folded his arms across his chest. "Let's not get carried away. I'm sure lots of European businesses go back that far."

"What's going on?" Maria set the mug down too hard and its contents splashed over the lip of the cup. "I mean, I'm in this just as deep as the two of you. Only I don't know *why* you're in it."

"It's a long story," Winters said.

"I've got nothing but time right now."

His stomach churned. Actually, they *didn't* have time. This whole thing was becoming more dangerous by the minute. If they were dealing with psychos he was going to have to anticipate every move, and that was impossible to do unless he knew his enemy inside out.

"Dad."

Winters shook himself and looked up at her. "We'll explain it all to you—we will. But right now, I need you to tell me everything you know about this brotherhood thing."

Maria gave him one more narrow-eyed look before she said, "Okay—from the fourteenth century on they were financiers, importers, that kind of thing. Tejada called them 'A group of Barcelona businessmen.'"

Sophia leaned toward her. "Those were his exact words?"

"Yeah. Like I said, he has all these paintings of them and their descendants in his house and some on the walls at Catalonia's office, but they've never published pictures of the board. You can't find them anywhere on the Internet, not even on their website, which I found completely weird."

Winters found it almost too incredible to believe. But he did.

"I told you about the mystery deal that Snowden was involved in," Maria continued. "About Elena finding out about it and trying to cover it up—I know that's why Molina had her killed."

"I am sorry," Sophia said.

"But I didn't really believe Tejada was part of that, and I still don't know for certain that he was. It seemed like it was all Molina. He was the one I saw with Schlesinger."

Winters' head came up from the chart. "Schlesinger? CIA Schlesinger?"

"I didn't tell you this part?"

"What part?" He knew his voice was sharp, but the more Maria revealed, the more worried he became.

"After my initial trip over here, I went back to DC briefly. My assistant met me at the airport and we stopped for lunch on our way to the office. Molina and Schlesinger were in that restaurant having lunch together. They were at a table in back. I took notes on my cell phone but I left that in the apartment." Her eyes opened wide with a look of realization. "Oh," she gasped. "They've seen that by now."

"It doesn't matter," Winters said with a shake of his head. "They're coming after us anyway. Do you remember any of what they were talking about?"

Maria's face had gone pale, leaving only the faded traces of childhood freckles across her nose. Fear rose inside her but she pushed it aside, took a deep breath, and continued. "Apparently Molina had done Schlesinger some favor in Kenya and he was asking Schlesinger for a payback. Something about whatever had been intercepted in Chechnya, something that was now in a secure location."

Winters fought against the familiarity of this as he strained to hear every word she said.

"Whatever Molina was asking him to do was 'insane,' at least in Schlesinger's opinion. But it sounded like he'd committed some kind of indiscretion in Copenhagen that involved pictures of him with Danish schoolgirls. That part I learned later, on my own."

"Molina was blackmailing him," Winters said.

"He doesn't know how to do anything else," Maria said. "Except kill people."

Winters pumped a clenched fist as he paced back and forth at the end of the table. "Did you hear anything else?"

"Yes. Something about someone picking up a suitcase. Someone named Jason Elliot. My assistant looked into that and found a Jason Elliot was killed recently. He'd been shot and then for some reason mowed down by a hit-and-run driver."

Winters stopped pacing and looked away. "John?" Sophia asked. "What is it?"

Winters' eyes closed and his mind whirred as snippets of information dropped into place. The prophecies—the journal—the ancient brotherhood—the idea of an Antichrist that seemed so outrageous. Until someone believed he was the one. Until he resurrected what had been intercepted in Chechnya on its way from Moscow to Tehran and hidden for forty-five years.

In a suitcase.

"Dad—you're freaking me out," Maria said.

"I'm freaking my*self* out." He looked at them with his eyes wide and his cheeks ashen. "I know what they're doing."

✦ ✦ ✦

When Tejada arrived in El Masnou, darkness had overtaken not just the somnolent city but Abaddon's room. The old man, seated in his chair, was silhouetted in the window by the thin light of the moon, making it impossible to detect the expression on his face. Tejada was sure that was intentional.

"I came as soon as I could," Tejada said.

"No, you did not." Abaddon's voice was not stern, as Tejada had expected, but it had the unexpected edge of excitement, as if something long anticipated had come to fruition. "You came when I summoned you, Emilio. You could have come sooner."

"When was that, my lord?"

"When you knew that the plan as you saw it would not be fulfilled."

"I do not know that yet. Another day of trading will—"

"Will do nothing," Abaddon interrupted.

The fury Tejada had dreaded came alive for an instant but died in a single breath. Abaddon's next words were soft, coaxing. "You still hold out hope that our one-world currency—our first step to the global government you will rule—will come about by acclamation."

Tejada stepped forward, hoping to catch Abaddon's face in the light, but the old man thrust out his hand. It was best to tread carefully. This was his last chance to stop this.

"Well?" Abaddon said.

"It is preferable to the alternative."

"The alternative. You mean the ultimate solution I gave you."

"Yes."

"That is because you still harbor a soft spot for human beings."

Tejada felt a chill run through his body. "I am one of them," he replied.

"No!" Abaddon retorted. "You are not one of them. You are mine. You are one with me."

"The Russians will agree—"

"No, they will not. Koslov has his own scheme for world power, but unlike you, Emilio, that is not his destiny. Yet unlike you, he has no tenderness."

Abaddon turned his head, creating a dark, featureless profile against the window in the background. Tejada's chill ran deeper.

"You must put aside tenderness in all its forms," Abaddon continued. "You have already seen how it weakens you—in this turmoil you feel over Maria Winters."

"She is gone," Tejada said.

"And you plan to go after her."

Tejada was speechless, not from Abaddon's perceptiveness, but from Carlos Molina's betrayal. He should have known this the moment Molina quoted Abaddon to him.

He should have known many things.

"There are some who seem to be more loyal to me than you are," Abaddon said, confirming what Tejada already knew. "But I see through them—and that is what you must learn to do. You must sense things before you are told."

The old man's words were dizzying.

"But that does not matter at this moment," Abaddon said with a dismissive gesture. "It is time for the solution."

"I had hoped to avoid—"

"It is too late. The device is in place?"

"It is, my lord, but—"

"Then do it."

"Because we have been unable to retrieve the journal?"

"Because Molina is a pretender." Abaddon jabbed a gnarled finger in the dim light. "You, Emilio, are the only one I can trust to do as I say. When the documents are recovered—and they soon will be—they must be destroyed, along with the people who possess them. *All* of them. Only then will you be secure in taking your rightful place."

Abaddon paused to draw a long, rattling breath. "The Americans must be crippled so that you can ascend. They have not been handicapped by the efforts you've made so far."

Slowly Abaddon leaned forward and his face emerged from the shadows. At the sight of him, Tejada took a convulsive breath. The old man's skin was thin and tight along his cheek bones. His eyes were sunken and when he smiled his lips pulled back to reveal the blackened roots of his teeth.

"It is time," he said. "You will do it. You will give the order to detonate. And the bastion they call Wall Street will be demolished."

The energy of Abaddon that had always infused Tejada's soul and raised him to the heights of charisma and power now seemed instead to be sucking his soul out of himself. Tejada tried to pull away from the corpse of a man who now drew closer, but even his eyes could not move. Abaddon's were locked on his with a hideous force Tejada could not resist.

"You are one with me," Abaddon said in a low, raspy voice. "You are one with me."

That idea was not new. Tejada's complete revulsion was. Drawing on his last reserve of strength, Tejada nodded, bowed his head, and backed away. With words that had been drilled into him all his life he said, "It will be as you have said."

Only then did Abaddon release him. And only then did Tejada take leave of the man he had called "Master" . . . and whom he now knew was completely deranged.

45

Within a matter of hours, the airy, white-walled house that overlooked the tiny village was transformed from Sophia's retreat to a lockdown facility for the two women Winters loved most.

Curtains were drawn and shutters closed. Doors were locked and reinforced with bureaus and armoires, while emergency exits were fashioned from windows and a laundry chute. Sophia's driver brought in new burn phones for all three of them, and then she dispatched him to a separate location—close enough to collect them on a moment's notice but far enough away to put off anyone who might have followed him.

Winters had gathered every implement that could be used as a weapon and instructed Sophia and Maria on how to use them to defend themselves. At the same time, he also stressed the need to follow his orders without question, knowing secretly that he wouldn't let either of them wield so much as a rolling pin against Tejada's people.

With their physical security addressed, the most vital remaining issue was that of contacting Rebhorn to alert him to what Winters was certain Tejada and Molina planned to do. Then the appropriate agencies would go into action and he'd be out of it. More important, so would Maria and Sophia. But contacting Rebhorn was the tricky part. He already suspected Winters was crazy. If Winters didn't have hard evidence to convince him, Rebhorn would simply write him off as lost and that would be the end of it—the end of his attempt to stop Tejada and Molina, and the end of his career with the Secret Service.

But hard evidence was something he lacked.

Winters still wasn't sure he knew the true nature of Maria's relationship with Tejada. She'd told him many things, none of which implicated her in any way, but every time she mentioned him a light went on in her eyes and the look on her face softened. It might matter—it might not. But he was going to have to wait for the right moment to ask her. She was vacillating between uncanny strength and an uncharacteristic vulnerability, and Sophia had advised him to gauge his approach carefully.

And truth be told, his mind was otherwise occupied. He sat now in the dimly lit nook off the kitchen, half-listening to the murmur of female voices upstairs as he went over what he knew. He had to be clear before he called Rebhorn.

Winters pushed the notes he'd made into the yellow arc of light on the table. He was born about the time the so-called suitcase bombs had been intercepted on their way to Iran in the early seventies, but their existence was well known among the ranks of the Secret Service. Several of them had supposedly been hidden in secure locations around the United States. Speculation about those locations was a popular late-night topic among agents as they shared a beer after a long day. Rumor had it that the CIA had one or two that they kept for archival purposes—secured in a vault at Langley or in the fifth level of the Pentagon basement, depending on who recounted the story. Others suggested they were poorly constructed and leaked radiation, so it was a mystery to him why the CIA would have insisted on keeping them. He'd always suspected they'd forgotten where they'd put them—or that the rumors of their existence were unfounded—but apparently not.

He tapped his pen on the name Schlesinger and recounted in his mind the conversation Maria overheard. He could be totally wrong about what it meant. But the part about him having a dalliance with Danish schoolgirls was a no-brainer. Schlesinger was a sleazeball and should have been replaced long ago.

Winters stirred in his chair.

Schlesinger was obviously being blackmailed, but was he vulnerable enough to allow someone to talk him out of a radioactive bomb just to protect a reputation that didn't exist? There had to be more to it, but that really didn't seem to be the point. From the gist of the conversation, Molina had a nuclear suitcase bomb. That was the point. And if Molina did have a bomb, Winters had to assume he was going to use it.

And if these people would kill for a five-hundred-year-old journal they could have had for the asking, why wasn't it plausible that they'd detonate a bomb? It would be nice to know why, but the essential question was . . . where?

Winters scowled at his notes. Nothing Maria remembered gave him so much as a clue. Still, he went over the list again, looking at each item from as many perspectives as possible, asking new questions—trying to read between the lines.

Everything in him wanted to call Donleavy to see if he'd heard any buzz, but he didn't want to run the risk of Rebhorn finding out his friend had helped Maria. He had no choice but to call Rebhorn and hope to convince him with what he had. Mention of a threat like the one he thought they faced—detonation of a nuclear bomb at a location inside the continental United States—was too catastrophic to ignore, even if Rebhorn thought he was crazy. He might scream and shout in response. He might tell Winters he was fired. But after the phone call, Rebhorn would calm down . . . and then he would get curious. And then he would call the right people to look into it. Hopefully before Tejada and Molina discovered where he and Maria and Sophia were hiding.

And Winters had no doubt that they could.

Few people had Rebhorn's personal cell phone number. Winters was one of those few. Rebhorn answered on the first ring. But his greeting set Winters back in the chair.

"Winters," he roared. "Where the—where have you been?"

How had he—oh. The Barcelona code. "Long story," Winters said, as casually as possible. "I'll give you the short version."

"Don't give me any version. Just get your—"

"We're talking bomb, sir," Winters said, interrupting, then he plunged into an account of all he knew about the threat they faced.

"I have two things to say to you, Agent Winters," Rebhorn said when Winters finally paused. "One, you are obviously more unstable than Archer says you are. And, two—"

"Sir, I know it sounds crazy, but I'm as certain of this as I've ever been of anything."

"If what you said was true—and I've always doubted those suitcase bomb stories—but if it were true, you'd be talking about a forty-five-year-old bomb. Do you understand that, Winters? A forty-five-year-old leaking, deteriorating device."

"I know it sounds like a long shot."

"It sounds like the ravings of a madman."

"Yes, sir," Winters said. "But I think—"

"The second thing I have to say to you," Rebhorn continued,

"is—get yourself back here within the next forty-eight hours or you are fired. Permanently."

"See, that's the thing," Winters said. "I'm stuck in—"

A tone sounded indicating the call had ended, followed by nothing but dead air. Rebhorn had hung up.

✦　✦　✦

Maria could only sleep in short, fitful increments and she was just drifting into an uneasy doze when a vibration near her head alerted her to a call on her cell phone. She reached for it on the pillow and sat upright on the bed. The call was from Donleavy.

"Maria—Taylor here," he said when she answered.

The rest was chopped up. Maria pressed the phone to her ear—as if that were going to help the connection. "You're breaking up," she said.

"—heard another—Tej—Lou—"

"You heard Tejada and Molina talking?" she asked, trying to make sense of the garbled conversation.

"Not Mol—you left it set up—couldn't find you—got in—"

"What did they *say*, Taylor?" She leapt from the bed and moved to the opposite end of the room, hoping for a better cell phone signal.

"—Wall Street—"

"What about Wall Street?" she pleaded.

"—timate solution—"

"What?"

The phone beeped and went dead.

"No!" Maria poked at it but the signal was gone. "No! Donleavy, come back!"

She didn't realize how loudly she was yelling until her father appeared in the doorway with a meat cleaver in his hand.

"Dad?" she said. "What's a 'timate' solution?"

✦ ✦ ✦

Tejada was almost to Barcelona and he still hadn't carried out Abaddon's order. He picked up his phone three times en route only to toss it back onto the car seat. It was inevitable, of course. There was no doubt he would do it. He believed in the plan and had always seen himself in control of a global government. It was what he was born to do. The focus of his entire life. All he had to do was place one phone call and it would be his. Still, he couldn't bring himself to give the order.

Back then, it had not mattered that masses of people might die to accomplish his goal. Before, when he had not known how loss could feel, it didn't matter the consequences. Didn't matter that thousands of people might die. They were nothing to him. But that was before . . . before Maria had entered his life and turned his world upside down.

Near the city limits Tejada pulled over and walked to a wall that bordered the beach. The sun was sinking toward the horizon, promising a soft Mediterranean night. The beauty of it burned in his chest as he cupped the phone in his hand. Anyone within blocks of the Wall Street financial district would be disintegrated. If he made the call, he would have to live with the deaths of all those people. And the rest of it too.

"But that is the way it must be," he said softly. "It is the path I chose long ago. And a destiny I cannot avoid."

With a flick of his thumb against the keypad, he placed the call.

46

I s there anyone you *don't* know?" Winters asked Sophia.

"I try to be accommodating."

Maria slipped out of the kitchen, leaving her father and Sophia staring lovingly into each other's eyes. Maybe if they hadn't been in this situation, she would have told her father to kiss the woman already.

The plan Sophia proposed was for a friend to meet them at an all-but-abandoned airport about fifty miles away and see that Maria and her father were flown safely to New York. How she knew someone who could do that, Maria didn't know. But it was a gift she was glad to receive. A way out without having to face Tejada . . . or Molina. And in the meantime, Winters had reached Donleavy with a better connection. According to him, Tejada and Molina did in fact possess a suitcase bomb and they intended to detonate it somewhere on Wall Street. That was the "ultimate solution," according to Donleavy. Someone had to get there and stop him. Maybe Rebhorn would send an agent. But if not, Winters was determined to act on what he knew, if they could find a way to get to New York. That's when Sophia offered to contact a friend. And that's when the plan for them to leave came together.

Maria's job had been to procure a safe house for their arrival. One phone call to Nathan Todd at the church in Maryland had accomplished that. She toyed with the phone again now. She needed to call Austin. To hear his voice and the comfort it brought. Because she was scared to death.

Austin's cell phone went straight to voice mail. "Sorry I've been *incommunicado*," she said. "I need your help. Call me?"

Maria glanced at the phone once more. She hesitated to call Austin at the office. She'd been out of touch with Snowden, and for all she knew he was in on this too. But she had to hear Austin's voice so she dialed the number from memory.

"Gump, Snowden and Meir. How may I help you?"

Betsy Smythe. Maria silently cursed the fact that the firm was one of the few that still used an actual receptionist.

"Austin Faulkner, please," she said, in what even she knew was a lame attempt at a Southern accent. It would be a miracle if Betsy took her for some relative of Austin's. The uncomfortable pause was a sure indication that it hadn't worked. Until Betsy said, "Mr. Faulkner is no longer employed here."

"Since when?" Maria asked.

"I am not at liberty to divulge that information." Betsy's voice slid out of protocol mode. "Is this—"

Maria ended the call.

She tried to resist the fear that pressed so closely, but with all that had happened lately, what was left but the worst possible scenario? They'd found out he was helping her get Elena away from Molina, she concluded. That was all there was to it.

Maria could hardly breathe.

Stop, she told herself. She had to stop, or she wasn't going to make it through what she'd already made up her mind to do. In fact, now was the time to inform her father. Now or never.

Winters and Sophia were sitting in the nook, saying nothing. Just staring at each other the way they had all morning. A plate of churros waited, uneaten, between them. Her father looked up first, his eyes filled with tears.

"Sorry to interrupt," Maria said.

"No, please—join us." Sophia pushed the plate toward the empty place at the table but Maria didn't sit down.

"I got the safe house," Maria said. "We can go there whenever we need to."

Just as she'd known it would, her father's face darkened. "You'll be going there straight from the airport."

"Yeah, well, that's the thing. I'm staying with you."

"No, you're not," he responded forcefully. His finger jabbed the air in her direction, punctuating every word. "It's too dangerous."

"I know."

He waited, eyebrows arched, while Sophia excused herself from the room.

"That's it?" Winters asked with a wry tone.

"I'm not going to try to talk you into it, Dad, because I don't need your permission. This is my battle too. I started it and I'm finishing it."

"You're going to disarm a bomb."

"No. And neither are you."

"I know who to talk to—"

"I can help—"

"You can help get yourself killed!"

"Dad—stop. For once, just listen. Not to what I think. Not to what makes sense. Just to what I feel."

Winters looked away and Maria slipped onto the chair Sophia

had vacated. "I can do something," she said. "I don't know what, but I can contribute. What I can't do is just stand by and watch another 9/11 happen to us."

Winters swallowed hard. "You are your mother's daughter," he said softly.

"No," Maria said, taking his hand. "I am my father's."

47

Carlos Molina didn't speak a word until the Catalonia jet touched down in New York City. Louis had slept the entire flight. Tejada sat behind them, papers spread around as he pretended to work. But as the wheels screeched on the tarmac, Molina turned to Tejada and said, "It was not in the plan for you to come. The Master did not order it."

"And yet here I am." Tejada kept his eyes on the documents as he tucked them into his briefcase.

"I am still to take down Winters?" Molina asked.

Tejada could feel Molina's gaze boring in on him. He smiled, without looking up, and said simply, "Your task remains the same. Winters has the journal. You watched the Conte woman give it to him when he left Málaga, yes?"

"Yes."

"So retrieve it and take it to Abaddon. Do what you will with Winters."

Molina gestured toward Louis, who was blinking at the early sunlight. "And him?"

"He will assist you. There are two named Winters, are there not?"

"I thought you—"

"I have had a change of heart."

Molina's eyes narrowed. "Then may I ask why you are here?"

Tejada looked him full in the face. "Let us just say I have trust issues."

Molina seemed caught off guard by the comment, but Tejada pushed on. "Do I have reason to believe you have carried out my orders regarding Wall Street? Including the change?"

"Yes," Molina said.

"The trail of evidence will lead back to Iran?"

"Perhaps not. I had it in place for the carrier to be an Iranian student. Now that you've ordered a—"

"Aside from that, the trail will hold? With the CIA's cooperation?"

Molina's eyes narrowed with resentment. "When the Americans conduct an investigation, *yes,* they will find their information points them to the Iranians. The story was originally concocted to protect the CIA from its own operations." Molina clenched his teeth. "It would be airtight if you had not changed the carrier."

"I had my reasons, which are no longer your concern." Tejada nodded in Molina's direction. "You will send the text on my command. In my presence."

"Yes," Molina said and he took a cell phone from his pocket.

✦ ✦ ✦

Winters didn't open the note from Sophia until the cargo plane made its final approach into LaGuardia. He knew what it said and was certain if he read it sooner he would order the pilot to take him back to Spain. Maybe he was as crazy as Rebhorn said he was.

John,
I know I must accept that our time together may have come to an end. Separating is far harder to do than anything else we have been

through, and that is saying a great deal, isn't it? Now my prayer
vigil begins and it will not end until you have safely done what
you must do. But please know, Agent Winters, that if you return
to Spain, I will not be so gracious about letting you leave again.

Te amo,

Sophia

"You're in love with her, aren't you?"

Winters looked over at Maria, seated in the sling next to him.

"It's okay," she said. "I think Mom would like her."

Winters nodded. "How's your Spanish?"

"Probably better than yours."

"Do you know what '*te amo*' means?"

A slow smile—the first he'd seen—spread across her face. "Looks like the feeling is mutual. It means 'I love you.'"

Moments later, the plane bounced onto the runway in New York. It was time to do this thing. And now Winters had twice the reason to stay alive.

According to the man Maria referred to as "Sophia's guy," they were to meet their escort just inside the cargo terminal. He'd be in a brown work uniform with an orange *Transporte Internacional* logo above the shirt pocket. It would be identical to the ones Winters and Maria changed into during their flight. They had matching caps too, and Maria's hair stuck out beneath hers in every direction. It wasn't much of a disguise. Anyone who knew her would recognize her from the hair alone, but to Winters' relief they crossed the tarmac and stepped inside the terminal without incident. Their *Transporte* clone was waiting as promised, and led them through the hangar toward a door on the far side.

This guy could have a real future in the Secret Service. Serious lack of facial expression. Monosyllabic answers. Even the shades he donned as he opened the door were standard issue.

"Louis?"

Winters went immediately on alert. Maria stopped short in front of him and he stepped on her heel.

And then it all went down in triple time. Maria's elongated scream. Her body slung over Louis' shoulders in a fireman's carry. Her body landing on the backseat of a car. Tires burning rubber as they sped away.

All the while, Winters lunged for Louis but he dove into the car after Maria with an agility that belied his heft. The door flapped as the car fishtailed across the pavement with Winters in pursuit on foot. As they pulled away, Maria appeared in the back window, waving him off and mouthing the words "Go to Wall Street."

This was exactly the scenario that had terrified Winters. Fighting against a sense of panic, he turned to their escort, who stood helplessly at the hangar door, cell phone in hand.

"You want me to call nine-one-one?" he asked.

"Where's your car?" Winters barked.

The guy broke into a run toward a silver SUV parked a few yards away. Winters followed. The cell phone he was digging out of his pocket rang and he jammed it to his ear.

"Winters," he said in a huff.

It was Donleavy.

"I've been listening to the chatter in New York," he said. "Just in case."

"And?"

"The pilot of an airborne RadNet radiation detector flying over Manhattan has picked up a spike in gamma rays."

Winters climbed into the SUV and motioned for the driver to follow the car that was now turning onto the main road on the other side of the security fence.

"They've narrowed the radiation source to a four-block sector of Lower Manhattan," Donleavy continued. "But nobody knows what they're looking for."

"A suitcase," Winters said. "Call them. Tell them to look for someone carrying a suitcase."

"I tell them I heard it from you and they'll put *me* in the psych ward. I thought you were headed down there."

"I can't! Those thugs just took Maria." Winters grabbed the dashboard with one hand as the driver careened the SUV out the gate. "They went left!" he shouted to the driver.

"John, listen to me." Donleavy's voice was calm and even. "They're not going to kill her. I heard the conversation myself. Tejada told Molina to make sure nothing happened to her."

"This wasn't Molina. It was some guy. Louis, I think." Winters gestured to the driver again. "Take a right—cut across that lot!"

"Even better," Donleavy said. "According to Maria he's further down the food chain. He'll do whatever Tejada said— "

"I can't just let them take her—"

"And you can't just let them blow up Manhattan. Get to Wall Street. No one will believe me if I tell them. I'll find Maria. Did you get a license number?"

"A license number?" Winters cried indignantly. "I didn't have time to—"

The driver rattled off a series of numbers and letters. Winters asked Donleavy, "Did you get that?"

"I'm on it," Donleavy said. "Keep your phone on."

Winters shoved the phone into his pocket and scanned the road ahead of them.

"What do you want me to do?" the driver asked.

Winters watched the traffic swallow the car and gave a heavy sigh. "Take me to Wall Street," he said with resignation. "And get there as fast as you can."

48

When the SUV turned onto Bleecker Street, confusion was already taking hold. Police were setting up roadblocks that pedestrians sullenly disregarded, while red-faced drivers leaned on their horns, stuck their heads out of windows, and shouted obscenities.

"You know any shortcuts?" Winters asked.

"A few."

"Get me to the corner of Broadway and Wall Street—"

"Done," the driver said and made an impressive U-turn into an alley barely wide enough to walk down. He appeared unruffled by the pile of empty pallets he clipped and, in fact, seemed to enjoy the excitement.

Winters wished he could say the same.

Sweat had already formed salt rings under the sleeves of the brown uniform shirt, and his eyes burned from the strain of searching the sidewalks for signs of someone carrying a suitcase. The streets were clogged with briefcase-toting men in business suits, but none of them were the right size. A 1970s-era Soviet suitcase bomb wasn't really a suitcase but more like a golf bag or an oversized duffel. Small by comparison to a bomb dropped from an airplane but hardly as small as the suitcase the moniker suggested.

Winters felt rusty and unprepared too. It had been months since he'd put his observational skills to a test like this. Yet something was kicking in. Something familiar. He glanced at the driver as they made the corner onto Broadway. "What's your name, pal?" he said.

"Alejandro," the driver said. "But you can call me Al."

"You're a prince, Al." Winters pointed to the right. "Drop me here."

"I can take you around the block."

"This is safer. You don't want to be anywhere near here, so—"

"I'll wait."

"No, man," Winters said as he opened the door. "You don't understand—"

"In that alley across the street." The driver pointed to the left. "I will wait for you there."

"We're not actors in a movie, Al—"

"You will need me to get to your daughter. After this is over. I will wait," he insisted.

Winters didn't have time to argue. Another barrier was going up in the next block. Soon he would be hard-pressed to get anywhere near the New York Stock Exchange.

"Okay," he said, finally. And with a nod to Al, Winters left the SUV and ran down Broadway.

Though no doubt weakened by time and lack of maintenance, a suitcase bomb would still carry enough force to create a blast radius of six or seven blocks. Much larger than the four-block area Donleavy said the police were focused on. Either way, it was an area much too large for a single person to effectively search.

If the stock exchange really was the target, it would have to be attacked from outside. A layperson would have little chance of getting inside the building with a case that large. And besides, security at the entrance would stop them immediately. If they used a layperson.

What if they had someone on the inside? A trader or technician. They could enter the building a different way. But surely, even employees go through the security checkpoint—don't they?

Still, Winters threaded his way through the foot traffic and hurried toward the stock exchange building. He had no option now but to try. And hope for the best.

As he made his way down the sidewalk, he craned his neck over and around the oncoming crowd, eyeing every attaché and tote bag on Broadway and stopping only to check the alleys and side streets. He was about to circle back to the other side of the exchange when he took a cursory glance down Exchange Place. It was virtually empty, except for a lone figure standing at the far corner with his back to Winters. Holding an oversized metal case.

The man was about Winters' height but even from a distance his muscular build was obvious. His black jacket strained at the shoulders and his beefy arms hung at his side as if he'd spent every day in the weight room.

If the man had any moves at all he'd have the upper hand physically. Winters wouldn't be able to wrestle the case away from him. He'd have to talk him out of it.

As Winters started toward him, the man with the case reached into his jacket with his free hand, took out a cell phone, and thumbed a text message. That was a good thing. If they had to fight, maybe Winters at least would have the advantage of surprise.

And, from the way he flexed his arm, the guy seemed to be getting tired. That case—if it was the bomb—wouldn't be light and the longer he stood there the heavier it would get. That was the thing with weight lifters. They were strong but they seldom had any stamina.

With a few more steps to go, the guy still didn't seem to realize Winters was coming up behind him. He stuffed the phone in his pocket and shifted the case to the other hand. That was *not* a good thing. If he'd been holding it for that long, time was running out.

"Excuse me," Winters said. "Could you tell me—"

The figure whirled around to face him and in an instant he realized—the man with the case was Ben, his brother.

"What do you think you're doing?" Winters shouted.

Ben took a step backward, both hands white-knuckling the handle of the case. "What are you doing here, Johnny?" he asked. "You're supposed to be somewhere else."

"I asked you first, Brother," Winters replied, his mind reeling with shock. Nothing he had planned would work.

"Go away, Johnny," Ben said in a sullen tone. "This is my gig. I don't need your help."

"Your gig? With who?"

"The Service. They sent me."

Ahh. The Service. Winters knew the angle now.

"Well, look, buddy. Change of plans," Winters said. "I have orders to take over from here."

Ben shook his head and held the case closer. "Whose orders?" he asked. "The Service isn't even using you right now. You've got PTSD." Ben took another step back.

"I'm over the PTSD," Winters said. "Look, you've done a great job up to this point, but they sent me to take over. I know what to do with it."

"No, man! Why does it always have to be you? *I* know what to do with it!"

Winters scanned the case for a button, a switch, anything, even as he gave Ben a nod.

"What are your orders?"

"I get the text, I set the case down here. Not until then."

The switch was on the bottom. Winters forced himself not to lick the sweat off his upper lip. Ben had no such self-control. He released the case with one hand to pull off the watch cap and mop his high forehead.

"That's the deal with these ops," Winters said. "You have to be flexible. Last-minute changes happen. They knew you would trust me, which is why I'm here."

"They told me *not* to trust you." Ben's voice was high-pitched and tremulous and he had trouble getting the cap back on with one hand. "They said you might show up and try to mess with me, but not to let you. It's part of my training."

Forget everything he'd thought about Tejada's choice of a carrier. The man was a genius.

"I have orders, too," Winters said. "They sent me on purpose to try to mess you up—just the way they sent you to mess me up. You know, the whole thing with the laptop?"

Ben's blue eyes now showed fear, but Winters forced a smile. "It's part of the training game, Bro. No worries. But you see, what they've done here is pit us against each other, to see how you handle it."

"I know how I'm gonna handle it. I'm not putting this down until they tell me to."

"Even though I outrank you?"

"Yeah," Ben said defiantly.

Winters shrugged. "You can do that, but do you know the penalty for disobeying a direct order from a superior?"

"*They're* my superiors."

"Who? Give me some names."

Ben's face went blank. "They never told me their names."

Winters smirked. "They took that approach, huh? This way it doesn't come back on them."

"What doesn't?"

"Look, Brother, this isn't just a training mission. There's some serious stuff in that case. This goes down wrong and heads will roll, including yours."

"So," Ben said, pleading. "What do I do?"

"You show them that you know the protocol. You have no way of knowing what rank these people have, but you know mine. And it trumps yours. So, hand me the case and do it gently. You got it?"

Ben nodded, lifted the case to hold it with both hands, and offered it to Winters. Winters reached for the handle—and Ben's cell phone buzzed.

The case slipped and they both went for it. Ben grabbed it once more and clutched it against his chest, then turned away as he fumbled for the phone.

"Ben, give it to me," Winters demanded. "Give it to me now."

"They said to set it down and I'm doing it. This is my chance, Johnny." He held the case out to his side and began to lower it.

As Ben stooped to put the case on the pavement, Winters thrust his hand behind Ben's arm and swept it away from his body. At the same time, he grabbed it with his other hand and slammed his full weight against his brother's body. Ben staggered to the ground. His head smacked against the sidewalk.

Winters held the case at arm's length and stared down at him. Ben looked like the kid brother he'd once seen beaned by a baseball. "Don't move," Winters said to him. "I mean it."

Ben groaned.

Holding the case in his arms, Winters turned away and walked back toward Broadway. All he needed was a cop, a firefighter, anybody to take this thing off his hands. He had to get to Maria.

Before he reached the end of the block, he spotted two members of the bomb squad heading toward him in hazmat suits.

"This what you're looking for?" he said.

They stopped a few feet away.

"Agent John Winters, Secret Service," he said, barking the words in an authoritative tone. "Got it off a Middle Easterner." He nodded over his shoulder. "Took off toward the river."

The bomb squad guys looked stunned.

"Here," Winters said, thrusting the case in their direction. "Take it. And don't set it down. The trigger is on the bottom. I'm available for questioning later but I have another matter to take care of."

The great thing about guys in those squads was that they were interested in only one thing—the bomb. No one came after him or hailed him as he sprinted back up the alley, and helped Ben to his feet. When Ben was standing, he slung an arm over John's shoulder and the two of them made their way up the alley, away from the bomb squad.

"Where did you pick up the case, Ben?" Winters asked.

"Why should I tell you?"

"Because I think the same people who set you up to *bomb* Wall Street have taken Maria. You say you want your chance? Here it is. Tell me where they are."

As they emerged onto Broadway, the silver SUV nosed to a stop right in front of them. Winters slammed Ben against the passenger side. His head thudded on the glass and Winters leaned in close. "You tell me now. Or I'll leave you in this alley and you can take the fall for everything." When Ben didn't respond, Winters shoved him again. "Are we clear?"

"I got it in the parking garage. At the law firm."

Winters frowned. "What law firm?"

"Gump whatever. I don't remember the name."

"Gump, Snowden and Meir?"

"Yeah! That's it. They told me to meet them there. In the parking garage. That's where I got it."

Winters stuck his head into the SUV. "Al, you mind babysitting my brother while I borrow your car?"

"I was just going to suggest that," Al said.

49

Louis parked himself in a chair across the table from Maria and popped open a can of Coke. He shoved a second one toward her, but she shook her head.

"I don't drink with people who kidnap me," Maria snarled.

Louis took a sip of Coke but didn't answer.

She'd never been able to figure out whether he actually spoke English. He definitely understood the universal language of fingernails down the cheeks. She noted with some satisfaction the angry claw marks on his face. But she had to hand it to him, though. He hadn't even blinked.

"So what are you, stoic?" she asked.

He stared at her a moment, then turned away.

"That answers that question." She shifted positions in the chair. "Here's another one. What are we doing here? Why don't you just kill me and get it over with?"

"We are waiting," Louis said at last.

Maria grinned. "So you do speak. Who are we waiting for?"

Louis took another sip from the can.

"If you tell me we're waiting on Molina, I'm going to beg you to just put that gun to my head right now."

Louis just looked at her. And from the set of his jaw, she knew she wasn't getting any more information from him.

The room in which they sat was more like a vault, and she'd never known about it. After nine months with the firm she didn't even know it existed. Of course, there was a lot she didn't know—like the fact that Bill Snowden was in league with terrorists. But she couldn't go there, because from that place her mind went straight to Tejada—and she was still finding it hard to believe that he would mastermind an attack like the one her father was trying to stop. Shrewd, underhanded business deals—that she could see. But this . . . from the man she'd almost fallen in love with?

No. Don't go there, she told herself. *Not even for a moment.*

Trying to appear bored, Maria slid low in the chair and glanced around once more. No windows. No sound. In a basement she hadn't known existed. One door, with a handle like ones she'd seen in banks. No other furniture except the round metal table where they sat. And only two chairs, both with hard plastic seats. Nothing on the stark white walls. Gray concrete floor.

Maria let her head fall over the back of the chair and peered at the ceiling through half-closed eyes. Rows of fluorescent lights were no help. There must be a ventilation system. The chill she felt had to be coming from someplace besides her own fear.

After a moment she located a vent, on the ceiling above the door. It was just about big enough for her to crawl through. If she had a screwdriver to take off the cover. If she had a way to get up there. If Louis were unconscious on the floor.

She sat up and watched him crumple the can with one hand. Okay, so much for that idea.

Her only chance was to get out the next time that door opened, and the only way to do that was to divert everyone involved. But if "everyone" included Molina, she would be out of luck. She'd gotten away from him once, and he wouldn't let that happen again, no matter what instructions Tejada had given him. She could only hope Molina wasn't coming. But then, if it wasn't him, who were they waiting for?

Maria pulled the Coke can to her and rolled it between her hands. "So why the change of plans, Louis? Why you instead of Molina?"

Louis stared at the crumpled can, but did not reply.

"Well," Maria said, "I'm glad we have this opportunity for a chat because I've always wanted to make sure there are no hard feelings about me not wanting you as a bodyguard. The thing is, I didn't want anybody. I thought I could take care of myself." She shrugged. "Looks like I was wrong, huh?"

"*Señor* Tejada's orders."

"I'm sorry?"

"*Señor* Tejada sent me for you."

Interesting. Maria leaned on the table. "So what's Molina up to, then?"

Louis shook his head. He actually looked—uneasy?

"Whatever it is, you don't like it. Right?"

No answer.

"Or do you just not like Molina, period?" She leaned in further. "I'm right there with you on that one, Louis. I personally can't stand the guy. He's rude, boorish—truculent."

Louis looked at her quickly and then glanced away.

"Truculent," Maria said. "It means, like, combative. That doesn't help you, does it? Okay—he turns everything into an excuse to be violent, know what I mean?"

Louis nodded.

"That's why Tejada sent you instead of Molina. Because he knew

Molina wouldn't be able to resist knocking me around, no matter what Tejada ordered." Maria leaned back in the chair and hugged her knees into her chest. "You, on the other hand, won't lay a finger on me if that's what Tejada told you. I'm right, aren't I?"

Louis nodded again.

"But you can see how I'd be concerned, right? If Molina is coming, I have a problem. You get that?"

"No problem."

"You're going to protect me from Molina."

"*Sí.*" Louis nodded. "Yes."

Maria closed her eyes, hoping Louis would see that as relief. Truth be told, she needed a minute to sort it out. She wanted to ask, *For how long?* But she was afraid of the answer. When she opened her eyes, she said instead, "Just one more question, Louis. How are you going to protect me? Reassure me."

Louis looked again at the crushed can, and Maria wondered if she'd gone too far. And yet she couldn't stop. "If the two of you were put in a ring with no weapons," Maria said, "my money would be on you all the way. But that Molina is always armed. I bet he takes a bath with his AK-47."

Again there was no answer from Louis. But he opened his jacket and revealed a holstered pistol at his side.

"Gotcha," Maria said. "I feel better."

Okay, so what about the plan to escape? Knock out Louis with the Coke can, grab his gun, and wait for whoever to show up? Any attempt to do that would just make him mad. An angry Louis? Yeah, all bets were off then.

Louis toyed with the can he'd crushed, rolling it back and forth in his hand. Finally Maria said, "What do you see there, Louis?"

He gave her a sheepish look.

"Really," she urged. "Tell me what you see. I want to know. If you're like me, you see weird stuff in everything."

"*Pietà*," he said.

"Like . . . Michelangelo's *Pietà*?"

Louis' face reddened and he covered the can with his hand.

"I can see that," Maria added. "I just didn't know you were into art."

Louis nodded.

"So have you actually seen the original? At the Basilica?"

He turned his head toward the door, and Maria stiffened. She heard it now too. The lock was turning. The anxiety she'd kept at bay surged and she grabbed the Coke can. While Louis sat focused on the door, she arranged the can like a missile in her hand and hurled it at his temple. Without so much as a flinch he slumped face-first on the table.

"Oh, no," Maria groaned. "What have I done?"

The lock continued to turn, slowly to the right.

Maria flung herself across the table and yanked the gun from Louis' holster and jammed it into the waistband of her pants. She had no idea how to use it but it felt heavy and cold against her skin. She had to be safer now, right?

Then the door came open and Molina appeared. He took in the small room in two short steps and lifted Louis' head by his hair. At the same time, Maria saw the door open.

"Is he dead?" she said.

Molina gave a disgusted grunt and leaned closer to Louis' face. Willing herself to move slowly, Maria picked up the crumpled "*Pietà*" and pretended to be looking for a trash can. Molina was still swearing in Spanish over the unconscious Louis as she made her way toward the door.

Then Molina let out a curse with a different tone and she glanced in his direction to see he was holding the Coke can. A look of realization dawned on his face. Without waiting to see what happened next, Maria bolted for the open door. But as she reached it, Molina grabbed her from behind. She kicked and screamed and flung her arms from side to side in a desperate attempt to break free, but he only held her tighter.

Holding her up to keep her feet off the floor, Molina backed away from the door and turned to kick it closed. She couldn't let that happen.

With her mouth wide open, she chomped down on his forearm and held on until she tasted his blood. Molina's hold loosened and she got free of one arm. Her feet touched the floor, but still he dragged her back and reached with a foot to push the door shut.

But something else pushed back.

And seconds later, her father stood in the doorway.

Molina was startled by Winters' sudden appearance and let go of Maria. Free of him, she rushed toward her father, but just before she reached him, Molina grabbed her again and pulled her tight against him, his arm across her neck holding her in place. She didn't have to see the gun to know it was pressed against her temple.

"Don't move, Maria," Winters said. "Just stay calm. He isn't going to shoot you."

"That's easy for you to say," Maria choked.

"Shut up!" Molina ordered.

"Make me," Maria said.

"I love your fight, honey," Winters said, "but let me handle this one, okay?"

"Let's make this easy," he said to Molina. "I'm the one you want. Maria was just the bait. Am I right?"

Molina pressed the gun harder against Maria's temple. "You have *la revista*?"

"The Columbus journal?" Winters replied. "Yeah, I have it. Not *on* me," he added quickly. "I didn't want to carry it with me to Wall Street—seeing how it might have been blown up today."

"You bring the journal," Molina growled. "I release the woman."

"No, Carlos," said a voice at the door. "Those were not my orders."

How her father kept from turning around, Maria didn't know, but she knew that voice. And then Tejada appeared.

The arm around Maria's neck went slack and she tried to duck under it. But just as quickly Molina choked her against him again and pressed the muzzle of the pistol against her head once more. "Let her go," Tejada said. "The father is yours. Give me the daughter."

"He does not have the journal," Molina said, breath hot and rank against Maria's cheek.

"He will take you to it," Tejada assured.

Winters held up both hands. "I'll go willingly, Carlos."

The journal, Maria knew, was with Sophia, in Spain. The envelope they'd made a production out of taking with them from Málaga contained an old copy of *Don Quixote* from the retreat house.

"No," Molina said, shaking his head. "She dies too."

Tejada's glare hardened and he drew a pistol from beneath his jacket. "Let her go."

"You have not followed Abaddon's plan," Molina insisted. "Nothing you have done has worked because you have not followed his orders."

"Abaddon," Winters said. "Now that's a name I'm not familiar with."

"Do not speak it," Molina demanded.

"I will fulfill the plan on my own terms," Tejada said. "Abaddon is dead."

Molina gasped in disbelief and his grip on Maria's neck slackened.

Without warning, she pushed his arm away and dropped to the floor.

Just then, a shot rang out.

Maria screamed and covered her head with her arms, as something heavy crashed to the floor beside her. When she opened her eyes, she saw Molina's body lying beside her, his eyes blank with a lifeless stare.

Before she could move, Winters was beside her. Gently but firmly, he slipped his arms beneath hers. "Come on," he said. "We have to go."

He helped her to her feet and turned toward the door. Tejada stood there, the gun still in his grasp, the barrel trained on them.

"I appreciate you saving my daughter," Winters said. "But I can take her from here."

Tejada stared at them a moment, his eyes fixed on Maria. "I have something to tell you," he said finally.

"I don't want to hear it," Maria retorted.

Tejada smiled. "For a while I thought I was capable of love. Do you think that is true, Maria?"

"I think you *were* capable of love, Tejada," she said. "But now you have given in to evil."

Tejada lowered his head as if in thought. While he was distracted, Maria took Louis' pistol from her waistband and handed it to her father. He slipped his fingers around the grip and waited.

"Then this is it," Tejada said, raising the pistol to fire. "I am sorry it has come to this."

Suddenly, the deafening report of Louis' pistol—the flash—the look of surprise on Tejada's face—all happened in such rapid succession Maria could barely move as Winters shoved her toward the door.

"Is he—" she gasped. "Did you—"

"Come on." Winters pulled her after him. "We have to get out of here."

Maria looked down at Tejada, who was writhing on the floor, helpless for perhaps the first time in his life. And yet there was the gun, just within his reach on the concrete.

"Dad!" she screamed.

Tejada's fingers closed over the pistol. Winters flung Maria aside and turned to shoot. "Run, Maria!" he said.

But before she could move, a hulking form came to life at the table. With a heave Louis dropped on top of Tejada and pinned him in place.

50

The sun crept into the room that overlooked El Masnou, like fingers strangling the darkness. Tejada went to the window and cursed it beneath his breath. He knew now why Abaddon had spent so much of his time in the shadows. There was too much to accuse him in the light. Perhaps if he remained here he would come to believe as the old man had that the truth lay in the dark.

He moved to the chair in the middle of the room and turned it slowly in a circular motion, facing each of the cushions arranged on the floor. All were just as the Brotherhood had left them that day Abaddon had passed his power down to Tejada.

Now, so much had changed.

Molina was dead. Snowden had been found hanging in his office, a chair lying on its side beneath him. The rest of the board had scattered when the news began to spread that Catalonia Financial was behind the attempted bombing of Wall Street. As for Abaddon himself, Tejada was not convinced he died naturally in his sleep. Abaddon seldom slept, and the vial of aconite he kept was empty.

Tejada turned to the old man's self-appointed throne. "You did it to give me no choice, wily one. And here I always thought I had one." He smiled slyly. "But you knew that. As you knew everything."

Almost.

He looked again at the circle of cushions lying at his feet. Abaddon was wrong. The choice remained. It was true that Catalonia could regain its footing under another name—as it had done so many times through the centuries. The journal had gone back underground, and he now knew where to look for it. As long as he lived, the Brotherhood could have life and achieve its purpose.

But one choice remained—to prove Maria Winters wrong. To look to the root of goodness inside himself and see if it had indeed been choked out. It was there before him as clear as the shaft of sunlight that shot insistently through the window, undaunted by his wish for darkness. He could take it. He could follow where it led.

Outside, he heard the toll of bells as they rang in the church tower, beckoning to the people of El Masnou, calling them to worship. But they had no idea that the Antichrist stood above them.

He must choose, and he must choose now. There could be no reluctance in embracing the role. It must be all, or it must be nothing.

Tejada walked to the window and leaned out. Nothing did not mean chasing after a self that might still exist at the root of him. It meant . . . nothing. It meant allowing himself to drop from this window, against the rocks that beckoned below.

"Lord Tejada?"

Tejada stopped breathing.

Heavy footsteps resounded in the room. Tejada held up his hand. "A moment, Louis," he said. The steps stopped. Tejada closed his eyes and let himself see her one more time. The outrageous hair. The bright, intelligent eyes. The smile that illuminated the soul he'd forgotten he had.

She was the only one who knew him. Only she could know . . . the evil had cut to the root of the good. And so, it must be the truth.

Slowly he turned from the window. Louis sat on the cushion just to the right of the chair, waiting. Louis, who had kept him from killing her.

Tejada took his seat and looked down at his brother.

"*Nos comprometemos nuestras vidas y nuestras fortunas con el maestro,*" Louis said.

✦ ✦ ✦

Winters ended the call and rested the phone against his cheek. Maria crossed the hotel room and sank into the nondescript chair across from him.

"So," she said. "When are you going back to Spain?"

"Not until the Service is done with me." He gave her a thin smile. "With us."

Maria pushed a hand through her hair. "How many times can they ask us the same questions?"

"You have no idea," Winters said shaking his head. Then he looked up with a sarcastic grin. "You don't like being quarantined here with me? How often do you get to stay in a suite like this, huh?"

"I'd just like it to be my choice." Her eyes softened. "But no, it isn't that bad. We haven't talked to each other this much since—"

"Uh-oh," Winters said, cutting her off. "I hear it coming. 'Dad, we need to talk.'"

"What else do we have to do?"

"I could teach you to play poker."

"I know how to play poker," she groused. "I'm serious, Dad. We need to talk about what you're going to do."

Winters knew she was right. Although she was feisty and smiling again, back to doing that thing with her hair, she had circles under her eyes and when she thought he wasn't watching, her gaze drifted off and her mouth trembled before she tightened it back in line.

They'd talked about everything from her mother to her sense of betrayal by Snowden to her longing for her friend Austin, whom she still couldn't find. She'd poured out her grief over the girl Elena, and her anger at Ben—whom he knew was undergoing questioning that made theirs pale by comparison.

But she never mentioned Tejada. He'd seen the sparks that flew between them even when guns were drawn. Winters had watched her struggle that day to answer his question—was he capable of love? She had at the very least been on the verge of love with him, but she wouldn't talk about it. He wanted to tell her she would discover the kind of relationship he was finding with Sophia—but they hadn't talked about her yet, either. Where they were was here, with Maria staring at him with her wide brown eyes, waiting for the answer to a question he hadn't heard.

"Hello?" she said. "You with me or what?"

"Hit me with that again."

"What are we going to do after this?"

Winters rubbed his chin. "You're not talking about jobs."

"No." She shook her head. "I'm talking about the journal—the prophecies—all of that. And about Sophia."

"We've got you hooked too."

"How can I not be? I'm Columbus' descendant too."

Winters motioned for her to go on.

"Sophia told me what that guy in Jerusalem said to you."

"Jacob Hirsch."

"I don't think you can ignore that, not after all that's happened. You didn't kill Tejada and I know he's not done. I saw it in his eyes as we were leaving."

Winters nodded. He could almost feel the knot in her throat.

"So you can't be done either," Maria continued. "Hirsch told you that deciphering the message of the prophecy is your task and now we know it's true."

Winters felt a thickness in his own throat. "'We'?"

"Yeah." She curved toward him. "Do you know how close I came to letting myself get pulled into that evil? And that's just me—one individual. Thousands of people could have been killed if you hadn't stopped it. This is our destiny."

In another time, a former place, Winters would have told his daughter she was being a drama queen. But these weren't the hyped-up ideals of a teenage girl. This was a woman, a passionate woman, his grown daughter who was confronting him with the truth.

Just as she had tried to confront Tejada.

"We might have the key to unlock the code," he said to her. "Hirsch says it's buried in the journal."

Maria spread her hand on her chest. "And not just the journal, Dad. I think it's buried in us. But are you in?" Winters looked into those wide brown eyes, where he saw her mother, and where he saw himself. And where he saw the truth. Slowly he nodded. "Yeah," he said. "I'm all in."

ACKNOWLEDGMENTS

First, I want to thank you, the reader, for picking up *The Columbus Code* and taking the time to read it. With so many other things vying for your attention, it is an honor that you dedicated time to read this novel.

A huge thank you to Worthy Publishing for seeing the spark in this novel and getting it out to readers. A special thank you to Worthy's CEO, Byron Williamson, for leading such a wonderful team of people, and Jeana Ledbetter for her dedicated support and guidance on this project.

This book would still be editorial chaos if it were not for the keen eye and guiding hand of Kyle Olund, the executive editor on this book. Thank you for making this final product the best it could be.

I am thankful for my agent, Ted Squires, and his passion and vigor for getting this book to Worthy. He has a gift for seeing potential, and I am appreciative to him for seeing potential in me.

Thank you to Doug Preudhomme for taking this novel to the next level of exposure with your marketing expertise.

My deepest gratitude and sincere thanks Joe Hilley, for his amazing gifts and talents, and to my executive assistant, Lanelle Shaw-Young, both of whom work diligently to help me accomplish my vision. Thank you to Arlen Young for his invaluable help.

Above all, I thank my wife, Carolyn, and family. They are the light that keeps me going. It would take an entire book to list all the things my wife does for me and what my family means to me.

ABOUT THE AUTHOR

MIKE EVANS is a #1 *New York Times* best-selling author with more than 25 million copies in print, including *Christopher Columbus, Secret Jew.* He lives in Fort Worth, Texas.

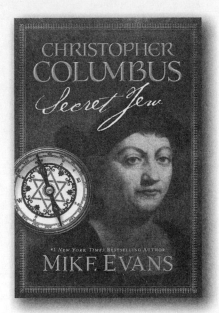

IF YOU ENJOYED THIS BOOK, WILL YOU CONSIDER SHARING THE MESSAGE WITH OTHERS?

Mention the book in a blog post or through Facebook, Twitter, Pinterest, or upload a picture through Instagram.

Recommend this book to those in your small group, book club, workplace, and classes.

Head over to facebook.com/worthypublishing, "LIKE" the page, and post a comment as to what you enjoyed the most.

Tweet "I recommend reading #ColumbusCode by Mike Evans (@JerusalemPrayer) // @worthypub"

Pick up a copy for someone you know who would be challenged and encouraged by this message.

Write a book review online.

Visit us at worthypublishing.com

twitter.com/worthypub

worthypub.tumblr.com

facebook.com/worthypublishing

pinterest.com/worthypub

instagram.com/worthypub

youtube.com/worthypublishing